FREEWATER

AMINA LUQMAN~DAWSON

A James Patterson Presents Novel

Little, Brown and Company

New York Boston

Copyright © 2022 by Amina Luqman-Dawson
Star art copyright © ArtMari/Shutterstock.com
Paper art copyright © Didecs/Shutterstock.com

Cover art copyright © 2022 by Cozbi A. Cabrera.
Cover design by Tracy Shaw. Cover copyright © 2022 by Hachette Book Group, Inc.

JIMMY Patterson Books / Little, Brown and Company
Hachette Book Group
1290 Avenue of the Americas, New York, NY 10104
JimmyPatterson.org

First Edition: February 2022

JIMMY Patterson Books is an imprint of Little, Brown and Company, a division of Hachette Book Group, Inc. The Little, Brown name and logo are trademarks of Hachette Book Group, Inc. The JIMMY Patterson Books® name and logo are trademarks of JBP Business, LLC.

The publisher is not responsible for websites (or their content) that are not owned by the publisher.

Library of Congress Cataloging-in-Publication Data
Names: Luqman-Dawson, Amina, author.
Title: Freewater / Amina Luqman-Dawson.
Description: First edition. | New York : Little, Brown and Company, 2022. | Audience: Ages 8–12. | Summary: After fleeing the plantation where they were enslaved, siblings Ada and Homer discover the secret community of Freewater, and work with freeborn Sanzi to protect their new home from the encroaching dangers of the outside world.
Identifiers: LCCN 2021016150 | ISBN 9780316056618 (hardcover) | ISBN 9780316056748 (ebook)
Subjects: LCSH: African Americans—Juvenile fiction. | CYAC: African Americans—Fiction. | Slavery—Fiction. | Brothers and sisters—Fiction. | Communities—Fiction.
Classification: LCC PZ7.1.L865 Fr 2022 | DDC [Fic]—dc23
LC record available at https://lccn.loc.gov/2021016150

ISBNs: 978-0-316-05661-8 (hardcover), 978-0-316-05674-8 (ebook)

Printed in the United States of America

LSC-C

Printing 3, 2023

To Zach,
and to generations of enslaved children
each of whom deserves a voice in this world

Some escaped the treacheries of enslavement by going North. But there were also those who ran away to the deep swamps and forests of the American South. There, in secret, they created free lives.

This is a tale of what might have been.

Prologue

SANZI HAD BROKEN YET ANOTHER RULE, BUT she didn't care. It was night, and she was alone and on the forbidden edge. To make matters worse, despite her mother's numerous warnings, Sanzi crossed right over, leaving behind the safety of her swamp island home. *Just a peek*, she thought. That's all she wanted, then she'd go back. Down the muddy hillside she slid to a single tall tree. She climbed it, hopping from one craggy branch to the next, higher and higher.

On the highest branch, moonlight hit Sanzi and made her nutmeg skin shine silver. From her perch she looked out. A sea of swamp mud, muck, and tangle lay before her. To her disappointment, fog rolled in from the east, covering her view like a white feather blanket.

She strained to see beyond the muck and fog to the plantation lands. She was a free child of the swamp and those lands were a mystery to her. It was a miracle her parents and the others had run from there and found this piece of elevated swamp land, small and dry. Their own secret island in an ocean of mud.

Tales had spread among the swamp island children like herself about what lay in plantation lands: two-headed men, turtles without shells, and skeletons that rose from the dead. Although she was twelve and almost grown, at least in her mind, Sanzi still wasn't sure how much of it was true, but she did believe that dangers lay out there.

As Sanzi contemplated that danger, she took a walnut-shaped stone from her sack, placed it in the well of her sling, and spun it overhead. The whir of the leather sling whispered in the air like children sipping hot soup. *Sssip, sssssip, ssssip.* She aimed toward the plantation lands. With a dream of adventure and a flick of her wrist, she released the sling and watched the stone soar high in the air, catch the moonlight, and disappear into the cauldron of fog below.

THE
JOURNEY

Homer

DOGS BARKING IN THE FOREST IS EXTRA SCARY.

All their growling and yapping hits the trees and makes it sound like they're coming from every direction. Stokes had sent out the whole pack. He knew we'd tried to escape, and his knowing had me to blame.

But Ada didn't say that. Eyes wide open with fear, Ada's skinny arms held tight to a tree trunk. She was huffing and puffing to catch air.

"Homer!" She howled it in that way that said, *You're my big brother—now what?*

I didn't have the breath nor heart to answer her. My mind was still on where we'd come from. Where were Mama and Anna? How could we keep going without them? Mama had gone back because of me, and now they were both gone.

"Homer, they're coming!" said Ada.

Paws crushed dead tree branches. It was enough to bring me back.

"Run!" I said. But it was too late. In the moonlight I spotted dog ears that pointed straight up. Funny thing was, I knew this dog. Even in the dark, I could see its face, big and round like one of Mama's iron pots in the Big House kitchen. Stokes had me feed that big head when he was away watching the fields. I had to do it with my morning work, after collecting milk and eggs, but before watering and brushing down the horses. The dogs ate just about the same food rations they gave us—lucky dogs. Yet they always stood there, yapping mean and angry—ungrateful dogs. Now here, this same dog came running at me like it didn't even matter he'd had the food from my hand. We were strangers. I was the slave and he was the dog sent to catch me.

He sank his teeth into my ankle. Ada screamed. She didn't need to. I was so scared I didn't feel anything but the hot wet of his tongue. With my other foot, I kicked him in his head. He let go, whimpering, then backed away, maybe waiting for his friends before coming at me again.

I grabbed Ada and we ran.

There was water nearby—Mama had told us about it. *If you don't see me come back, get to the river*, she'd said.

I didn't take much heed of her instructions at the time. We were going North, and Mama and Anna were coming along with us.

Mama said there was a river, but she hadn't told us it wasn't a thing like the sleepy one we knew by Southerland. We heard the water before we saw it. It was night, but this river was awake. We stood on the bank with barking behind us and roaring water in front.

"It sounds like a hungry monster!" Ada likened every-thing to monsters and angels. But she was right. The water spilled downhill and grumbled like a belly waiting for food, its tongue licking this way and that as it turned and twisted toward the foggy swamp. Lord only knows what happened when it got there. But there was no time for wor-rying about that. If those dogs met us again, they weren't going to be any nicer.

"Ada, you know that dream you have about flying?" I asked. Even with dogs on our heels, her face was kind of happy that I'd remembered her dream. She nodded.

"Well, now you get the chance to fly, like you did in that dream. We're gonna fly right off this riverbank."

Ada considered. "Into the water?" she asked.

I nodded. The sound of dog paws hitting soft ground came closer.

"But Homer, I can't swim." She said it more with sadness than anything.

"That's all right, you can do it," I said.

"But Homer, *you* can't swim," she said.

Before I had a chance to think about that fact, I grabbed Ada's hand and ran toward the riverbank and jumped.

Homer

WHEN MINGO DIED LAST SUMMER, THEY SENT over a coffin to our quarters. It was a simple wood box, narrow and short. I didn't know him well. But you don't forget a man you help put in a coffin. He was tall. When we folded his long legs to fit in that short wood box and nailed on the lid in the middle of the summer heat, I remember being scared that he wouldn't be able to breathe in that thing.

In the river, a flash of Mingo came to me. That's how being underwater felt, like lying in a coffin. I couldn't breathe, see, or move. I'd swear that water felt like pudding—heavy, wet, and smooth.

I stopped, pudding still until Ada's dress swiped my foot and woke me up. I took hold of it and started kicking and chopping at the water like I was fighting that big-face dog all over again.

Everything went swirling and finally I hit air. Water filled my ears and slapped my face. In my arms Ada was swinging at the night, reaching for things that weren't there.

"Homer!" she coughed.

The water pushed us downriver into a churning fall. Over we went, and down under again. My head hit rocks on the river floor and clanged like a cowbell. Everything went black. I awoke floating in the water, and Ada's arms were gone.

Then I heard it. A scream. Ada had made that same scream the last time she'd been around Mistress. That scream had set Mama's mind on taking us North.

I fell back into the ugly water. This time, I used it to help me get farther downriver, to Ada.

Ada's got a color on her, oak brown with lots of spots. I only ever seen spots like that on Master Crumb. It's those spots that led to troubles and the scream with Mistress. In the moonlight, her spots caught my eye. Ada was pressed to the riverbank, water smacking her this way and that. I kicked and fought my way to her. She grabbed on to me.

We reached for roots poking out from the bank and clawed our way out of that river. When we hit land, I lay there with my head heavy and pounding. Ada coughed and spat.

"I don't think we flew that time," she sputtered.

"No, I reckon we didn't," I said.

"I think we mighta needed to be running faster when we started, not just go jumping like that," explained Ada, like she was the one who was twelve, not me.

Even at seven, Ada holds tight to her dreams. I'm the

opposite. If it didn't work the first time, there was no way I'd be trying it again.

"What you reckon is gonna happen now?" she asked.

I looked around, hoping for an answer. Thin, tall, starving-men trees stood at attention. Huge, fat ones with knotty trunks rested on their sides. All were covered in a tangle of vines, brush, dreamy fog, and darkness.

I coughed and the whole swamp answered with a heap of grunts, growls, tweets, and squawks. The swamp heard me, and I felt anything but safe.

I had my rules back at Southerland; the most important was being invisible. Invisibility was how I survived. I'd learned that all attention, even the good kind, could be dangerous. I'd go a full day without anyone or anything even knowing I'd been there. Fetching milk, brushing horses, tending the flower garden, getting eggs, all of it done without so much as a *moo* from a cow or a *cluck* from a chicken, or anyone saying my name. I was nowhere, I was nothing. When I did it right, I felt safer. But the swamp didn't abide by my rules. This swamp saw me.

My head sank into the spongy wet ground. It smelled of old tea.

"Homer, you hear those monsters?" asked Ada.

She leaned over me. Her wild curly hair touched my nose. Ada liked to do things close. Sweat made her spots shine like tiny coins in the moonlight.

"It's animals you're hearing—ain't no monsters, Ada."

Her eyes got dark, almost as brown as mine. They were the only thing about us that looked alike. She exhaled. Her breath already smelled like the swamp. Ada had a way of soaking things up.

"That's what the monsters want you to think," she said, like it was me who was talking without good sense. "Mrs. Petunia told me they'll eat you alive. They just step out from one of these trees and swallow you down whole," she said.

"Mrs. Petunia was trying to scare you. There ain't nobody living in these here trees," I said.

"You think we could get up North from here?" Hope shone in Ada's eyes as she said it.

"North?" The word didn't seem right in this place.

"Mama said we were going," Ada reminded me.

Hearing talk about Mama made me rub my hurting head and almost cry from shame and sadness. I was set on going back for Anna. Anna was my friend and she needed saving. I tried to go, but instead Mama went in my place. And when no one came but those dogs, we did like Mama said and ran for the river.

"Ain't no heading North in this here swamp. Besides, we can't go North without..." My ending hung in the air. *Mama.*

"I was only wondering. Mrs. Petunia would whisper about the North. She said there were people free like birds there. I'm thinking if there's ever a place where people can fly, it's in the North. Going there we might even learn to fly ourselves, then come back here and fly Mama away."

Sometimes Ada's dreams burned so bright I didn't have the strength to put them out.

"I don't know," I muttered.

Ada smiled at me. She found that a good answer.

Mama was a finder. An egg tucked under the hay of the chicken coop, a tick lodged behind my knee, wild mint left over from planting three years past, my favorite rock, she could find it. She was good at finding me and especially Ada. When Ada was small, she was always wandering into trouble. Ada's foot stuck in a ditch, her hair caught in nettles, or she was lost in the forest. From the kitchen, Mama would know to go find her just in time. Mama had told us to run for the river. Maybe she could find us. The thought made me sit up.

How would she know where on the riverbank? Head pounding, I got two sticks, went to the bank, stuck them into the ground, then leaned them onto each other to make a point.

"What are you doing?" asked Ada.

Mama could find that, I thought. Then, as if the swamp said no, the damp ground pulled at the sticks and they fell flat. A second try and they fell again.

"Nothing," I said, digging my toes into the spongy earth. "Nothing." Still, if Mama slid down the river like us, she'd probably stop in the same place we did, then she'd climb up the bank and there we'd be. It was possible. She could find us.

Tired by the thought of it all, I sat down and everything began to swim. Blood ran from a cut on my temple. The swamp, Ada, and the river were spinning around me.

"We need to stay here for a minute," I heard myself say, and I laid my head back and let sleep come over me.

Stokes

AS OVERSEER OF SOUTHERLAND PLANTATION, Stokes prided himself on three things: driving enslaved souls in the fields until they could hardly stand from exhaustion, his instincts for knowing when one would run off, and training dogs to hunt and return those runaways to Southerland.

On the evening of Rose, Homer, and Ada's disappearance, Stokes's instincts were slightly dulled. Situated at the start of a dirt path that ran through the quarters was the overseer's shed. Inside, a poker game had his full attention. His two newly married brothers-in-law, Rick and Ron, who also served as his overseers in training, were with him. Having hired them as a favor to his two sisters, Stokes tolerated their dim-witted ways.

Yet, there was one favorable thing about Rick and Ron for which he could rely on—losing at poker. That night, Stokes was well ahead in the game and was contemplating what to do with his winnings, when his luck turned and he found himself caught with a less-than-fortunate poker hand. What to do? In frustration, he said he needed to pause the game to check the quarters. An unusual request, but one he felt would gain him enough time to consider his next card move. Happy to oblige their older in-law and employer, Rick and Ron settled into a game of balancing playing cards on their noses.

The first cabin door Stokes swung open proved unremarkable. He was almost set to return to his losing poker hand when something made him stop before Homer's cabin. He swung the door open. The floor was empty of three souls.

"Runaways!" he shouted down to the overseer's shed. Rick and Ron stuck their heads outside.

"What you say?" they asked in unison.

"Runaways! Get the dogs," ordered Stokes.

"Right now?" asked Rick.

"No, next Tuesday, you idiot!" yelled Stokes.

"In the night?" asked Ron.

"What? You afraid of the dark?" yelled Stokes.

"No." Rick shook his head.

"I ain't, either. But we're gonna take torches, right?" asked Ron.

"Get the dogs!" said Stokes, with steel in his voice.

Rick and Ron jumped into action.

They released Stokes's young dog first for the quick catch. It was fast and loud but unsuccessful. Now Stokes unleashed his older trained dogs, their noses set on the scent of human fear. Only the river churning and the dogs' murmuring pants could be heard as they went left then right, moving back and forth, meticulously covering the forest ground, thirsty for a scent.

Their torchlights splashed shadows on the crackly trunks of the forest trees, catching the shine of waxy leaves. Time passed, the terrain became more difficult, but they found nothing.

"Maybe something's wrong with the dogs," Ron said.

"No," Stokes answered, straining to keep the insult from his tone. "I've had these—"

Then all at once the dogs stopped, pointed their noses west, and took off running.

"They've got a scent," said Stokes. They scrambled in the direction of the barking.

"We've got 'em!" Rick yelled.

· 4 ·

Homer

I AWOKE DAZED WITH ADA LYING TUCKED UNDER my arm, her eyes scanning the swamp trees in the early morning gray.

"Finally, you're awake." Ada hugged me.

"Yeah," I muttered, but my heavy head said different.

"I tried waking you, but you didn't move one little bit," moaned Ada.

"You see anybody?" I asked, peeking around.

"Nope. But I was wondering, you think Two Shoes tried to go North and ended up here, too?" asked Ada.

I didn't like thinking about Two Shoes.

"Why?" I asked, even though I already knew.

"He up and ran off and nobody caught him. I figured he got away North, but maybe he got away to here," she said.

Two Shoes was the talk of the quarters. He was different. He didn't work in the house nor was he a field hand. During harvest and planting time he worked in the fields, but mostly he did Mr. Crumb's bidding—from fetching food to fetching people. Then there were the shoes. Once he got them, we all called him Two Shoes. They were castoffs from Mr. Crumb.

14

Old leather with worn soles, Two Shoes spit shined them until they shone. It was unusual for the quarters to have such shoes. Shoes kept you from thorny branches, snakebites, and all sorts. Plenty folks had tried running off but most were found and brought back. But Two Shoes had made it, and we all figured it was on account of his shoes.

Most folks suspected he'd run off on account of Desmond, his only son. When Mr. Crumb sold Desmond, Two Shoes changed some. But Sally, Two Shoes's wife, changed the most. Sally had been a light in the quarters, but when her boy was sold, her flame went with him.

"I bet he lost his shoes if he went in that river," said Ada.

"I'm pretty sure when he ran, he didn't run for no river," I said. "What does it matter anyway?"

"I was thinking is all," said Ada.

Unlike most folks, I was kinda happy after Two Shoes was gone. I'd heard him one early morning with Mr. Crumb. I was by the side of the house and he was there on the back porch whispering about Wilson, who'd lived in the quarters and had run off.

"You know where Wilson gone to?" asked Mr. Crumb. Two Shoes was quiet a long while.

"Come on and tell me—we're gonna catch him one way or another," said Mr. Crumb.

"Yes, sir," Two Shoes said. "I heard he went over to McGrath's plantation. I heard McGrath had bought Wilson's brother."

Master Crumb spit his tobacco.

"I suspect he'll be back, once he's seen his brother," said Two Shoes.

Master Crumb spit again.

"You best get on back to the fields. Stokes will be needing a hand," said Master Crumb.

"Master Crumb, thought I might ask—" Two Shoes went silent.

Another splash of tobacco hit the porch.

"I reckon this harvest is coming out good," said Two Shoes.

Spit.

"We said that with a good harvest we might try...we might try getting Desmond back?" The words came out like a maybe.

Spit.

"Only...Sally has been missing him so," said Two Shoes.

Spit.

"Now ain't the time to be thinking about that," said Master Crumb. "Get on back to the fields."

I took off running around the side of the house toward the quarters, but my feet didn't act as fast as my head. Next thing I knew, I tripped and found myself rolling downhill. Muddy, I looked up and there were the shoes.

"What ya doing over this way?" asked Two Shoes as he pulled me up.

"Getting something for Mama," I responded. His stare was hard. "She's waiting on me," I said as I ran off.

The next day, after he was found at McGrath's, Wilson was whipped. Whippings are terrible. No matter how many you've seen, you're never ready for the next one. They always made us watch.

Two Shoes stood behind Mr. Crumb, his face kept to the ground.

Something howled, then came a squawk, and the swamp woke up in a clatter. Ada sat up and watched the trees as if they were monsters on the attack. A thin trickle of blood ran down my face. I crawled to the riverbank and dipped my fingertips in a puddle, then rubbed the cool water on my hot head. I didn't have to see the bleeding to know I had to stop it.

So what you waiting on? That's what Old Joe back at Southerland woulda said to me. Yes, he was old as dirt. He was even old when I was little. He'd been with Master Crumb since Master Crumb was a child. Master Crumb's father had made a gift of Old Joe to his son on his wedding day. I'd seen many kinds of ways we moved from one place to another. We were sold, loaned, taken, and ran away, but gifting was the strangest. Gifts sound nice, but slave moving was always ugly. It didn't seem right to call it gifting.

Old Joe was a serious person and had survived years on the plantation. I'd learned plenty from watching him. I'd seen him tie off bleeding cuts. Now I took hold of my pant leg and tore a long piece of the wool, wrapped it twice around my head, and tucked in the end. I started to see about the bite on my ankle when Ada caught my attention.

"You hear that? I think they're coming for us." Ada's face went tight, and she stood up.

"Ada, ain't no monsters coming for us." I leaned back. She spun around with her ear cocked to the foggy sky.

"I ain't meaning monsters. The dogs," she said.

• 5 •

Homer

BETWEEN THE CHIRPING AND SWAMP RAUCOUS, there was barking.

"Far off?" Ada whispered.

"If we're hearing it, not far enough," I said. High bushes and walls of thick knotted vines surrounded us. "Come on," I ordered, pulling Ada toward a small opening of leaves.

"What about the monsters?" Ada asked.

"We go through here, or we go back off that riverbank. Which you think will keep us?" She stared down the bank at the running water.

"You think if we run faster we'd be able to fly this time?" Ada asked.

That was Ada, she wasn't one for giving up on dreams.

"Ada, get on this way." I pulled her through the small opening and deeper into the swamp.

With so many plants, trees, vines, and bushes, there was no clear path for running—you hardly knew which way to go anyway. Pushing through was the best we could do. Which way? Whichever way made the dog barking get quieter.

With no shoes to speak of and the ground so wet, we thought the muck would swallow us whole. Squawks and growls died down as we moved. It was like the swamp shut up and decided to watch us. I stepped and felt the muddy ground give way under me. A sinkhole. Mud and muck took my feet and then my legs.

"Homer!" Ada yelled. Arms flying, she reached out to me, but the hole kept pulling me down.

"Get something, Ada!" I called to her. "A stick, anything!"

Ada spun around, heaved back the weeds we'd come through, and disappeared. Each time I moved, the ground pulled me in more. In the muck, my leg caught a vine and the more I fought, the tighter it got. Mud swallowed up my waist.

"Ada!" I yelled. *"Ada!"*

I swear it was ten tobacco plantings before I saw the bushes shake. "I got a stick!" Ada called. It was more like a fallen branch, heavy and long. She shoved the branch my way, and I grabbed hold.

"Ada, get me up," I begged.

"All right!" she said.

I could hardly see her little body behind the bushy branch as she yanked.

I didn't budge.

"I'm sinking!" My chin was touching the muck.

"I'm trying," Ada cried, but I was going under all the same.

Then she braced the branch on a tree and pulled. I started moving. The vine around my leg gave way a little, and Ada hauled me from the water until I hit dry land.

"You did it!" I huffed.

She ran around the tree and climbed over the branch to me. I smiled but Ada didn't look happy. Instead, her mouth hung open.

"Your leg," she whispered. I didn't understand.

"What do you mean?" I asked.

"Homer, look." She pointed.

I looked down at my vine-tangled leg and saw no vine there at all. Coiled around my leg, thick as two fists put together, was a snake. Its head was raised, and it was considering my thigh, while its body, dark brown and shiny, tightened around my calf and foot.

I opened my mouth to scream, but the air in my chest disappeared. So Ada screamed for me.

The snake, maybe tired of fighting with my leg, maybe tired of my screaming sister, squeezed its coiled body tighter and opened its fanged mouth.

I didn't see the arrow coming, but I did hear it whiz through the air. It was like the zip of a hummingbird. So fast you couldn't see it, but you knew it was there.

I sat up. Beside me the snake lay dead with its fangs separated by an arrowhead.

Its body still held my leg tight, like it had plans for me even in death. I kicked it loose as Ada ran to me.

"You all right?" Ada asked.

"Uh-huh," I panted.

"An arrow got the snake." Ada said it like arrows falling from the sky was how it was meant to be.

"But who had the arrow?" I asked.

Overhead, fog clung to the trees. It was the fog that made him appear to be sent down like a bird from some other world, someplace…magical.

When he came through the cloud above Ada and me, his long arms and legs were outstretched like a hawk. He was free-falling, plunging through a path between the tree branches. Silent, he dropped until he neared the ground, where he grabbed hold of one branch then another to slow his fall and land on two feet before Ada and me.

I jumped back, almost rolling over the snake beside me. Ada didn't move a bit. She stood there, eyes wide open.

Homer

HE WAS THE MOST DIFFERENT PERSON I'D EVER seen. His skin was a sweet, deep, glowing hickory brown, with hair locked into long ropes that hung over his wide shoulders and down his back. His shirt was white, or it had been at some point, with a bit of ruffle cloth on the collar, and torn to tatters along the bottom. Across his chest was a fur strap that mounted to his back a bow and a quiver filled with snake-killing arrows. Around his waist were strange ropes I'd never seen before, like braided vines.

We were right in front of him, but he didn't even look at us.

Say something! I thought. But my voice was choked by all my thoughts. Ada broke the silence.

"You fly here from the clouds?" she asked, like that was the most important question.

He walked past her and stepped over me with animal-skin shoes. Grunting, he pulled the arrow from the dead snake, rubbed the bloody point on his pant leg, and placed it in his quiver.

Ada walked over and looked up at him.

"You fly other places? You ever fly North? We were going North, but then the dogs were after us and we couldn't fly so we got washed away by the river, then we came here," explained Ada.

Silence. Maybe he couldn't hear.

No matter, Ada pressed on. "You live in the swamp? You seen any monsters living in—"

His hand went up in front of her face. Where there should have been three fingers, there were smooth nubs, leaving only a thumb and its neighbor. Ada stopped in the middle of her thought and stared at the half hand in front of her. Then he motioned quiet to us both.

"Dogs," he whispered.

Through the thick bush came echoes of barking and shouting. "Come on back, darkies. We know you're in here, and these dogs are gonna find ya."

It was Stokes. I'd have known his voice anywhere.

Ada grabbed hold of me.

"Do we have to go back?" she whisper-shouted in my ear. Blood drained from Ada's face. We both knew what happened when you didn't do what Stokes told you.

"He's coming," she said.

Ada ran for a thick wall of bushes, tripping and falling as she went. My first thought was to join her, but curiosity made me peer back at the man.

He hadn't jumped at the sound of Stokes. Anyone with sense was scared of Stokes. But the man's face hadn't changed. Instead, he whipped his two-fingered hand out and caught hold of Ada's dress. Before she could say a word, he tore off a long piece of her hem. He made two thin strips, took two arrows from his quiver, and wrapped the cloth around the tip of each. From his pocket he brought a sticky brown lump of something and put a bit of it onto both arrowheads. From his other pocket he took out a match and put the wooden end of the stick into his mouth.

"Little darkies! Don't make me have to come in there and get you out!" yelled Stokes.

"We come after you and we'll tan you good!" Rick yelled.

"Quiet!" I heard Stokes say.

Southerland had come to the swamp.

The flying man still didn't run. Instead he turned to Ada and me and said, "Stay."

Stay! He must be crazy. But Ada and I didn't move an inch.

"If these dogs come in there and find ya, they'll tear ya to pieces. Come on out and I'll keep them off ya," Stokes promised.

The flying man pulled rope from his waist, lashed it around a tree trunk, and fast as a squirrel, he climbed up, disappearing into the leaves and branches.

"You see him?" asked Ada, her head craning upward.

"No," I said, listening for Stokes.

"You think he's coming back?" asked Ada.

"He has to come back—where else is he gonna go?" I said.

"Maybe he'll go flying off again," said Ada.

"I don't know, but I think we need to get out—"

I was trying to make a plan, then Stokes said, "We've got your mama, you little darkies." Ada took hold of my hand and squeezed until her nails cut into my skin.

"I know ya want to see your mama again, so come on out of there," Stokes said. Like the swamp heard him, hidden animals started chirping and hollering.

"He's got Mama," Ada said.

I heard him! my mind screamed.

"I don't wanna go to Stokes, but I want to see Mama," said Ada.

It seemed the flying man was gone, but then I saw a flame high in the tree, small as a pinhead flickering in the fog.

"It's him," I said, pointing for Ada to see. A flaming arrow arched over us and struck dry leaves. Smoke came first, then came fire, big and orange. It licked the trees, releasing a swarm of birds into the clouds. Another flame flew overhead, lighting a dead tree, sending up plumes of black smoke that scratched our noses. The air smelled like Mama's kitchen when the chimney needed cleaning.

"Swamp fire!" yelled another man.

"Get my dogs out of there!" yelled Stokes. "Get on out of there!" His voice trailed farther away.

Ada and I stood breathless. We knew we'd seen something unimaginable: a man even Stokes feared.

Homer

"HE SCARED OFF STOKES," BREATHED ADA. NO one scared Stokes—it was Stokes's job to do the scaring. But the flying man was unconcerned about what he'd done. Instead, he came down from that tree, tied his long, locked hair in a knot, pulled a small ax from his pouch, and started cutting a path through the plants, heading deeper into the tangled thicket.

He turned back, seeing that we weren't following him.

"How'd you learn to do that?" Ada called after him.

"Who are you?" I asked. "What are you doing in this here swamp?"

He shook his head and kept hacking away. Then he stopped and for the first time he stared right at me. A chill ran down my spine. He saw me.

"None of those are good questions," he said. "Here are some questions: Can you spot bear tracks in mud? Do you know how to keep snakes off you at night? Do you know how to hunt?"

"He doesn't know any of those things," chimed in Ada.

"Hush up!" I said, knowing she was right.

"Well, you don't," insisted Ada.

"Then you best follow me," said the man, and he went right back to his hacking.

Follow you where? Who knew where this man would take us? If Stokes had found us, as soon as Mama got away she could, too. Staying meant we'd be here when Mama came for us. This was all too much to explain to this snake-shooting, fire-starting man, and even harder to explain to Ada.

"We might as well go on," said Ada, and off she went running behind him.

"Ada!" I called.

I saw the man's head bobbing up and down in the bush, and right before he went out of sight, he said, "Suleman. My name is Suleman."

8

Anna

THE NIGHT HOMER AND ADA RAN FROM SOUTH-
erland plantation, Anna awoke with a start from the bark
of the dogs. Four others—a mother, father, and their two
children, also asleep on the dirt floor across the cabin—did
the same. They all knew what the sound meant. Runaways.
Someone had tried to escape. The four peered through the
cabin's small window. Anna went outside. She stepped into
the night as Stokes and two men ran past with the dogs,
their noses already sniffing the air.

"Get back in your cabin!" Stokes barked at her.

"Get back in there!" Rick and Ron echoed, running
behind Stokes.

Anna moved into the doorway's shadow and waited for
them to pass. *Who ran off? Sarah and her father? Or maybe the
two tall men, Clive and Henry? No.* Candlelight flickered in
their windows. In fact, there was light in each cabin apart
from one.

Can't be! she thought as she pushed the door open to
Homer's old home. Moonlight rushed in and shone on

elderly Mrs. Petunia, still snoring on the floor, with three empty blankets beside her.

Homer was gone. They all were.

A memory flooded her mind. In the early days, when she first met Homer, he hardly spoke or even looked at her. But she knew they'd become friends because in the quiet times his words would come. She knew that she was his best friend when he shared his secret.

They were alone one afternoon, sitting at the river's edge fishing for dinner.

Homer leaned in and whispered, "I can make myself invisible."

"What's invisible?" Anna asked. *Is that like making yourself happy or angry?* she wondered.

"It's when no one can see me," Homer said. Anna stared at him, her brow furrowed in confusion before stating the obvious.

"Homer, I can see you."

Homer sighed. "It's not like that. I do it when I need to."

Anna saw that he believed it. He was her friend, the only one she'd ever had. Maybe she should believe it, too.

"I could show you how," he said.

"All right," Anna said slowly.

Homer inhaled and his face went still. His lips moved only the slightest bit.

"You have to think yourself into nothing. Be where you are but don't see yourself there. I do it hard enough and most times no one even sees me," Homer explained.

Anna squinted her eyes at him.

"Are you doing it now? 'Cuz I still see you," she said.

"No, I'm not doing it now," said Homer, turning to face the water, his feelings crushed. "I do it back there." He gestured toward the plantation. "I was thinking you could use it with Mistress. Maybe it could help you." Homer threw a stone into the water.

"I suppose," said Anna, wanting to make things right with him.

"If she can't see you, maybe she won't get at you like she does," said Homer.

Anna exhaled.

"I don't know. As soon as she gets in one of her ways, I become..." Anna thought. "What's the opposite of invisible? Red? Yeah, I'm like shining red, and she hits me." She let out a sad laugh.

"Yeah, I suppose you're right." Homer laughed, too, so as not to let her laugh alone.

Anna smiled at the memory, gazed about the cabin, then whispered his name.

"Homer."

When no one answered in return, apart from Mrs. Petunia's snore, she knew Homer wasn't invisible. He was gone. What's more, Homer had been wrong. He couldn't make himself invisible. An invisible boy couldn't have men and dogs chasing after him in the middle of the night. Even if Homer didn't know it, he was real.

She closed the door, silently forgave Homer for leaving her behind, found the North Star in the sky, and wished her real friend well.

9

Homer

AFTER TRUDGING THROUGH THE SWAMP FOR much of the day, I felt sweat soaked through my shirt. Ada had gone silent. Only thirst, hunger, or fear quieted Ada.

Finally, we came to a small clearing with water. Ada and I ran to it.

The water was still and bright green as a new spring leaf.

"You think we can drink it?" Ada asked.

"Green water is better than no water," I said, sounding more sure than I felt. I put my hand in, and like the skin on hot milk, the green broke and tea-brown water poured through. I filled my hands and drank. It tasted of the earth on a cool day.

Ada watched then followed me, gulping a few times.

"This brown water tastes good. It looks all old, but it tastes like a clean forest," said Ada.

Suleman joined us, gulping loud and strong, then pouring water over his face and atop his hair, and again, he glowed.

Before I knew it, he was down on one knee right next to me. His sweat smelled of ripe fruit.

"Let me take a look," he said, touching my bandage.

My stomach tightened, but I let him. Cool fingertips brushed my forehead as he unwrapped the cloth. A warm breeze hit my raw flesh.

"Homer, it's all red and pink," moaned Ada, turning pale.

"They hit you?" he asked.

I shook my head. "It was the river."

"It needs cleaning." He tilted my head down and scooped water onto my cut. It stung, but the cold felt welcome as it dribbled down my neck and back.

"The cut's wide, but not deep. I suspect that was a hard hit. You'll need to watch yourself," he warned, wrapping the cloth back around my head.

The water felt so good, I dipped my sore, dog-bitten foot into it.

I was wondering what would come next when Suleman stepped into a thicket beside the water and pulled. Like magic, we saw a cut-down tree trunk, rounded with the insides scraped out. With a push, it went right into the water and floated like a leaf.

Ada gasped. "It's a tree boat," she said. "I never seen a tree boat. You suppose we're gonna ride in that tree?" As she said it, you could tell she was excited. I wasn't so sure.

"Get in." Suleman said it like there was no question that riding in a tree was a good idea.

Ada and I waded over. Lying in the boat's bottom were long sticks. I picked up Ada and put her in the well. It was deep enough to swallow up half her body. Suleman helped me in, handed me a stick, then he started rowing.

"It works! We're moving like a twig in water. When we go North, I want one of these," said Ada.

I watched Suleman and taught myself to row along with him. We moved between trees that grew up from the water, with not a scrap of soil in sight. Great big lily pads lay side by side like floating tablecloths. Birds swooped down, stood on the pads, and watched us. Drips and spots of light sprinkled through the tangle of vines, knotted wood, and leaves.

"Mrs. Petunia never told me about the flowers," said Ada, picking a yellow one about the size of her hand from a lily pad as our boat passed by.

Flowers were growing right out of the water while others spilled down from tree branches: Tiny white ones clumped together like a cloud on land; big orange ones sprang out of the riverbank.

"It's pretty," Ada said. "Not pretty like we know, swamp pretty."

I wished Mama could have been there to see. She loved flowers. Maybe she would see them when she came to find us.

Forest, river, vines and bush, watch for the sinkhole, more vines and bush, green water, then the tree boat. Those were the steps. I whispered them to myself. If we could get here, she could, too. All I needed to do was remember the steps.

Dark holes and shadows were all about, with strange noises and echoes coming from them. Snakes slithered in the water. *Maybe monsters were real.*

Soon the waterway became narrower and the brush so thick it made an impassable wall before us. There was nowhere to go. Suleman stopped rowing, took his bow and arrows off, and unwrapped the vine rope from around his waist. Then, like it was nothing, he dove headfirst off the boat and into the tea-water.

"Hey!" I shouted. But it was too late. He'd already disappeared.

"You see that, Homer? You think he can swim?" Ada asked.

"Well, I suppose he wouldn't have jumped in there unless he could," I said.

"But there ain't no place to swim to," said Ada.

We studied the water around the boat. Nothing.

"What if he sunk down to the bottom? What if he doesn't come back or he decided to go off North by himself, seeing as how he can swim and fly?" said Ada.

"Why's he gonna leave us here with his tree boat?" I asked, trying to make sense of it myself.

"That's true. I sure enough wouldn't want to leave behind a tree boat, even for going North," said Ada.

"Look." I pointed.

The wall of brush in front of us shook and shimmied, and before long its middle swung open like the door of a chicken coop. Suleman stood inside the small waterway, tied the branch door open, then swam to the boat and jumped back in.

"That's your secret door?" Ada asked.

For the first time Suleman glanced back at Ada and answered her question.

"Yes," he said with all seriousness.

10

Homer

FOREST, RIVER, VINES AND BUSH, WATCH FOR THE
sinkhole, more vines and bush, green water, tree boat, lily pads,
secret water door. The secret door would be tricky. How
would Mama know where to find it? Hmmm. She'd find
Suleman first, then Suleman would help her find the door.
He'd found us, he'd find her.

We ducked down and floated through the doorway.
Suleman tied the door shut behind us. The rest of the day
was spent rowing, then walking through swamp when the
waters grew shallow, then rowing some more.

Before long, it was dusk, and fog was settling on the
water.

"It's like rowing in the clouds," whispered Ada.

Through the mist came a bank of dry land.

"We sleep here," said Suleman.

Here! Big trees with long weeping leaves made a half
circle around the bank. Darkness was coming. If monsters
were real, this would be where they'd come for dinner.

Suleman walked past me, his bow and arrow in hand.

"Now that you're free, there's much for you to learn," he said.

Free. That sounded strange. There was no North, no pretty houses, no Mama. I didn't even know there could be freedom without Mama. My heart sank.

Suleman loaded his bow, pulled it tight, aimed toward Ada across the way, and fired. As the arrow went whizzing toward her, I remembered we were in the middle of nowhere with a flying man we didn't even know.

"Ada!" I yelled. The arrow passed so close she could have kissed it.

Behind her, a weasel was pinned to a tree by Suleman's arrow.

"You got something!" Ada clapped like it was a trick.

In no time, Suleman had the weasel skinned, on a stick, and ready for cooking.

"You gonna start a fire?" I asked.

"Not out here," he said.

He touched the biggest tree, felt along the trunk, then pulled. The bark came off to uncover a hollow inside.

Suleman entered.

"A secret tree hideout!" Ada said, running to it.

"Wait!" I said. "Who knows what's in there? Maybe this is where Suleman takes all the kids he finds and eats them!"

Ada giggled. "Now *you* sound like Mrs. Petunia."

A fire pit was dug in the middle. Bows hung on a wall of roots.

Suleman brought some dry shrubs and sticks to the fire pit.

"It's nice." Ada pulled me inside. "Why don't you use your matches?" Suleman rubbed the sticks together, then blew a little until smoke started.

"My matches are for work," said Suleman.

"Which plantation do you belong to?" asked Ada.

"No plantation ever had me. Not here." Suleman pointed to his head. "I ran three times." He held up his two-fingered hand. "The overseer took one each time. Now, plantations belong to me," said Suleman.

"How long you been in this swamp?" I asked.

"More time than I know to count," said Suleman.

"What do you mean, plantations belong to you? How do you get a plantation?" Ada couldn't understand it, and I couldn't either.

I'd seen folks try running away. Seen 'em caught and lashed until you couldn't tell skin was ever smooth on their backs. I swear I could feel my own back go hot and bleed, like I'd been hit myself. I learned how hurting can be caught, like a cold, or the pox. That's the thing about plantations: Even if you stay away from being hit, you can't keep away from the hurting.

"Which plantation had you two?" asked Suleman.

41

"We're Master Crumb's at Southerland," I whispered.

"Is that right?" Suleman took the weasel on a stick and stuck it into the fire. "You still his?" Suleman asked, looking at me with iron eyes.

My face went warm. That's why I didn't like saying things, because too many times what you said could turn out to be the wrong thing. I shook my head. "I s-s-suppose not," I stuttered. I half expected Stokes or Master Crumb to jump out, but nothing happened.

Instead, Suleman nodded and gazed into the fire along with me. "I know which place you mean," said Suleman. "Old Joe stays there."

"You know Old Joe?" Ada's eyes got wide.

I'd spent most of my life following Old Joe, learning this, helping with that, and never once did he mention Suleman. *What else didn't I know?*

"I know people all around those parts. It's my work to know things. I get to know plantations and take what they don't have any right to," said Suleman.

"How you do that?" I asked.

"I have my ways. I know I like Crumb's shirts." Fire flames danced in his eyes as he said it.

"Here," he said, tearing off two pieces from the weasel and passing them to Ada and me.

"You're wearing one of Master Crumb's shirts." As I said it, I knew it was true. If he'd have been wearing a shirt made of gold, I wouldn't have been as surprised. I recalled when this particular shirt went missing; Crumb had cursed. Stokes had searched the slave cabins. I'd seen many things in the past day, but seeing this flying man wearing Master Crumb's shirt was a sign that there was more to the world than I'd ever known.

That night I closed my eyes tight to block out the strange howls, buzzes, and whines of the swamp. I whispered the steps for Mama in my head. If I said them, she'd know them. *Forest, river, vines and bush, watch for the sinkhole, more vines and bush, green water, tree boat, lily pads, secret water door, tree hideout.* I said it to myself once, then a second time, as I fell asleep.

11

Nora

FROM THE MOMENT NORA OPENED HER EYES that morning she knew something was wrong. Her window let in the bitter smell of things burned, not the scent of fresh-baked biscuits she was used to.

"Nora! Nora!" Her mother's voice bounced up the stairs and along the walls and ceiling of Southerland's Big House until it met Nora's room at the back end of the hall.

"Nora, are you up? The dressmaker will be here any minute. Don't have me come up there to get you!"

Nora gave no answer. Despite her being eleven, none was expected. But she didn't want to wait around for her mother.

"That child, we can't have this today!" Mrs. Crumb complained.

Nora went to her window and observed the kitchen. About twenty yards from the house, the squat, odd-shaped structure had tendrils of smoke coming from its open window and door. Out of the kitchen came Petunia. Old age had hunched her over. She shook flour from her apron, wiped sweat from her deep brown brow, rubbed her cataract-filled eyes, and coughed into the fresh air. Before long,

Petunia caught her breath and wobbled toward the dairy shed.

Age had taken Petunia out of the kitchen years before. *This morning is all wrong*, thought Nora. *Where is Rose?*

Nora pulled a gingham dress from her wardrobe and tugged it on. As her head came through the hole of her dress, she caught her reflection in the mirror. Brown hair fell past her shoulders. She combed strands over the left side of her face. The gesture hid her red strawberry mark.

"Your lucky number must be eight," her father used to joke. "'Cuz your mark is just like the eight legs of an octopus."

She'd pulled him to the library and motioned for him to show her. He'd obliged and shown her a drawing in one of his books. Sure enough he was right. An oval-shaped octopus head marked her temple, and from it sprang eight curving marks. Two that stretched to her left eyebrow, another three that unwound along her cheekbone, and another three that traveled down her jawline. The image was so exact that some might have considered it a talisman, a unique mark for a unique person. But that was not the case for Nora. That bit of strawberry had set the path for her upbringing.

When Nora was born, her mother was shocked by her daughter's coloring. Mrs. Crumb examined the perfectly unmarked face of her other daughter and declared her new baby was unwell and in need of special care.

Rose was ordered to wean little Homer and directed to care for Baby Nora. Rose became Nora's wet nurse, and a bassinette was moved into the kitchen. In between preparing meals, Rose fed little Nora, first from her breast, then from the simmering pots of soups, stews, and meats she prepared each day. Eventually, a small room was built onto the kitchen for Rose. Apart from Saturday when she slept in the quarters, Rose slept in that room.

Time passed and no moves were made to end the arrangement. Contrary to her mother's predictions, Nora grew strong. A tutor was brought in to help with Nora's studies. She was quick to learn to read and write. First she read the entire book her father had shown her about sea creatures. Soon she knew that the octopus was highly intelligent, able to hide in plain sight and sneak into just about any space. It was mischievous. Nora liked to think that she could be all of those things. Perhaps she was an octopus.

That first book led her to many more. She spent her days in the kitchen with Rose, face buried in the pages. Mrs. Crumb lamented about Nora's ways and reasoned that books had taken her daughter's voice, because Nora never had words to speak. Doctors had been brought in to check the child's health. There was no medical reason for her lacking voice. She simply chose not to speak. Perhaps she was afraid that she would not be heard.

Mrs. Crumb hoped the mark would fade and with time Nora's words would run fast like a river. But now that she was eleven, it was clear the mark would not budge, nor would her tongue.

The back stairs near Nora's bedroom were dark, narrow, and meant for servants to come and go without notice. Nora considered them hers. She counted the steps as she eased down. *Step one, two, skip three (because it creaked), four,* and so on.

"But Mama," whined Viola, "the wedding's only a month away. How can Rose be sick?"

"Don't you worry yourself, Viola sweetheart. We'll be sure Rose is here for the cooking. The wedding will be perfect. Nora!" called Mrs. Crumb.

Nora listened and waited.

"We have the dressmaker coming, and if I don't get that girl up, she won't be presentable for anything," Mrs. Crumb groaned.

"Presentable? The whole county's going to be here. Between that mark all over her face and her acting dumb and sitting at the front table for God and man to see, Mama, it's gonna be nothing but embarrassing! Why can't she stay in the kitchen?" whined Viola.

"Now, stop fretting. We're gonna cover that mark, and

your sister will be needing to be on her best behavior for your wedding. Don't you worry, she *will* be," said Mrs. Crumb.

Step five, step six, went Nora, down the stairs. Opening the back door, Nora slipped out and walked the twenty yards to the kitchen.

It was empty. Spilled flour, melted butter, and eggshells littered the table and floor. Nora shook her head. Rose would be livid at the sight. A metal tray of burned biscuits sat at the end of a wooden table. Nora bit one, breaking the hard, dark exterior and sinking her teeth into a raw dough center. *Awful*, she thought. With a slow chew, Nora swallowed it. Seeing nothing more to eat, she ate two more.

Tucked behind the far kitchen wall opposite the stove was Rose's room. A floral scent of roses wafted from it. Dried flowers, picked off the ground by Rose, lined the walls of her small domicile. The cot against the wall was empty. Nora knew it well. She went over and sat on it and wished for Rose's return. During the night, when bad dreams or loneliness became particularly intolerable, Nora would come to Rose's room.

"You sleep here," Rose would say, giving her the bed and rolling out a mat for herself. "Lord knows what Master would do if he found you sleeping on the floor." And Rose was right. There were nights when Papa discovered Nora in Rose's room. He always took her back to bed. Thankfully, he never told anyone.

Nora examined the empty space and anxiety welled up inside of her. *Where was Rose?* To her further dismay, when she came out of Rose's room, Anna was in the kitchen sweeping up flour. Hot embarrassment came over Nora for having been caught in Rose's room. It was a secret that she even went in there. But since Anna came, with her watchful eyes, the kitchen didn't feel like Rose and Nora's anymore.

Out the kitchen door, down the hill from the Big House, Nora ran toward the quarters. Before long, she heard her father's raised voice coming from one cabin.

Through the slats of the cabin, Nora peeped in.

"You're gonna have to salt these lashes before infection sets in," Crumb grumbled. There was a long moan.

Nora gasped. Rose was there.

"Yes, sir," said Stokes.

"Now!" barked Crumb.

"You heard him—go get the salt and water," ordered Stokes of Rick and Ron. The two hurried out of the cabin. Crumb leaned over Rose.

"God knows she won't be any good to work for a time, and we've got the wedding coming," he huffed. "You do this, Stokes?"

"I had the boys, Rick and Ron, take it on. They're learnin' to do things properly," said Stokes.

"Y'all got me in a heap of trouble with this, you see. And if she can't work? You think about that? Sure, slaves need whipping, but you need to know how and when!" said Crumb as he spat in frustration.

"I did her like I would any other runaway. They need to learn," said Stokes.

"Yeah, but I have a wedding coming and a Mistress who ain't gonna care about nothing other than getting this one back in the kitchen to cook for it," said Crumb.

Soon, Rick and Ron came through the door, one with a pail of water, the other with salt spilling from a large burlap bag.

"Papa, Papa, breakfast!" Viola called in the distance.

Crumb went to the cabin door. "We'll be there directly, Sweet Pea," he yelled.

Rick and Ron stood with their heads bowed to the ground.

"And the boy and girl?" asked Crumb.

"They'll turn up," said Stokes, rocking from one foot to the other. "We had a good chase on them, had to stop when fire broke out. I'll get right back out there."

"How's a boy and a small girl manage to escape? I've seen many grown men caught by now," asked Crumb.

"We'll find them," chimed in Rick and Ron.

Crumb shook his head in disapproval. "Stokes, get those wounds cleaned," he said and exited the cabin.

Stokes pulled Rose onto her stomach. Her shirt was torn. Rivulets of blood streaked across her back. Nora gasped again.

Then came the salt and a bloodcurdling scream that rattled through every cabin on the path in the quarters. Nora ran. When she reached the top of the hill she stopped. Her stomach tumbled and twisted. She grabbed her knees and heaved up every piece of dry biscuit she'd eaten. It took some moments to catch her breath. When she did, she saw Anna standing outside watching her. Without a word, Anna walked back to the kitchen.

• 12 •

Homer

I DREAMT OF ANNA. SADNESS SPILLED FROM her eyes as she said over and over, "You promised me. You promised me."

Anna, I said. *I'm sorry.*

But that didn't change her chant. Her words rang in my ears and left my chest so heavy I couldn't move.

I awoke to Suleman's hand over my mouth, his palm pressing on my lips, and the sting of his two fingernails cutting into my wet cheek. Raindrops dripped from an open hole above us in the tree trunk.

Ssshhhh. Suleman motioned. He awoke a drowsy Ada, and silent as ghosts we left the tree hideout.

Anna's face haunted me as we got back to the boat and rowed on without saying one word. She was my friend and I'd made a promise to her. It was the sort of promise that made my heart ache.

A few days before Mama woke us up in the dead of night to go North, I was in Southerland's flower garden in the July heat, fetching water for thirsty plants meant to be kept per-fect for the big wedding. It was dreadful hard work. But the flowers were blooming and covered each bush in red, pink, white, and yellow.

As I watered, I heard Mrs. Crumb's shrill hollering in the Big House. The back door slammed. Anna, who always moved with a sure foot, wobbled down the stairs and hid herself under my biggest rosebush. Her deep brown skin was wet with tears. Pink roses hung all around her face, which was swelling to one side, and blood began collecting in one of her amber eyes.

"I hate that wedding," said Anna. "She told me to move Miss Nora's dress from the wardrobe to the bed, and I was doing it. I didn't even see that it had caught on something."

"Here," I said, taking a small rag from my pocket and dipping it in my bucket of cool water. "Put this on there, before it puffs up."

Anna didn't even try reaching for the rag. Instead she stared straight ahead at the garden.

"I wish fire would rain down from the sky on that lady," said Anna. She was quiet a long while, then as if she'd made up her mind about something, she said, "When I'm gone, you be sure to remember me. I ain't been many places long enough to be remembered."

"What do you mean gone?" I asked, but she didn't say a word. Her eyes were far away.

"I told you, I'm gonna find my way North," Anna promised the damp hot air as she rubbed her arm. I half believed she would.

I wet the cloth again, folded it, and dabbed her eye. It was round as a walnut.

"You could come with me," she whispered. "When I find a way, I could tell you. If you find a way, you could tell me."

I'd have said anything to make her better.

"What about Mama and Ada?" I asked.

"There's bound to be all sorts of fine places to live in the North. We could find one for all of us."

"All right," I said.

"Promise," said Anna, serious as sin.

"I promise," I said, to make Anna feel better and mostly because I didn't believe it could happen, not then, maybe not ever. I didn't know Mama was thinking to have us run off.

Now here I was. I'd lost Anna and Mama.

It was the second morning since we'd run off. We rowed and watched the sun wash the clouds away.

"Suleman, you think we should've stayed in the tree hideout?" asked Ada.

We stopped at the water's edge, put the boat under more shrubs, and set off walking again.

"You'll be needing a place to stay" was all Suleman said.

Stay? Out here? I thought. A ghost wouldn't be caught dead out here. But Ada and I followed along. We got to a clearing, where Suleman stared into the leaves overhead. With his two-fingered hand in the air, he motioned for us to stop. An arrow shot from the leafy heaven above us. It zipped through the air and landed at Suleman's feet. I grabbed Ada and pulled her to the ground. Suleman didn't take cover. Instead, he looked into the trees and let out a call, a high-pitched whistle.

Like a breeze swept through the clearing, leaves shook and danced on the trees, swishing and fluttering at once. Then as if by magic, the trees came alive. Branches turned into legs, then arms, and leaves into faces.

They came down from the trees and landed on the ground before us.

· 13 ·

Nora

THAT SAME RAINY MORNING, NORA HAD GONE
back to the quarters to peek at Rose through the cabin slats.
Rose was deep in sleep with Petunia at her side. Not wanting to be heard, Nora backed away from the cabin and
caught wind of bickering coming from Stokes's shed. Peering in she saw Rick and Ron, the two men responsible for
Rose's pain.

"You carry the water jug!" said Rick.

"Why do I always have to carry the water jug? You carry
it, and I'll pack the pocketknife," said Ron.

"You're the one who's gonna be complaining about thirst
as soon as we step foot in that swamp," said Rick.

Back and forth they went as they prepared for their
return to the swamp to catch Homer and Ada. They'd never
chased runaways deep in the swamp, and Nora watched as
they packed just about anything they could think of. Some
matches, string, a blanket, a towel, a hat, a rifle. They'd
probably need a long knife for cutting wood and other
swamp things. They'd have to get a proper one from the
toolshed. That would take some doing.

Nora went to the kitchen in search of something fitting for Rick and Ron's first runaway-hunting trip. After all, they'd hurt Rose. Mrs. Petunia didn't see and Anna didn't comment when Nora reached for two fist-sized cuts of raw meat awaiting the evening meal. She wrapped them each in an old sock and as Rick and Ron were commandeering a long knife, Nora stealthily placed a meat-filled sock in the bottom of each of their packs. Nora had her octopus ways.

Stokes

KNIVES ACQUIRED, RICK AND RON STRAPPED their heavy loads to their backs. When Stokes saw the two of them and their oversized packs, he shook his head.

"We ain't going camping," he said.

"You think it's too much?" asked Ron.

"No," sneered Stokes, "unless you've got a tent in there."

"We don't! Just a blanket," assured Ron.

Stokes shook his head again.

"Since we got the mama already," Rick announced, "I'm thinking we'll get the rest for sure this time!"

Ignoring him, Stokes gave orders to his overexcited in-laws.

"We head back to where the fire started—we should find a scent from there," said Stokes.

By the time they made it to that place, Ron had toppled down a riverbank and been pulled from two mud pits, Rick had been bitten by a shower of mosquitoes, and they both stunk. All three of the runaway chasers' clothing had been torn by prickly bushes and vines.

Exhausted, Ron and Rick asked in unison, "Stokes, how much longer you suppose we'll have to walk?"

Stokes didn't answer. He sent his dog one way, then another. It took some time to realize the dog had led them in a circle.

"Wait." Stokes stopped. He pulled at nearby vines and brush and held them up. Freshly cut ends caught the light. "This way," he said, and let the dog lead the way through a new path that ended at green water.

"Who ever heard of green water?" Rick asked as he splashed it on Ron.

"Hey, cut it out!" yelped Ron.

"Quiet, the both of you!" hissed Stokes.

Odd sounds and howls echoed from the dark shadows of the swamp. The three men stared into the swaying leaves overhead.

"Look here." Stokes pointed. There were prints in the mud. Several small ones, but one set that was deep and wide. Those prints went from the water's edge and off toward a thicket of brush. Growling, the dog pulled the leash hard toward it. The thicket shuddered.

"Somebody's in there," Rick said, moving forward.

"I'll get him!" whispered Ron.

"No, I'll get him!" argued Rick.

"Wait, fellas!" Stokes whispered.

Each convinced that this was their heroic moment, Ron and Rick pounced, pulling back the thicket.

"We've got you now!" they shrieked.

The black, furry head of a bear met Rick and Ron. Having been rudely disturbed, it confronted the men nose-to-nose, teeth bared, eyes angry, and growled.

Hot bear breath warmed their shocked faces. In unison they both screamed. *"AAAAHHH!"*

The bear joined them. *GGGRRRRAAAHHH!*

"Run!" Stokes shouted. The scent of meat in their packs hit the bear's nose and it charged, catching hold of Rick's pack and digging its teeth in.

"It got me!" Rick yelped as the bear pulled the pack from his back, then it went after the next pack.

"Murderation, it got me, too!" Ron yelled.

Rick and Ron took off hollering. Stokes watched them and shook his head in disapproval.

• 15 •

Homer

WHEN I WAS LITTLE AND I STILL LET PEOPLE SEE me, I took to playing in the mud. I would wipe the cool, cinnamon-brown mud all over myself and pretend it was a new skin. Then I'd run up to the kitchen and peek my face in the window. Mama would get so upset, she'd pull her pots from the fire and take me to the water's edge.

She'd wet my legs, arms, and face, and rub her hands up and down my skin, pushing away mud that didn't want to leave. I'd sit there smiling. It would be just the two of us, in the middle of the day. That was our mud time.

When my skin was slick with water, she'd put my face in her hands, kiss my forehead, like she always did to me and Ada, and say, "You be sure to keep clean, and get on back to the quarters." I remember running back always feeling light as a feather.

As I eyed the three people in front of me, that mud time came to mind. Deep rust-colored mud covered their skin. Leaves and branches, strung on by vines and rope, looped around their heads and hair, down their bellies and to their toes. They were trees come to life, with no telling where leaves and mud stopped and where their bodies began.

"Tree people," Ada whispered. "You think they're the monsters Mrs. Petunia talked about?"

"Suleman," the shortest tree man said, smiling through his face of leaves.

"David," Suleman said back. They hugged.

"Everyone will be happy to hear you're living free," said David.

Suleman smiled for the first time. "Is there any other way to live?"

Ada walked over to the tallest of the tree people. "Y'all nice tree people?" she asked.

"Ibra," said the tall tree man. He put a leafy hand on his chest as he said it. Ada pulled Ibra's arm until the tree bent down to her height.

"Ada," she said, patting her chest. "I knew there'd be monsters in the swamp."

"Did you?" said Ibra. His branch head tipped to one side, confused. Ada didn't even notice.

"Don't you worry, I won't tell one soul about you," said Ada.

"Good," Ibra said.

"And these two?" the third tree person asked. A branched hand pointed my way. A tree woman. She was dipped in mud with thick, deep green leaves covering her from head to toe. A nest of braided vines wrapped about her head, and two amber eyes watched me. They were the same color as Anna's. But where Anna's had a million years of patience, this tree woman's eyes were full of salt and vinegar.

"These two found their own way out," Suleman said.

"Have we had two so young come to us on their own?" Ibra asked, his dark tree eyes watching us.

"I'm seven," Ada piped up, like she was grown. I tugged her arm to quiet her.

"No," said David. "They're brave little ones."

Who were these people? They didn't know I'd ruined everything and that it was my fault our mother wasn't with us. Ada stood there looking at me. She knew. Even with all her talking and questioning, she didn't say anything. We may not look a speck alike, but she never felt more like my sister.

"Trackers?" the tree woman asked Suleman.

"Yes, with dogs," said Suleman.

"More will come," said the tree woman.

"Daria, we have our patrols. We'll be watching," said David.

"They won't settle for two children running off. Makes it look like more could run. Each time they track, they come in farther," said Daria.

Suleman nodded in agreement.

"We should move," she said.

"We will," said David; still, he paused and touched Suleman's shoulder. "Were you able to bring back things?"

"No. These two came," said Suleman.

"Yes, right, of course, of course," said David. "We need tools. The swamp provides, but the tools help us grow."

"None this time," said Suleman.

David nodded. "All right, we'll go. But come with us. We'll have a wedding soon. Come and be safe."

Suleman shook his head. "I don't care for being safe."

David smiled. "Suleman, you have enough courage for all of us," said David. "Take this." From a leafy sack, he pulled a chunk of stiff yellow cake. "We expect a good harvest this year."

Suleman took the cake, tore off a piece, and chewed. The rest he put in his pack as he headed back toward the bush. Ada ran for him.

"Suleman, you're leaving us here?" she asked.

"It's okay. You go with them." He motioned.

"You got somewhere else to fly to now?" Ada asked with seriousness.

"In a way," said Suleman. In time, everyone found it easier bending to Ada's view.

"You think they're gonna make us into tree people?" asked Ada.

"They're aiming to take you someplace safe. Maybe tend to that head," Suleman said, glancing at my bandage.

I looked around. There were all kinds of words the swamp made me feel, but safe wasn't one of them. And where did Mama fit into all of this? The farther we went, the harder it would be for her to find us.

"Now, you go on with them," said Suleman, almost out of sight.

"Hey!" Ada called after him. "Bye," she said, pulling down three fingers and waving goodbye with the two left over.

Suleman returned the two-finger wave, then he was gone.

Homer

"WE MUST MOVE," SAID DARIA AGAIN ONCE Suleman had disappeared into the bush.

"Come," said David, and with a gentle hand he put Ada and me in a line with the tree people. First Daria, then David, then me and Ada next, and Ibra in the back. We set off, one behind the other, but not going straight forward. Instead, we moved like a five-person snake sliding through the swamp. Even when the brush was low enough to walk straight forward we'd turn, walking this way, then that way, zigzagging on a veiled path. It was the strangest thing. *Is this how tree people walk?* I wondered, but I didn't dare ask.

Ada got tired or bored and started to tarry, hanging back a little longer and not following as close. I could tell Ibra didn't have any little sisters because he didn't know what to do. He fell right into Ada's *What's this?* trap.

Ada would stop and touch this leaf or that plant or this tree bark and ask, "What's this?" Ibra, who I now knew was a nice, patient person, was entertaining every question.

"What's this?" Ada would ask in her singsong voice.

"It's a sweet gum."

"What's that?"

"Them's blackberries," and sure enough they started to fall behind.

"What's this?"

"Them's maple leaves."

Finally, I'd had it.

"Ada, you come on!" I called to her.

"All right!" Ada said. But she'd lost sight of our mysterious winding path, and before Ibra could stop her, Ada went running straight forward.

"Wait!" Ibra shrieked. Ada went charging into the underbrush.

It didn't take but a second before I heard her scream, high and thin, like a deer caught in a trap. Ibra jumped into the brush, and with one of his long arms, he lifted Ada out.

I started to run to get her, but David grabbed my shirt.

"Wait," he said. He leaned down and pointed to small white dots poking out of the brush. "Careful." He gently pulled apart the brush beside us to show that each white dot was the sharp tip of a wooden spear dug into the ground. I touched one of 'em and it stuck me good. "We put them here for the catchers."

A sea of white points spread out all around us, save for the small zigzag of places where we'd walked.

"The grass cut me," Ada whimpered. "I ain't never seen

mean grass." Ada's clothes were torn and crisscross cuts were all about her legs.

Ibra touched one of the deep cuts, then went back down the zigzag path until he got to one of Ada's *What's this?* plants. He tore a few leaves from it.

"Keep still," he patiently commanded Ada. Liquid sprang from the stems in his hands and Ibra dripped the plant water on the cuts. Then he pulled the vines, twigs, and branches from his back, lifted Ada onto it, and stood. Through her tears, Ada set out giggling.

"Look, Homer, I'm riding a tree!" cried Ada.

"You planning to have that girl on your back for this?" Daria asked Ibra like she didn't much care for the idea.

"I'll manage," said Ibra, patting Ada's foot.

With an impatient frown, Daria went back to zigzag walking.

I appreciated lining up after that.

We walked until we met a maple tree surrounded by soppy wet ground. There was space for us all to sit where its base of knotted roots rose out of the mud. Yellow cake like David had given to Suleman was passed to me and Ada. The cake crumbled in my mouth. It was corn. I'd need Mama with me to say what more it had mixed in, but I knew it was corn. *Oh, Mama,* I thought, looking about, *you would never believe this.*

Forest, river, vines and bush, watch for the sinkhole, more

vines and bush, green water, tree boat, lily pads, secret water door,
tree hideout, more rowing and walking, tree people, zigzag through
the brush, I said to myself. Mama would need to be careful.
She'd need to know she couldn't walk straight or the spikes
would get her like they did Ada. She might bend down and
notice the white dots, but maybe not. If she could get to the
tree people, they'd help her. She could find them, and then
they could find us.

"You think we'll keep on walking like this forever?"
Ada whispered to me.

The Big House and the fields aren't places for questions.
My way was to *see* what needed learning. That's how Old Joe
and I did. We could go half a day without saying no more
than a few words. But things needed asking at some point.

"Where are we going?" I put my question to David, who
seemed like knowing things was his business.

"We have to keep moving," he said.

"Where?" I asked again.

"Now, we go up," said David.

"Huh?" I asked.

"Up." He said it natural, like he was saying left or right.

"Up? Up where?"

"We best move. We want to get there before dark,"
Daria said. She took a vine rope from her waist, wrapped it
around the maple, and climbed into the tree branches and
leaves overhead.

"We're going up *there*?" Ada's eyes followed Daria up the tree.

Ibra and David unwrapped their vines as Daria did.

Ada pulled my arm and whispered, "They're gonna make us into tree people." There wasn't a pinch of fear in her voice.

"Wait!" I said. *He couldn't mean up there!* I didn't much care for the world down here, but at least I knew it. "I thought we were going someplace safe."

"Down here, the swamp owns us. Up there, we own the swamp," said David.

With that, he tied a length of rope around my waist, then lashed it around the tree. Ibra put Ada on his back and tied two lengths of rope around them both, like a shell on a turtle.

"Feel for the pegs and use them to climb," David said.

Then like there was nothing weird about it, he was up the tree, grabbing at pegs buried in the vines. I couldn't hardly believe it.

"Come on, then," called David.

"It's all right—keep your eyes up as you climb," said Ibra.

"It's all right," Ada repeated, like she knew anything about anything.

I half felt like I was starting to live in one of her imaginings with flying men, secret swamp doors, tree people, and now this.

I pushed my hand into the leafy trunk and felt rough pegs sticking out like small tree arms. I grabbed one and put my foot on another and pulled myself up, then I felt for more.

We climbed, and the swamp fog lifted as we got over the dark blanket of trees and leaves. Sunset from the west warmed my back.

"You think we're going right up to heaven?" asked Ada from below me.

"Not that far," Ibra said.

"Think we're gonna see birds flying up there?" she asked.

"Might be some," said Ibra.

"We're gonna go walking across the sky!" yelled Ada.

"Ada, quit all that wild talk!" I'd about had it with her imagining.

"But look, Homer!" Ada yelled.

You ever seen something that don't seem real? I've seen a few things. Like the time Jenny the horse had a little baby horse. I tell you I couldn't half believe my eyes when it came out. First it wasn't there, then it was, all big-eyed and wobbly. Old Joe said don't, but I touched it. I like to make sure of things.

I stopped climbing to be certain I was seeing right. Ropes knotted together and strung from our tall tree to some other far-off tree made a bridge.

"She's walking across the sky!" Ada pointed.

There was Daria on the sky bridge, floating over the swamp below. She was so far away she was like one of the small stick dolls Old Joe made for the children in the quarters. Daria stopped, put a horn to her mouth, lifted her face, and blew a long moan.

There, up high, without all the swamp trees around, I swear that sound went straight up to heaven.

· 17 ·

Homer

THE BRIDGE WAS THREE SIDED, LIKE AN UPSIDE-down triangle. The bottom was a thick rope a little wider than my foot. From it came two sides, with thinner rope connecting it to the base and ending at just about my waist, where you could hold on. You'd have to move like a tight-rope walker, one foot in front of the next, to make it across. It rocked back and forth, swaying with each step Daria took or every breeze it caught.

"What if I fall?" I asked David. I'd be smashed like an egg on the swamp floor.

David put his tree face right in front of mine. Through the branches, his dark eyes were calm. "Don't fall," he said, like it was a choice I needed to make. "Hold the sides and look straight to the end, nowhere else. Remember, you've done harder things than this to get here." He pulled me onto the sky bridge.

My heart thumped straight through to my feet. *Boom! Boom!*

Each beat and step were thunderclaps roaring through

73

my body. I'd seen the sky every day of my life, but being up there in it, I saw that it was so big, it went on forever.

"Look to the end!" David called back to me. *Boom! Boom!* My heart clanged as I stepped forward.

I'd learned most everything in my life by watching. From studying Old Joe, I knew how to shear a sheep of all its hair, change a horseshoe, prune roses, and more. Now I watched David.

He had a limp on his left side that made him dip a little each time he stepped on that foot. He walked sure of that bridge like it was dry ground. I dipped to one side, walked sure, and copied it all.

Then I let my mind remember the steps. *Forest, river, vines and bush, watch for the sinkhole, more vines and bush...what's next...green water.* How could I forget the green water?! *Tree boat, lily pads, secret water door...tree hideout, more rowing and walking, tree people, zigzag through the brush, sky bridge.* Again. *Forest, river, vines and bush, watch for the sinkhole, more vines and bush, green water, tree boat, lily pads, secret water door, tree hideout, more rowing and walking, tree people, zigzag through the brush.* Got it. Mama would get it, too.

"I'm flying!" Ada yelled.

There she was, strapped to Ibra, her face all red and happy peeking around his shoulder, arms straight out, flapping.

"Flying like a bird!" called Ada.

When my feet touched the end of that bridge, I almost flapped my arms like Ada. The bridge finished at a landing. On it was a man, sitting there in the sky, natural as anything.

"Evening, Gus. Watching over things for us?" asked David.

Gus nodded and kept his eyes on the bridge. "Climb down," he said, pointing out pegs for us to hold. As we started to descend, I heard him call to us, "Welcome to Freewater."

"What's Freewater?" asked Ada.

That's exactly what I wanted to know.

18

Nora

ABOUT THE SAME TIME HOMER AND ADA WERE descending into Freewater, Nora was sitting on the Big House porch when Stokes, Rick, and Ron returned from their unsuccessful runaway capture. At first, she wasn't quite sure it was Rick and Ron. Their clothes were torn and muddy, their packs were gone, their eyes were bloodshot red, bug bites pockmarked their faces and arms, they were each missing a shoe (lost as they ran from the bear), and they were fussing.

"Ain't no way I'm going back in that wretched swamp again," said Rick, scratching his bug bites.

"Me too, the devil himself couldn't live in that place," said Ron, pulling a wet sock from his foot.

"Stokes, those two little darkies are most likely dead," said Rick.

"That's right, dead," echoed Ron. "We saw all those footprints right around that bear. I'm thinking it got 'em. If that didn't get 'em, the snakes did, or they drowned in all that mud."

Nora bit down on her lip. They thought Homer and Ada were dead. What would happen to Rose?

"Shut up, the both of you. The last thing Crumb will want to hear is that he lost his property to that swamp," said Stokes.

Just then, Mr. Crumb came to the door and surveyed Rick and Ron.

"I see you all came back empty-handed," he said, shaking his head. "And what in heaven's name happened to them?" Mr. Crumb asked Stokes.

"They're still learning," Stokes said with clenched teeth.

"Well, they need to learn quick because we've got ourselves a runaway problem. I don't have time for boys running games in the swamp!" Crumb huffed.

Rick and Ron averted their eyes to the ground and remained silent.

"We were tracking them," Stokes started. "We ran into some…some troubles. We were on them. It ain't just the little darkies out there. They have knives, maybe an ax. They cut the vines somehow, and we saw tracks. We'll get cleaned up and get back out there right away."

Rick and Ron looked up in protest but didn't say a word.

Mr. Crumb stared in the direction of the swamp land and spat off the porch. "Not yet. We'll get back in there soon enough. But the next time we go, we'll do it properly, with the right men and everything we need to smoke those runaways out. If they're living in there, it won't be for long," he promised.

FREEWATER

SKY HAD FOUND IT.

The perfect branch—high, wide, and strong. With her back against the trunk, she sat upright on her branch, legs outstretched before her. Sky's camouflage of leaves, mud, and vines allowed her to flawlessly disappear into the swamp canopy. Since the dark of sunrise, she'd been neatly settled into that very spot, thinking about the meal she'd make upon returning to Freewater.

As she considered acorn cakes and stewed fish, she heard panting breaths. Not loud. Nothing more than a heavy exhale. Most ears would have missed it. A patrol would not. She listened. The damp, muffled sound of footsteps. The crackle of crushed twigs underfoot. The person was close.

"I swear, this place is hell on earth. But it's got plenty of trees good for shingles," the man called out as he swung at the mosquitoes around him.

"I'll mark these trees!" he said. "You do the ones we passed on the way here."

"Right," a voice came from the distance.

The man had a metal bucket of black tar and a coarse

brush. Printed across the bucket were the letters *DSSL*. With the tar-covered brush he went about placing an X on one tree after another, even on Sky's tree.

He stopped. Feeling watched, he surveyed his surroundings and even stared up at the very branch where Sky sat.

"Come, let's hurry up and get this done!" he yelled. "This place gives me the creeps!"

Then he walked on, X-ing trees as he went.

19

Sanzi

JUST ABOUT THE TIME HOMER AND ADA WERE awakening in Suleman's tree den, Sanzi awoke in her cabin with a start. She'd had a dream. She'd finally caught the beast.

The dream felt so real, her skin tingled all over. It tingled in a way that said today was the day. Of course, *he* wouldn't be there, but that didn't mean she couldn't do something big.

She was up early. Everyone was. Rains had come the night before, and the word was out before first light: *Big Tree had blossomed*. That meant it was Remembering Day.

From behind the wooden divider separating her sleeping room from the kitchen came the hiss of the hearth fire. Steam rose to the rafters of the cabin, touched the dried herbs and flowers that hung from above, and perfumed the air. Sanzi stepped over her sister's empty mat and peered around another wooden partition between their space and their parents'. Her mother's mat also lay vacant. Sanzi's heart sank a little at the sight of her father's mat. It was neatly rolled and tied against the wall, as it had been for days. Her papa still wasn't back. Before he left, they'd talked about the man appearing in Sanzi's dreams, her beast, and her thirst for adventure. She wanted her papa home now— today, Sanzi would do something big, and she wanted him there to see it.

Around an even larger partition, Sanzi peeked and saw her mother, Mrs. Light, bent over the hearth. Her gray hair glimmered silver and orange in the firelight. At the far end of the cabin, Sanzi's older sister, Juna, knelt beside bowls that lined the walls. As if in a dance, the two moved in unison.

Whip, whip. Juna stirred a bowl with herbs, acorns, and berries.

Then *shoop, shoop* went Mrs. Light's wooden spoon as she added hot broth to each bowl.

Whip, whip, shoop, shoop, they went, filling each bowl because it was a special day.

"Keep going, while I fetch more acorns and berries. Everyone will be there—we'll need much more than this," said Mrs. Light.

"Yes, Mama," said Juna. Their mother ducked out of the cabin.

It's time, thought Sanzi. Unless she wanted a day of *whipping* and *shooping*, she'd have to leave now. Sanzi silently dressed. Given her dream and her mission, what she wore mattered. A slight disappointment washed over her as she pulled on her shirt. It wasn't made of white cloth, which would have made it perfect. Instead it was a leather patchwork, but the pieces did form a sort of ruffle at her collar, and she'd shredded the shirttails to make them look even more authentic. Close enough. She cinched a belt of braided vines and animal skin about her waist. That would be essential for today. Her shoes were better, animal skin. Almost perfect was the fur strap slung across her chest and over her shoulder. It was just like his. Did he wear it on the left shoulder or right? She couldn't recall. The quiver it held was a miniature replica of what she remembered of his. Her hair wasn't in ropes, but she used a piece of rope to tie her thick, kinky hair into one large puff above her head. She looked at her hands. Five fingers on each. There was nothing she could do about that.

"Sanzi, oh no you don't!"

"What?" Sanzi jumped at the sound of Juna's voice.

"You know what! Not today with your crazy games, Sanzi." Juna stood behind her, shaking her head. "I see what you're wearing. You'll be out there running about the swamp and you'll come back late. You can't do that today of all days!" said Juna. She ran to the divider and spread her arms to block its opening.

"Don't worry. There's plenty of time. I'll be back," said Sanzi.

"Mama's gonna get so mad if you go. You know you have to be here for the memory circle at Big Tree. If you aren't here, I'll get in trouble," said Juna.

Sanzi sighed. Juna was only three years older, but sometimes she sounded a million years old, or at least as old as their mother.

"You won't get in trouble. I'll be back before she even cares I left," said Sanzi. She felt along the cabin wall and her hands touched the most important part of her ensemble, her bow, only meant for use on special occasions such as this.

"If you aren't there, I'll have to do everything!" said Juna.

"You're always doing everything!" said Sanzi. "That's why Mama thinks you're so great."

"Oh no, not the bow!" said Juna.

"I have to have the bow," said Sanzi, as she stuck it in her quiver along with a handful of slender arrows. She cinched it all tight around her shoulder. For good measure she tied her sling across her chest and slung a small pouch of stones over her shoulder. She looked herself over. She was ready.

"I'll be back, and everyone'll be happy when they see what I bring with me." Sanzi smiled. She ducked under Juna's arm and ran for the door.

"Sanzi!" begged Juna. But it was too late.

Of course, Juna didn't believe in her mission, Sanzi thought as she pulled back the flap door on their cabin and ran. Juna hadn't had the dream. Her skin hadn't tingled. How could she understand that today was the day?

20

Sanzi

THE INK BLUE OF THE NIGHT SKY WAS TURNING to morning gray as Sanzi stepped out of her cabin. There was hustle and bustle along the sole path that stretched the length of the village. Each cabin was at work, making their own contribution to the Remembering Day celebration. Many took a moment to see for themselves that Big Tree had fruited and to taste a bit of its new acorns. It was said to be good luck to do so at the first bloom.

But Sanzi didn't need the luck of Big Tree that morning— she'd already had her dream. Besides, going anywhere near Big Tree would mean being seen by her mother, and there was nothing lucky about that.

Determined not to be distracted from her mission, Sanzi headed in the opposite direction. She needed Billy. A little help from him and she was assured success. Down the path she raced, toward a cabin a few doors away from hers. She didn't bother going to the cabin's door, as she already knew no one would be there. Billy's father, Ibra, had gone on patrol with her own father. Mrs. Faith, the older woman who also lived with Billy and Ibra, would be at Big Tree. The woodcutters would soon come knocking, so Billy wouldn't be inside his cabin. The woodcutters were the last people he'd want to see.

Sanzi went around to the side of Billy's cabin. In the shadows she almost tripped over his long legs as he leaned against the cabin's mud wall.

"H-h-hey," said Billy in a nonchalant way, as if hiding between cabins at daybreak was the most normal thing to do. At fourteen, he was the tallest of the young boys in the village, yet the deep hunch of his back made that fact forgettable. His gangly arms held two nervous hands fumbling a stone carving tool in one and a wooden bracelet in the other. Wood chips were scattered about his feet. Often where you found Billy, you found wood chips. For someone who didn't like woodcutters, he loved wood.

"I'm going," said Sanzi. "Come with me. I think we can get it today." Of course, *we* had been her and Suleman in her dream, their arrows aimed and fired together. Billy would have to do.

Billy looked over Sanzi's attire and shook his head.

"O-o-oh no. L-l-last time we went t-t-trying, we g-g-got in s-s-so much t-t-trouble. Mrs. Light still l-l-looks at me f-f-funny," said Billy.

Sanzi sucked her teeth. "She made a big thing out of

nothing," she said. "My arrow hardly even scraped Gus. He shouldn't have even been in that part of the swamp in the first place."

"He was g-g-getting plants, for y-y-your mother," said Billy, shaking his head again. Then he got quiet. The sound of whispering and chatting floated toward them. As the footsteps came closer, Billy shrank into the wall.

"What are you doing?" asked Sanzi, even though she already knew.

"N-n-nothing," said Billy.

"Why don't you go? At least they ask you," said Sanzi.

Billy put a finger of *shhh* up to his lips.

It was a small group, only two men and a woman. They stopped in front of the cabin. One of the men came to the cabin flap and called, "Billy!"

When no one answered, the group moved on.

"I wish I could go," said Sanzi. "Even if it's only for cutting a few trees. At least you'd get to leave Freewater and see something new. Me, I can't go anywhere. Ever." She kicked the wood chips beside her.

"I'll g-g-go s-s-sometime, I just d-d-don't feel up to it t-t-today," said Billy, scraping the thinnest sliver of wood from his bracelet, then smoothing it with his shirtsleeve.

"You never feel up to it. But that's all right, and besides, today we have more important things to do anyway," said Sanzi, hoping her enthusiasm would be contagious.

Unmoved, Billy shaved a few more paper-thin wood pieces from his bracelet.

"You know, Juna's up right now, cooking with Mama. You could take her that bracelet," tempted Sanzi.

"I-i-it's not r-r-ready yet," said Billy, smoothing the already polished soft wood and slipping his gift into the pouch on his waist. He'd been making it for weeks.

"I know if you come with me and we come back like heroes, Juna might even want to wear it for the memory circle," said Sanzi.

Billy looked at her. A flash of ambition crossed his face.

"Come on, I had a dream about how to do it. Today is the day," said Sanzi as she ran onto the village path. Billy shook his head and followed her.

21

Sanzi

JUST AS THEY TURNED OFF THE PATH TO GO toward the river, she heard it, a laugh she knew all too well.

Not him! Her whole insides groaned. She didn't want him to see her, not today, not when her skin tingled, and she was on her mission.

"Where do you think you're going?" Ferdinand snickered. "Still trying to be Little Suleman?" His big teeth shone in a smile as he looked over Sanzi's outfit.

"I'm not little," Sanzi said, but instead of sounding stern, her words came out like a whine.

He laughed again and mimicked her voice. "You're just sad because your mama won't let you leave Freewater."

"You don't know anything!" Sanzi shot back. But the truth was that he was right. She couldn't leave—not her, nor Juna, nor any other child born in Freewater.

Ferdinand flashed his knife in the air. Although Sanzi believed Ferdinand was a pig-head, she knew his knife made him unique. He was maybe thirteen, and he'd come about four months earlier after running off from one of the swamp ditch-digger gangs. It was Suleman who'd found him and brought him to Freewater. Sanzi had spent most of her days imagining wonderful things about Suleman, but she couldn't understand why he hadn't left Ferdinand where he'd found him.

When he came to Freewater, the one and only thing Ferdinand possessed was that knife. How he'd commandeered it, no one knew. It was a great knife. A shiny blade with a nice, smooth wooden handle. It was newer and nicer than any knife they'd had in Freewater for years. And Ferdinand kept it stuck to his hand.

"I imagine he went through many hard times to get that knife. There's no need to take it from him. So long as he helps," said Sanzi's father, David. And help he did. Everyone liked Ferdinand because he was always there with his knife to save the day. Cutting wood for houses, clearing brush, digging holes. Although she wouldn't admit it for a million years, Sanzi wished for Ferdinand's useful popularity. But maybe that could all change today, once she caught the beast.

"Well, while y'all are playing in the trees, I'm going with the woodcutters," announced Ferdinand, flipping his knife in the air. He turned to Billy. "You coming? Or is your tummy hurting again?" whined Ferdinand, and he ran off down the path.

Billy's face melted.

"Shut your mouth!" Sanzi called after Ferdinand.

"He doesn't know anything," Sanzi reassured Billy. "I can't wait to see the look on his face when we get back!" Sanzi pulled Billy down the path.

• 22 •

Billy

BILLY FELL QUIET AFTER FERDINAND'S TEASING. It stung a little, but the thought of leaving Freewater with the woodcutters was a bad alternative. Out there, Billy was certain he'd be hunted.

Years before, when he'd run off with his father, they'd been in the swamp for days before they'd come to Freewater. In that time, they caught the notice of a runaway catcher patrolling the outskirts of the swamp. Ibra pulled Billy into the muck, and with reeds in their mouths, they hid just beneath the water's surface. They stayed still as the dead, breathing through their thin plant straws. The man passed close enough to reach out and touch them. From his watery grave, Billy watched the hunter's murky image.

It didn't matter that later David found and guided them far away, through the hidden wooden stakes, the secret door, and the sky bridge. For Billy, that slave catcher was still out there, hunting.

As time passed in Freewater, Billy imagined that hunter getting closer and closer each day. In Billy's mind, he was terrifyingly certain that the hunter was just outside of

Freewater's confines, lurking under every bush and behind every tree, waiting for Billy to leave Freewater.

Nope. Today was not the day to go woodcutting. Maybe tomorrow, maybe then he wouldn't be scared. Being with Sanzi helped Billy forget that feeling. But being with Sanzi created all sorts of other feelings, too.

At the bottom of the path, they came to the water's edge. Billy's head began to swirl as he listened to Sanzi's plan.

"I had a dream, clear as anything. I saw the beast and we got it," she whispered. "We'll wait in the lookout for it. When we hear it, you'll go down and chase it back toward me. Then I'll swoop in with my bow and get him!" Sanzi said her plan in a matter-of-fact way that didn't match the red flags going off in Billy's mind. By now his tummy really was beginning to ache.

They traveled a little farther along the water until they reached the spot where large bushes almost blocked their path. Sanzi pulled on them, and from behind came a boat. Her boat. He'd watched her spend the better part of a year finding the right tree and then carving out the trunk with fire and jagged stones. Granted, the outcome was crude, with it being more splintering bark than boat, but it worked. Sort of.

Oh no, thought Billy. The boat almost certainly meant they'd be getting into some sort of trouble.

"Do we h-h-have to take the b-b-boat? Can't we w-w-walk?" he asked.

"It rained last night, so the water's high. And besides, if we walk it'll take all day!" said Sanzi. "Come on!"

She pushed her craft into the water, waded in behind it, and swung herself into its well. Billy carefully put his long, shaky leg over the boat's edge. The boat leaned over, almost capsizing. Sanzi grabbed a stick paddle and leaned the opposite way to steady it. As they cast off, Billy's stomach turned, flipping and flopping with equal parts fear and seasickness.

As they rowed through the muck and further into Sanzi's adventure, one thought tugged at Billy's mind. Through the nausea he steadied himself and asked, "H-h-how am I going to chase the b-b-beast?"

"Run in his direction, use your sling. That'll be enough to scare him back to me," said Sanzi. A small part of Billy appreciated that Sanzi thought he could be that brave. However, every other part of Billy thought that using his sling and running toward danger didn't sound appealing. It sounded downright crazy.

Between the plan and the boat, Billy broke out in a cold sweat. He stopped rowing and wiped his brow.

"That s-s-sounds..." He paused, not wanting to squash Sanzi's dream. "Maybe we should wait until our f-f-fathers come back from p-p-patrol—they could help," said Billy, hopeful she'd reconsider.

"What's the point in that?" asked Sanzi. She frowned at Billy, a little insulted that he thought her plan and her bow were not enough.

"How do you know the b-b-beast will even come?" asked Billy, trying to keep the hope from his voice.

"That's what I saw in my dream. I was at the lookout and it came right past us!" said Sanzi. "You'll see!"

23

Billy

WHEN THEY FINALLY REACHED THEIR DESTINA-
tion, on the very edge of Freewater, Sanzi docked the boat
at a sloping piece of land jutting from the water. The two
stepped onto dry earth, and Billy's fears began to settle. For
him, this hill near the edge of Freewater was out of reach of
the hunter. This spot was his and Sanzi's.

Atop their hill, Billy watched Sanzi become the heroine
she dreamt of being. She bent down and dug her hands into
the moist ground. It wasn't long before she felt what she
sought, a stone. It had a sharpened point on one end. She
unwrapped the sling from her shoulder, loaded the stone,
and swung it beside her body—faster and faster. Wind
whipped like the hollow whistle of a bird.

"That tree," Sanzi said, pointing at a far juniper trunk
already chipped and marked from many other stones.

Sanzi spun her sling even faster, then released. The stone
shot out and popped as it hit the tree. Chips of bark flew off
and the swamp awoke with tweeting, chirps, and whistles.
Billy watched her and wondered if he could also be swept
up in Sanzi's tidal wave of courage.

She studied the canopy of leaves overhead.

"That was definitely like Suleman, huh?" she asked Billy expectantly.

"Yeah, I think s-s-so," said Billy, despite the fact that he'd never actually seen Suleman use a sling.

"Try yours," Sanzi encouraged.

Billy bent down and dug his hand into the soft dirt. He pulled one stone out, about the size of a marble. Too small.

"I d-d-don't know about using my s-s-sling," he said.

Sanzi ignored his trepidation. "Here," she said, handing him a larger, sharper stone.

Billy pulled a sling from his pouch. It was a stiff, clean leather rope, barely used. He loaded the stone and swung it overhead.

"Go on, shoot it," Sanzi called. Eyes squeezed tight, Billy released. The stone went high and slanted before it plunked into the water behind them.

Billy shrugged with embarrassment. *See?* he thought.

"Billy," said Sanzi, feeling her plan begin to slip away. "You have to believe you can hit something, if you ever expect to do it," said Sanzi. Her father had said that to her a million times. And she swung again to show him. "Believe it."

For Billy, Sanzi's confidence was contagious. The next time he swung his sling, it went in the right direction. After a few more tries, he added his own mark to Sanzi's tree.

"See! You're ready," said Sanzi. Even Billy had to smile.

"Let's check the ropes," said Sanzi, and she pulled a wide animal skin belt from around her waist, put it around the tree, and began climbing. Billy did the same with his belt and followed her. They climbed until they reached Sanzi's perch, a small wooden platform wedged between two thick branches and where ropes made of soft tree wood were knotted to the trunk.

The ropes were Sanzi's invention. There were four, each one in a different direction. Her very own network of sky bridges. From her perch, the ropes were placed at a downward angle that allowed Sanzi, using her belt, to zip down from her high tree to another far-off lower tree.

"I'm almost like Suleman, the way he swoops in to save the day and destroy the plantations," Sanzi said with dreams in her eyes.

"I guess," said Billy, touching the thin ropes.

With a few firm pulls on each rope, Sanzi made sure they were strung tight.

"I'm going to swoop in and that beast won't know what got him," said Sanzi. "Come on, let's wait on the high bench."

Billy's face lit up. Going up to the high bench was Billy's favorite part about coming to their island hideaway. Up about ten feet higher than the small platform was another piece of crudely wedged wood. The two friends settled on it.

Billy exhaled, taking in the lush green blanket of swampland trees around them. In the distance, he could see the raised outline of Freewater, like a bird's nest within a sea of trees. The only signs it existed in the bed of green were the gently sloping ropes of the sky bridges. They floated above the swamp canopy in each direction. He could also see the soldier-straight stalks of Freewater's cornfields. In the far distance beyond the bridges, there were miles more swamp where even Freewater's dwellers had never ventured.

As was intended, in the fifteen years since it began, even the best of slave catchers couldn't spot Freewater. Billy was filled with that truth each time he went up to the high bench.

Sanzi took her bow from her back along with an arrow from her quiver.

"When the beast comes, I'll be ready," she said and practiced loading her arrow. Hoping to turn her attention away from the worrisome plan, Billy asked a familiar question.

"Y-y-you think Suleman will come back?"

Sanzi nodded, afraid that if she said it aloud, a soft breeze would blow her wish away. Instead she began the story she always told when they sat in the high perch.

"I was out with Mama, I was little, maybe seven," said Sanzi.

"Picking plants and s-s-such," Billy chimed in. He'd heard the story more than once and he didn't mind.

"Yes, you know Mama. She had her mind set on teaching me and showing every kind of plant. We were out getting sassafras and honey. She didn't notice that I'd walked off," said Sanzi.

"Weren't you s-s-scared?" asked Billy.

"No, all I remember was the butterfly. It was brown, blue, and orange and flapping all around my head. I went running after it. That's when I found this place. As I came up the hill, my foot caught on a sharp root and I was cut. I didn't cry. But I sat on that hill and I looked up. I swear Suleman was spread out like a spider on a web in the leaves up here," Sanzi said.

"He s-s-see you?" asked Billy.

"Yeah, he put up his hand and only two fingers showed. I think he waved, but maybe he was just letting go. Feet first, he swooped down, grabbing branches as he fell, and he landed right in front of me on that hill."

"You s-s-say anything?"

Sanzi shook her head.

"He didn't say anything, either," said Sanzi, "but he wrapped my foot with a piece of cloth from his shirt." Sanzi had sewn that same piece of cloth into her shirt. She touched it, willing even more of her memory to return.

"I touched his bow," said Sanzi as she ran her fingertips over her own bow. "It was on his back."

"Did he m-m-mind?" asked Billy.

101

Sanzi shook her head. "He took it off and let me hold it. It was smooth, almost soft," said Sanzi.

"He put an arrow in it and everything. Then he pulled my hand way back, swung me around, and I let it go. That arrow flew and it hit a water bird," Sanzi recalled. "I went to fetch the bird, and before I got back, he was gone, rowed away on his boat."

"When Mama found me, I was there with my foot wrapped and a big water bird next to me. Mama cooked it that night."

"'He's Suleman,' Mama said after I asked her. 'He lives on his own, raiding plantations. Taking from them and bringing to us. He helps us survive.' I remember feeling he could do anything in the world. Maybe even fly to the moon," said Sanzi, looking into the distance at the great beyond.

Billy shook his head, reminded of all the things Sanzi didn't understand.

"Not o-o-out there," whispered Billy.

"Do you remember what it's like?" asked Sanzi. Billy looked down into the swamp trees, fearful for the first time that his slave hunter's ears had just perked up.

Billy was quiet a long while. "Out there, it's like you can't b-b-breathe. But you don't even know you can't breathe until you leave it."

"If I could bring back all the things Suleman does, I don't

think I'd mind it too much out there," said Sanzi. Many times, her father returned from patrolling with small bundles sent by Suleman. Matches, flour, nails, a pan or bowl, sometimes even a shovel or knife. Every time they arrived, Freewater's inhabitants would celebrate and give thanks to their marauder hero, Suleman. Sanzi would touch each thing and feel the zing of adventure they carried.

"One day I want to come swooping in, full of things that everyone will want," said Sanzi.

Unsure what to say to make her understand, Billy thought a long while, then whispered, "Out there, even g-g-good things f-f-feel bad," said Billy.

"*Swoot, click, click, swooooot,*" came the call. They both fell silent. Sanzi felt the sound pierce a hole in her plan.

"It's y-y-your mother calling! We should get back," he said.

"Not yet!" said Sanzi. "She won't mind if we wait a little longer."

"*Swooooooooot, click, click, swooooooooooot,*" the call rang out again, filled with impatience.

"Oh n-n-o," said Billy.

Then came the sound, a splash in the water.

"The beast!" said Sanzi.

24

Sanzi

"LISTEN!" WHISPERED SANZI AS SHE PUSHED herself off the high perch and went down to her ropes. Billy took one last look at the serenity around him, then descended behind her.

There was another splash below, and from the water and muck ran not one wild pig but three. This was even better than her dream!

"Three!" said Sanzi, her eyes wide. Billy watched, filled with admiration for Sanzi's prediction and with fear for what it meant. He had to go down there.

The three wild hogs lingered on the small hilltop for a moment, eating the shrubs on its floor. Satisfied, they began a swift trot past the far hillside and toward a thicket of trees.

"Hurry, go down," said Sanzi. "Go that way and you can push them back to the tree rope." She pointed toward where one of her tree ropes ended.

Billy sat frozen on the wooden ledge.

"Don't think about being scared. Just think about what

it'll be like when we bring a beast on our shoulders back to the village. Everyone will think we're heroes."

Everyone included Juna, thought Billy.

"A-a-all right." He inhaled. Billy rappelled down the tall tree, his legs skidding and bumping the trunk along the way.

Confident her plan was finally underway, Sanzi unwound her belt and slung it over her tree rope. She steadied her feet on the wooden bench and waited for her moment.

At the bottom, Billy undid his sling, loaded it with a rock, and started running. A squeal came from the thicket as Billy spun his sling and swung. In the excitement he forgot to release the handle. Instead of catapulting the stone, the sling wrapped around his arm and the stone struck him in the head.

"Ouch!" he cried.

For a moment, Sanzi's heart sank. But Billy's scream scared the pigs and they began running right toward Sanzi's target tree.

He'd done it!

Sanzi grabbed the strap, swung her legs out, and began to slide down the rope. She swayed back and forth, wobbling slow and clumsy. For a moment she remembered that she was hanging from a thin rope over twenty feet in the air. Perhaps this was not the best idea. But soon she picked up speed and began swooping down just as she'd imagined.

As she reached the desired tree, she heard the call. Loud, screeching, angry. She'd have known it anywhere.

"Swoooooooooooooooooot, click, click, swooot!"

Startled, Sanzi lost her grip on the rope and went tumbling down into the thick mud below. Two pigs ran off. Undeterred, she trained her eyes on the one remaining pig some fifteen feet away. She pulled out her bow, loaded it, and just as she fired, she heard, *"Sanzi!"*

The arrow veered right, missed the pig, and landed close enough to send it running.

Sanzi turned to see her mother standing stern and livid.

25

Anna

THE DISAPPEARANCE OF HOMER AND ADA, NOT to mention Rose being sick, was a real irritation for the mistress of Southerland. Anna did her best to keep her distance from Mrs. Crumb, but she had chores. From emptying the chamber pot to fetching her washing, it had to be done.

Mrs. Crumb was in a foul mood, filled with *"Don't touch this"* and *"Go get that."*

At one point, Anna could not help but look at her. In a flash she saw the room burn down around this small woman, until she stood almost covered in a heap of ash. And there was Anna hovering over her in a dress made of the finest silk. The image gave Anna the sudden gratified feeling one gets after eating a good meal.

Mrs. Crumb saw Anna's peculiar, satisfied expression and she didn't know why, but she felt shivers run down her spine.

"What are you looking at? Go!" she commanded, ready to be rid of Anna.

"Yes, ma'am," said Anna as she backed out of the doorway.

For Anna the exchange with Mrs. Crumb was bad but was not unusual. Many other mistresses had been the same way. Something about Anna didn't suit them. It was the way Anna viewed the world. Anna didn't see things as they were—she saw them as she believed they were meant to be. That was a dangerous thing on a plantation. Real or not, those kinds of thoughts made a child uncomfortable to be around.

Anna had been sold off many times. Her former masters hadn't quite been able to put their finger on what was wrong with this cat-eyed girl. She did as she was told, but that prickly feeling she gave them made them want her gone. The more she was bought and sold, the more mysterious and uncomfortable she became for those she served. No one seller could speak for her—as none had owned her more than a year, perhaps two—so each made up tales about who she was and how well she'd serve her new master, just to be rid of her. Without any relations to be sold with her, Anna was a solitary being, connected to no one and nothing in the world.

Yet Anna knew differently. She had a mother. Not one she'd known, but one Anna was certain she was meant to know. One sentence of Anna's history had managed to pass from one seller and owner to another.

"The mother cut her something awful right before the woman was sold off," each of them said.

Anna knew this one bit of history by heart. She believed it wholeheartedly because she still had the scar. It was deep and large, stretching from her shoulder almost clear to her elbow in one straight line. At the top of the line, on her shoulder, were two smaller scars that came together to make the point of an arrow's head, pointing north like the needle on a compass. As this was Anna's only link to her mother, she concluded that her arrow scar was a message. Directions for where she was meant to find her mother once again. North. She'd cut her daughter so that Anna would always know where she was meant to be—everything else was a temporary stop on the way.

So Anna had always planned to go North. She figured that once she got there she wouldn't have to worry too much about finding her mother. How big could it be? Besides, all she'd need to do was show her scar and eventually someone would lead her to a mother who was looking for it.

Having Homer already gone North only strengthened Anna's resolve that she also would leave, and soon. The problem was, Mrs. Crumb called on Anna day and night with work of some sort, and it had only gotten worse with wedding preparations. Anna was even being made to serve drinks during the wedding itself. It made leaving unlikely.

Anna had seen others run, and nearly every time, their disappearance was quickly noted and the dogs were sent out. Like with Rose. Anna figured that she needed a moment when all the world was too busy, too sick, or too tired to notice her disappearance, and there didn't seem to be one. Regardless, Anna turned the thought of running over and over in her mind, sure that a plan could be hatched. It was meant to be.

She thought this thought so much, she smelled of it. Perhaps it was also the aroma of escape that made the mistress of Southerland less than pleased with Anna from the start.

Anna could remember that first day at Southerland quite clearly. She'd been brought in to meet Mrs. Crumb, and after a short once-over, it was clear the woman was irked.

"Where'd you find this strange girl?" she'd asked Mr. Crumb. He tried to reassure her, but Anna knew it wouldn't work. The only good memory she had of that first day was seeing Homer.

He was bringing fresh milk and butter for Rose. He was strange, and she liked that about him. Instead of bringing the milk into the kitchen, Homer stood under the kitchen window and whistled. *"Whee hoo, whee hoo."* Curious, Anna went to the window, leaned out, and there he was, his deep brown eyes meeting her amber eyes.

"What're you doing whistling under the window?" Anna asked.

Homer jumped, as if she wasn't meant to see him, before running off without a word. In a flash, as she watched him go, she saw large black angel wings on his back. They matched the very ones she often saw on her own back. Yes, they'd be friends for sure.

"You could bring it through the door," she said, watching him from the window the next day. Homer shrugged. On the third day Anna was outside waiting for Homer.

"I figure I may as well take it in myself. They call me Anna. What do they call you?" she asked.

Homer was quiet. Anna didn't mind. She had forever to wait for an answer. After all, their friendship was meant to be. Once he realized she wouldn't let him escape, he finally answered.

"Homer," he said. Anna stood in front of him with her eyes looking right into his.

"Homer." She repeated it close enough to make Homer step back. "How old are you?" she asked and turned him around, putting her back to his and touching his head to hers. "How old? Do you know?" she asked again.

More questions. She waited. She was patient.

"Twelve," Homer said. He was lucky to know. Old Joe knew his numbers and figures. He'd helped Homer and others on Southerland know, too.

"On the sale block, I heard Master Olsen call me thirteen, but then when your Master Crumb came along asking for a girl of ten or eleven, Olsen called me eleven. But I'm about as tall as you. I think I'm twelve," said Anna.

"What's your mama say?" Homer asked.

Anna shrugged. "I don't remember her," she said.

A long silence passed between them. Anna considered if she should share her secret. Then she saw his black feathery wings again, fluttering in the breeze.

"Look," she said, raising the sleeve of her dress, and showing her scar.

"What is it?" asked Homer.

"It's from my mama. She did it before we were sold apart. It points North, where she is. I'm figuring it's meant to help me know how I should find her."

"Oh, okay," said Homer.

That's all it took. They were friends. Now he was gone. But her mission remained. She'd find her way North.

26

Anna

ANNA WAS STILL WORKING ON HER RUNAWAY plan as she walked on the small path through the quarters toward home, when she saw the dim light in Homer's cabin. *How was Rose?*

She gently tapped on the door.

"Mrs. Petunia, it's Anna," she whispered.

"Come quiet, child," said Mrs. Petunia. Hot air, damp with the scent of herbs, met Anna at the door. The gurgle of boiling-hot water came from a pot in the hearth. Strips of wet cloth steamed just beside it.

In the shadows along the wall near the fire was Rose. She lay asleep on her stomach and looked small under the layers of poultice cloth of elderberry and sumac on her back.

Anna quietly made her way to Mrs. Petunia's side.

"Is she all right?" asked Anna.

"*Surrpp,*" went Mrs. Petunia, sucking her teeth and shaking her head. "They beat her something terrible, but she'll come through if we can keep the infection out and if she sleeps."

Just then there was a knock at the door, and in came Old Joe.

"She wake again?" he asked.

"Not as yet," said Mrs. Petunia.

Old Joe's hair was snow white and his skin was chestnut brown, smooth and etched with deep grooves of wrinkles.

Sparks, definite sparks Anna saw in Old Joe's eyes, despite his old age. Yes, like freshly lit matches in each eye. Old Joe felt Anna's stare and turned.

"Hello, miss," he said, tipping his head.

Anna liked that he addressed her like a young lady.

"What happened to Homer and Ada? You think they made it North?" Anna asked. If anyone knew, it would be Old Joe.

Old Joe shook his head. "Stokes says the little ones ran off into that swamp," he whispered. "When Rose comes around, she'd want to know," he said to Mrs. Petunia.

"*Surrpp,*" sucked Mrs. Petunia in more disapproval. "The swamp ain't no place for little ones like them."

Old Joe shook his head, but then there was that spark again. Anna saw it.

"I'm not staying," said Old Joe. "I'll give you space to care for her, I just wanted to bring you this." And he handed a small glass jar filled halfway with amber liquid.

"Made it myself," Old Joe said to Mrs. Petunia.

She smelled the contents and nodded. "Maypop water," she said.

"I crushed and steeped those maypop flowers two full

114

weeks in some of Crumb's whiskey. Don't think he'll miss it," he said.

"Whiskey. The way he drinks, I suspect not," Mrs. Petunia replied. "This'll do her good. She's gonna be in a heap of pain, ain't no way to get through it but sleep."

"I'll come by tomorrow to check on her," said Old Joe.

Then he tipped his head to both Anna and Mrs. Petunia and he was gone.

"What are you gonna do with that?" asked Anna, looking at the small bottle.

That's when Rose began to groan a deep mournful moan, then she awakened wailing.

"Homer! Ada!" she called out, tears streaming down her face. She tried to sit up and that only made her cry out again, "Homer! Ada!"

"Rose, you can't worry about anything just now except staying still for this here poultice," said Mrs. Petunia.

Rose cried out again and tried crawling off her mat toward the door. "My Homer! My Ada!" Sweat poured from her face.

"Anna, hold her steady!" commanded Mrs. Petunia.

Fear swept through Anna as Rose writhed in pain and grief. Anna took hold of her legs and hugged them tight.

"Come, dear Rose, come on. You can't do any running to find them today, you hear!"

As she spoke, Mrs. Petunia held Rose's face and opened the bottle of maypop water.

Rose cried out and thrashed in pain.

"Hold her steady, Anna! Hold her!"

Anna squeezed tighter.

"You need sleep, child," said Mrs. Petunia as she poured just a few teaspoonfuls into Rose's mouth.

"Old Joe came and said there's word the little ones are in the swamp," said Mrs. Petunia.

"The river, the river, the river..." Rose murmured over and over. Her voice grew softer, and by the time they placed her back on the mat and changed her poultice, Rose was sound asleep.

"She'll stay like that for a good long while, well past morning," said Mrs. Petunia as she stood and crossed the room.

Anna looked at Rose and saw sweet dreams of Homer and Ada hovering over her head.

"Come, help me get this last needle threaded," Mrs. Petunia called out. She was sitting on the floor before the firelight of the hearth with her sewing box at her knee and scraps of fabric in her hand and at her feet. A piece of fabric in one hand was held close to her face, while the other moved a needle and thread through it. In her youth Mrs. Petunia had been a seamstress on the plantation, making most any frock worn by Mrs. Crumb and her children. Now, with her eyesight nearly gone, she was tasked with making new clothes for the enslaved souls at the wedding.

Wool pants, a cotton shirt, and a hat for the men and boys, a dress with an apron for the women and girls. New clothes were given only once a year. This year, Mrs. Crumb waited until the summer wedding so the clothes would be new and suitable.

"Can't have you in tatters around my guests," Mrs. Crumb had said. Their clothing from the year prior had gone threadbare as they waited. Homer had been looking forward to the new clothes.

Now he wouldn't get them, thought Anna as she threaded Mrs. Petunia's needle.

"What are you going to do with Homer's?" asked Anna as she touched the crisp new fabric. "You know, since he's run off and all."

"Humph," grunted Mrs. Petunia. She was full of old lady sounds. Like old age meant words didn't much need saying to be understood.

"There's many folks who run off, most get brought back," said Mrs. Petunia.

Mrs. Petunia was right, the maypop water did make Rose sleep. Rose didn't wake once, not even the next morning.

That same day, Anna held the amber liquid up to the sunlight and felt a spark of a plan form in her head.

27

Sanzi

MUD DRIPPED FROM SANZI'S ONCE-PUFFY HAIR onto her face. Her prized shirt with the ruffled collar was now soiled, droopy, and sopping wet.

"You'll go just as you are," Mrs. Light said to her sullen daughter.

"It's Remembering Day, our most important day of the year, and you're running around the swamp swinging from trees. Everyone is there, waiting to start," scolded Mrs. Light.

Sanzi tried to hear her, but she couldn't. The pig was gone and all that was left behind was a dream that hadn't come true. She'd be going back to the village with nothing.

Billy walked beside her, not daring to say a word.

"I *almost* got that pig," said Sanzi. *I would have, if Mama hadn't come!*

As if Mrs. Light heard her thought, she stopped and swung around.

"You *almost* got hurt. What have I told you about those ropes?" Mrs. Light chastised. "A fall could break a leg or an arm or who knows what else, and none of my plants and

118

herbs might heal it! There was work to be done today and you weren't here to do it."

Freewater buzzed with excitement that traveled down the village lane and met Mrs. Light, Sanzi, and Billy as they walked toward Big Tree. Apart from David, Ibra, and Daria, much of Freewater was there and had formed a half circle under its blossoming branches. They parted to make room for Mrs. Light as she came forward and stood in the middle. Everyone knew their places.

"I h-h-have to g-g-go play," said Billy. He was a drummer and they always sat to the front of the circle. Since his father, Ibra, wasn't there, Billy would be the lead drummer of three.

Most of the children of Freewater, excluding the babies in arms, were gathered outside the half circle, forming a line, waiting for their turn. Each was neat—faces washed, hair combed, and clothes clean. Twelve children in all. As the youngest, the four-year-old twins Free and Hope were last.

Juna was there looking over each child, brushing off any bits of dirt, smoothing their hair, and handing each a bowl filled with berries and acorns. "Do you all remember your parts?" she asked. The whole line nodded in unison.

As the first child of Freewater, Juna took her place at the

front of the line. Just behind her, a space was open where her sister trudged into place, her face glowing with vexation.

"What happened to you?" Juna asked in dismay. Flowers were woven into Juna's braided hair, and the scent wafted over Sanzi. In every way that she was muddy, wet, and disheveled, Juna was clean and composed.

"We almost got a pig, a big one," whispered Sanzi.

Juna flashed a look at her. "You saw one?" It had been weeks since a good pig sighting.

"Three," said Sanzi. Juna's eyes grew wide.

"Three?" she repeated. Before admiration could overcome her, Juna inspected her muddied sister. She was a mess.

"I told you not to go. Mama was so mad. Take this off," Juna ordered, pulling the bow and quiver from Sanzi's back and placing it against a nearby tree. She tried rubbing some of the mud from Sanzi's face, but it only smeared down her cheeks and neck. Juna shook her head in resignation.

"Here, this one is yours. Don't forget to do your part," said Juna, and she handed Sanzi a bowl filled with berries and acorns.

"I remember," said Sanzi. Her heart sank at the thought of having to walk into the circle.

With one call from Mrs. Light, everyone quieted and sat down.

"We cherish Remembering Day," said Mrs. Light. Bits of

sunlight found their way through the trees and shone on her face as she spoke. Big Tree, festooned in white blossoms, blue berries, and caramel-colored acorns, loomed behind her.

"Each year, on the day Big Tree blooms, we form our Memory Circle to remember the miracle that brought us here and to thank those who came before us. The children of Freewater are the keepers of this story. It's for them to tell you."

Drumming began and the onlookers opened a pathway in front of Juna. With a bowl in hand, Juna stepped to the beat of the drum into the circle's center. Once there, she nodded toward Billy. He stopped playing and she began to speak.

"There were six of them," started Juna in a strong, clear voice. "Six who ran when they saw a chance. The man they called master was a gambler, in debt. One night men came to collect money owed, but the man they called master had none to give. They tied him up and went to his cabins. They took four enslaved souls and ran. The six left behind came together, gathered five blankets, two axes, bread, and six pieces of smoked meat, and ran for freedom. They were David, Mrs. Light, Suleman, Jupiter, Gus, and Mrs. Faith."

Juna stopped and Billy began to drum once again. She looked toward the line of Freewater children and motioned for Sanzi to come forward. Miserable, mud-soaked, and shoes squishing as she stepped, Sanzi came down the path and entered the Memory Circle. Even with her back turned, she recognized the sound of Ferdinand snickering as she stopped in the circle's center. Distracted from the task at hand, Sanzi's eyes scanned the crowd. There he was, outside the circle and beside the tree where Juna had left her bow and arrow. To her alarm, he held both in his hands. He smiled, then loaded *her* arrow in *her* bow.

Sanzi's face grew hot as a scream inched up her throat.

Juna gave her an impatient nudge, which brought Sanzi's attention back to the circle and to the expectant stare of onlookers.

Sanzi began. Her voice came out in a loud, angry squawk. "THE SIX RAN TO THE SWAMP. THEY RAN, BUT FOR DAYS THERE WAS ONLY WET AND MUD." Breathless, Sanzi rocked back and forth, fuming. Juna and Mrs. Light looked on in shock. Ferdinand smirked and aimed her arrow toward the sky. *Don't you dare!*

"Sanzi!" Mrs. Light whispered. Almost dizzy with anger, Sanzi continued.

"They walked and walked, and soon ran out of food. They drank from puddles and swamp water. They thought they would starve. But one day they found Big Tree," she recited.

Ferdinand pulled back on her bow. *He wouldn't*, thought Sanzi as she pressed on.

"Big Tree was large enough for them to sleep in, away from the bears and bobcats. They went to sleep thinking they might starve. But during the night, it rained. And in the morning when they woke up, Big Tree was full of berries and acorns to eat," Sanzi continued.

Ferdinand snickered again, then fired an arrow into the air. *He fired my arrow!*

"IT WAS A MIRACLE!" Sanzi finished, infuriated. Despite her angry tone, the circle of onlookers broke into resounding cheers and applause.

From there, each child from eldest to youngest came forward and added to the story of Freewater's beginning.

Ferdinand's shenanigans continued and no one noticed but Sanzi.

"On Big Tree's big trunk, the six marked each day they survived. With their axes, they cut branches into stakes and buried them all around the lowlands of Freewater, to protect it," said the next child.

Ferdinand climbed a tree, her bow in his hand. Sanzi gulped.

"When heavy rains came, water washed away mud at the base of Big Tree and there they found a small stone knife and a bowl left behind by Indians from hunting in a time before. That changed everything," continued another child.

With those words, each of the children came forward

with their bowls full of berries and acorns and placed them at the base of Big Tree. Mrs. Light took a weathered wooden spoon from her belt and held it up.

Little Hope and Free were last to enter the circle with bowls in hand. Nervous delight spread across their faces. In unison they spoke. Where one forgot a word, the other filled in.

"The things left behind gave them hope that they could build a village. That was the beginning of Freewater. Mrs. Light knew about plants. David and Gus knew about building. They built…cabins, one by one. They learned to make rope from poplar tree wood. They built the first sky bridge. When they found others lost in the swamp, they brought them here. And they had…us children," the two ended in unison. Again, the onlookers let out whoops of swamp sounds to cheer. The twins giggled in embarrassment and happiness.

Ferdinand fired another arrow! Sanzi couldn't take it any longer.

"*STOP!*" Sanzi shouted. Everyone went silent. Mrs. Light shot her daughter a glare that was so cold, Sanzi could feel small icicles forming on her ears. She pointed toward her offender. Everyone turned and looked, but he was gone. All that was left behind was her bow and a scattering of arrows.

"On Remembering Day, we give thanks to those who came before us and to Big Tree!" said Mrs. Light, waving her wooden spoon in the air. Everyone turned back to Mrs. Light and cheered again.

"Since that day we've welcomed forty-three newcomers and twenty-one children born here in Freewater." She turned, arms upheld, and smiled at the children in the circle.

"Today we celebrate by eating the berries and acorns of Big Tree, just as we did that first day," said Mrs. Light. "Please, everyone, feast on the food—"

Mrs. Light's festive voice was interrupted by the moaning call of a horn. Everyone stopped and waited. Then it came again. No words were said. Everyone knew what it meant. Almost in unison, they stood and began running, all in the same direction, with the same destination in mind.

28

Sanzi

SANZI WAS WITH THE GROUP UNTIL SHE NOTICED she'd left her prized weapon. How could she help defend Freewater without her bow and arrows? Almost at the cornfields, she turned around and ran back.

Filled with bustle and chatter and celebration only moments earlier, Freewater had now become a ghost town. The bowls were left behind. Ants had already begun eating the berries and acorns they contained.

Her bow lay on the ground abandoned. She claimed it and an arrow that lay nearby. She began hunting for the other missing arrow Ferdinand had shot. She spotted it. Relieved and incensed about her mistreated possessions, Sanzi was unaware when she was approached from behind. Turner wrapped his arms around Sanzi's waist and in one gesture pulled her from the ground and tossed her over his shoulder.

"Hey!" Sanzi yelled as her feet left the ground and her downturned head watched the arrows fall like a pile of forlorn twigs. "Put me down!" she shouted.

Turner's eyes showed no mirth, only fiery seriousness.

He said not a word. Instead he raised his hand to her mouth and began a swift jog with Sanzi bouncing on his shoulders.

Their destination: a plot of land also elevated like Freewater. It was quite small and protected by mucky water, making it a perfect place for a second field of crops, as well as a hideout. When they reached it, Turner set Sanzi down. She kept her head to the ground, mortified by her entrance.

A small circle had been left unplanted in the center of the corn patch. It was there that some fifty people now sat, faces upturned, silent and waiting. Hope and Free sat side by side with wide eyes and closed mouths. Billy's face was wet in a fearful sweat. Juna was stone-still.

The deep whisper of Mrs. Light's voice was all that could be heard. With one hand laid to the ground and one on her old stone knife, she repeated, "Mother Swamp, protect us as you have protected those who have come before us. Protect us from those who would bring us harm. May our traps hold steady. Protect the freedom we have found in your care."

It took hours. Hours of sitting. Listening. When the horn came, tooting once, twice, then a third long time, everyone exhaled in unison and stood up. There was much talk and laughter on the long walk back to the village.

Sanzi trailed at the back of the group, her mother not far from her. "Before we came to this place," began Mrs. Light, "when Papa and I were on that plantation, but before we were married, Papa lived in a cabin with a boy named Hansel.

Hansel came after we did. Scared as ever when he first got there. Papa helped him. Showed him things, and that boy followed your papa around, until one day he didn't. One day he ran off. Your papa didn't know where, but the overseer suspected Papa had helped him. Believed it so much, he beat your papa to get the answer he wanted. Then cut his knee to keep him from running one day himself. So, you see, if they come here and get even one of us, they'll use their ways to come for the rest of us. That's why your father thought to have this place and our rules. He knows what it means to have even one of us caught. One person can destroy all that we've built."

"I wanted my bow and arrows," said Sanzi. "If they come, I can help fight."

Mrs. Light stopped walking. She knelt down and held her daughter's shoulders.

"The first place we teach every child to find is this hideaway. We teach you to listen for that horn. We teach you our rules. Run with no more than what is in our hands. Run and don't look back. Turner went back to get you. I let him break our rule for you. You say you want to help Freewater. Well, start by not being the one who gets caught," said Mrs. Light. She watched tears well up in her daughter's eyes. Her face stiffened. "I am your mother in this hard world. My work is not to make you happy. My work is to keep you free. You best get up and come. We'll meet this evening," she finished, and turned to walk back to the village with Sanzi trailing behind.

29

Sanzi

SOUR FACED AND EMBARRASSED, SANZI SAT AT the back of the meeting. Billy soon joined her.

"Mrs. Light was m-m-mad?" asked Billy.

"Yeah, but she's always mad at me," Sanzi sighed. Longingly, she eyed Sky's ornate leafy camouflage. Everyone listened as Sky spoke.

"We were on patrol in the west. There were two men," Sky said, removing her foliage headdress at that evening's meeting. "They were walking about marking trees and talking. They came close to our western sky bridge tree, so I sent up the call."

"You did the right thing," said Mrs. Light, nodding her head toward Sky. *Mama thinks Sky is wonderful for being a patroller!* Sanzi sulked. *Why can't she see that I could be just like her?*

Everyone whispered.

"They're tree cutters and they're moving closer," said Mrs. Light. "They have their axes and they cut without any thought, only what will bring them money for shingles or lumber."

A fire pit burned in the center of the meeting room, and smoke left through a hole in the thatched roof.

"But we have our traps to the west, right?" someone called from the crowd.

"They could break the traps and come through," said someone else.

"They've come close," interjected Jupiter, one of the elders. "We may need to bring down that bridge and cast a new one deeper in the swamp leading to the lake. If we can get to the lake, we may have another way to escape."

Mrs. Light nodded in approval of Jupiter's idea and stepped to the center of the circle. Firelight made her silver hair shine metallic. She pulled her old stone knife from her waist belt and held it in the air to ask for their attention and permission.

"If you agree with Jupiter that a new bridge is needed, let yourself be heard," Mrs. Light called out.

Mrs. Light had asked for everyone's agreement and they obliged. Each person made their own swamp sound.

After a time in Freewater, some new arrivals could choose a new name and a swamp sound. Mrs. Light said she'd chosen her uncommon first name of *Mrs.* to inspire the respect she felt she was due and *Light* for what she felt in freedom. Children born in Freewater had names chosen for them. Everyone in Freewater could pick a swamp sound, something derived from the panoply of sounds the swamp emitted. Sanzi, after having seen the osprey swoop majesti-cally from the sky, had chosen its call.

Now, in response to Mrs. Light, the sounds of birds chirping, a growling bear, a purring bobcat, a snorting pig, the clap of thunder, the swish of wind in the trees filled the space and echoed into the distance. *That's another bridge I'll never walk on, another sky bridge I'll never even see because I'm stuck here!* Sanzi thought.

Obstinate, Sanzi sat silent. She didn't have the heart to make her sound.

"Will we need more rope?" asked Mrs. Light. "Billy, your father isn't here, but you can help us. How much rope and tools does Freewater have today?"

Billy stood up, nervous at the prospect of speaking.

Once a personal servant to the plantation owner, Billy's father, Ibra, had been tasked to keep track of stock and goods, human and otherwise. Ibra had been taught his num-bers. After arriving at Freewater, he set out to teach them to every child and many adults. Billy knew his numbers best.

Nervous, Billy pulled at his shirt hem as he reported. "Ummm, eighty-two lengths of r-r-rope, two a-a-axes, and t-t-two knives."

"Excellent, thank you, Billy," said Mrs. Light. *Yes, Mama likes everyone but me!* Sanzi lamented.

"We'll need at least one hundred and sixty lengths for a new bridge," called out Sky.

Grumbles of discontent went through the village. Heads shook. "I remember when we did our first bridge. We were still learning to make good rope!" said Mrs. Light. "It took us all, but we made it!"

Everyone nodded.

"It should be done quickly because the cutters move fast," said Jupiter.

"It's getting late. We've lost a day's work, but we can make a plan tomorrow. We must also talk to the other patrols," said Mrs. Light. "Sunny, tell us of our food."

Sunny was ready. "Twenty-three nets of corn and two nets of dried fish," she reported.

"As we do each day, we thank the swamp and we make our mark on Big Tree," said Mrs. Light. "We need someone to come up and make the mark." Sanzi liked being that person. It meant she could hold an ax and leave her mark. Sanzi raised her hand, but her mother looked right past her. "Billy, bring your ax, and you can make the next mark." *He hadn't even raised his hand.*

"I'm going," Sanzi whispered to Billy as he was about to stand. She'd had enough. She backed out of the meeting and pushed her way into the night.

She couldn't believe how terribly Remembering Day had turned out. That very morning she'd awakened with a tingling dream and now it was ending with a painful reminder that adventure would never find her, at least not as long as her mother had any say in the matter.

A horn sounded. Different than the noise earlier, it went up in a long wail and ended in a short bleat.

"The patrols are back!" sang Jupiter.

Whoops of happiness let loose. Everyone made their way to Big Tree and looked up into the canopy of leaves for them to come down.

Papa! thought Sanzi.

30

Homer

WELCOME TO FREEWATER.

The words rang in my head as we climbed down the tree. Several ropes latched on to the trunk to create more bridges, each connecting the tree we descended with other far-off trees. *What is this place?*

Down we went, leaving behind the big sky and entering a clatter of birds, thick leaves, and fog.

"You reckon this is the North? I always thought that you had to fly there, but maybe you just need to walk in the sky," said Ada from above.

"No, we ain't in nobody's North," I said. The truth was, if it wasn't the North, then what was it?

Chirping, howling, and more rose up to our ears. None of it seemed to bother Daria nor David. They kept climbing down, and before long they started making their own sounds. David whistled a bird song and Daria made the hiss of a snake. They sent their sounds down and a swell of swamp noises floated up to us.

Until my dying day, I'll never forget what we saw when we reached the bottom. Faces, like mine, talking and laughing, like it was the most natural thing in the world to live at the end of a sky bridge in the middle of a swamp. They swirled around me and Ada, patting our backs and smiling wide at us for no reason at all.

A girl with a bow and arrow tied to her back jumped into David's arms. He let out a big laugh. A woman with white hair hugged him.

"You're back early! Just in time for Remembering Day!" she said.

"I didn't want to stay away from this one too long," he said, smiling at the Bow and Arrow Girl.

His deep laugh mixed with the girl's giggling to make a sound so new to me, my ears tingled.

"Oh, Papa," the girl said as she hugged him.

"Suleman brought us these two," David said.

"Only them? Tools?" asked the silver woman.

"Only them," said David, setting the girl down.

Bow and Arrow Girl stared me dead in my eye. "You know Suleman?" Overwhelmed by it all, everything started to sway from side to side. I couldn't speak an answer.

"Hey! You hear me?"

"We saw Suleman," Ada piped up. "He waved to me like this." She showed her two-fingered goodbye.

"How'd you get those spots on your face?" asked the girl.

Ada shrugged.

"All right, let them be. My name is Mrs. Light. My little girl is Sanzi," said the silver woman.

"I'm not little, Mama," said Sanzi. She seemed pretty short to me.

"Welcome," said Mrs. Light. "Lord only knows what you two brave souls did to make it here by yourselves."

"We went in a river, and there was a snake, and I fell on this sharp grass, and I got this cut! Wanna see?" asked Ada.

Mrs. Light smiled a smile that said she understood.

"Yes, but what's your name?" she asked, bending down to Ada's cut leg.

"I'm Ada and this is Homer." Ada pulled up the shredded hem of her dress to show her injury.

"What you gonna pick for your new names?" asked Sanzi.

"Sanzi, don't worry them with that now. They don't have to choose new names. If they do, there is time. They made it here, that's all that matters," said Mrs. Light as she examined Ada's leg.

"I have something to help with that cut," Mrs. Light said. She studied me and reached for my head. "That bandage could use some tending."

I leaned away. *Who was this woman?*

"We'll give you time. Sanzi, go tell Juna that you'll both stay with Billy, Ibra, and Mrs. Faith tonight. I'll be needing to look after these two in our cabin." Then Mrs. Light waved her arms and everyone went quiet. "This is the first day for these two in Freewater. Every day, we mark Big Tree to remind us of how far we've come. Today, we'll have Homer and Ada make the mark!"

From her waistband she pulled a small stone knife, handed it to me, and guided everyone to the big tree's trunk.

"Homer, you see that tree?" Ada whispered.

I never wondered if a tree had a heartbeat, but I did as I studied this one. Knotted branch-arms came from the trunk, two big root-legs bulged from the tree's bottom, and a shower of shaggy hair-leaves covered the branches. From them hung small white flowers and acorns.

Markings like scars were etched on the bark, one lined up beside the next, so many it seemed they went back to the beginning of time. The day I'd helped bury Mingo, the day Mistress made Ada scream, every Sunday Mama left us for the week, Freewater had been here. My head pounded.

Mrs. Light pointed to an unmarked place on the bark. I could barely see through my pain and thoughts.

"Go on!" said Sanzi, reminding me that everyone was watching.

I let my arm swing, and that knife came down and landed crooked, then fell from my hand.

As if no one saw my failure, the whole swamp came alive with sounds. "Now, everyone, come up. Don't be shy. They need to feel welcome," said Mrs. Light.

One by one, they came up to us like we were special. Ada stood next to me and squeezed my hand. For once, we both weren't sure what to do.

"Welcome. I'm Wisdom," said one.

"I'm Ada," Ada kept saying to every person, like it was some kind of name game.

"I'm Jupiter," said another.

"I'm Faith," said an old woman.

Then in the middle of it all, my arms and legs went soft. The rock-hard pounding in my head turned to water and my eyes began to swim in it. I swayed to one side. As my head hit the ground, I saw them, gleaming leather from a fresh spit polish. Before everything went black, I heard Ada yell excitedly, "Two Shoes!"

31

Suleman

FIRE SPEAKS. IT STARTS OUT MURMURING, puffing, and sputtering: a whisper over the noise of silence. It searches for air and voice. The first yellow flame is a soft low note, hit perfectly. No one knows to pay it any mind. But it grows, gobbling up air, spitting out deep orange flames that holler and screech. By then there's little to be done but to listen to the screaming fire and watch its destruction.

Suleman yearned for this fire opera, knew it because he'd written it. He was the conductor. In the ink black of night, he watched the yellow flame sing on the tip of his arrow. He pulled his bow taut and fired. It hummed through the sky, arching high, flying over a cluster of side-leaning wood cabins, a neatly planted vegetable garden, then skimming the roofs of the dairy shed, the meat larder, and laundry. Then the arrow arched downward with a quiet swish. It made the barn flash bloodred and the hay pile beside it flash pale white. When the arrow landed, it hissed a tune.

Neighing horses and wailing cows sounded the alarm. Suleman waited. An overseer ran from here to there, fetching pails of water. The fire gobbled it, smoked, then bellowed again. The overseer ran for the cluster of cabins and banged open flimsy doors.

"Fire!" he yelled, more a command than an alert. Some twenty-five men, women, and children emerged. Sleep clung to their eyelids as they blinked at the screaming barn. Suleman watched.

"Move, you sorry wretches! Move!" the overseer shouted, then ran toward the barn.

Animals scrambled, buckets sloshed, dirt was shoveled and fetched to and fro.

Suleman descended from his treetop perch and melted into the darkness and mayhem. He reveled in it. He held the firm belief that fear, over clandestine theft, was the best medicine for the sickness that was plantations.

The laundry shed had no lock; there were soap, sheets, two shirts, and handkerchiefs. The swing of his ax on the larder's lock was unnoticed. Smoked meats, grain, matches, salt, and a tin cup—each item was folded into a make-shift sack from the sheets. All fit in a large bundle that hung across his back. Satisfied, he ran for the woods and waited. In time he heard frantic footsteps among the trees. Once they were close, he whistled. Even in the darkness he could see the frightened whites of their eyes. Three souls, a woman with a baby cinched onto her back and a man holding a stick at the ready. Suleman whistled again, put up his hand, motioning.

"Come, if your plan is to be free." Suleman beckoned.

The man and woman regarded the rickety cabins from which they had come and listened to the overseer yell. The woman grabbed hold of the man's hand and they followed Suleman into the darkness of the forest.

32

Nora

NORA STOOD ON HER FATHER'S CREAKY CEDAR library ladder. The smell of whale-oil polish mixed with the musty scent of old books. On tiptoes she reached for a plain green, cloth-covered book.

The well-worn pages were soft, smelled of the kitchen, and felt of things she understood. It was a book on plants and flowers. Rose loved flowers, so Nora often took the book and snuck to show Rose its pictures. The feel of its weathered cloth cover was a comfort in a world of confusion. Footsteps and voices coming down the hall made her tuck the book into her dress and hide behind the door of her father's study. After all, that's what an octopus would do.

Old Joe opened the door, entered, and set down a tray of whiskey and four glasses. Behind him came Nora's father, with three men in tow—Mr. McGrath, Mr. Boyd, and Mr. Ogletree. Nora easily recognized each one from dinners they'd had at the Crumbs' home to discuss business. For Nora, they reminded her of many boring evenings she'd spent hearing of their plans for their swamp business— Dismal Swamp Shingle and Lumber, the DSSL. The result promised profits for the group, and from those dinners Viola had met Mr. McGrath's son, who she was soon to marry.

Every time Nora saw these men, they'd try to make her speak, which made hiding the favorable choice to being seen.

"What happened last night was a disgrace. That fire dang near burned down my whole barn. Not to mention the three darkies that ran off," huffed Mr. Boyd.

Crumb swirled the brown liquid in his glass tumbler and waited a long while before speaking.

"How many you have run off this year, McGrath?" asked Mr. Crumb.

"Three. One went during planting, another two at summer harvest. We tracked the two and got them back. We never did get that first one. Suspect he's up in the swamp. Most owners talk about darkies running North. Well, some might, but what we've got down here is a swamp problem," McGrath grumbled.

"Them runaways stole from me. I know it was them. They got all sorts. It was awful," lamented Mr. Boyd.

"I can't believe you had two little darkies run off and you ain't found them yet!" McGrath said, frowning at Mr. Crumb.

"We expect to get them back soon," assured Mr. Crumb. He took a long swig from his glass.

Papa doesn't even know. Homer and Ada were probably dead, thought Nora. They hadn't told him about the bear.

"Fact is, they're both still out there loose, and the tale is spreading all over the slave quarters, ginning up insurrection. If a couple of little darkies could make it, won't be long before more try. Mark my words," argued Mr. Ogletree.

"Men, as partners in the DSSL we've been suffering losses from runaways in that swamp. We get the slaves out there for work only to have some run off, and we don't have the manpower to go after them. Not to mention the darkies that go there from our plantations. Runaways mean lost business and property. I say it's time we got in there after them," finished Crumb.

"Yes, we need to get in that swamp and end this thing," agreed Mr. Ogletree.

"I suppose it's time something was done," Mr. McGrath grumbled. He shifted the tobacco in his mouth and spit into the crystal tumbler in front of him.

"It's treacherous terrain. Mud and marsh for miles, snakes everywhere, and God knows what else," reasoned Mr. Crumb. "We need a guide, someone to lead us to the runaways' encampments, and I'm working on getting us one."

"A guide?" Mr. Boyd asked timidly.

"Yeah, I'm hoping for some word on these swamp runaways. I won't share as of yet. But I'll let you know," said Mr. Crumb, tapping his pipe. "We need a real militia in that swamp. I tell you, they won't run if they ain't got a place to run to."

"Militias mean real money," said a worried Mr. Boyd. "There ain't no guarantees. We sent a couple of hired men up into them swamps and lost one to snake bite, and after two days they got nothing. Going in there is risky business."

"No. If we're going to do it, we should do it right. Hire some trained militiamen. They'll get 'em out," argued Mr. McGrath.

"Well," considered Mr. Ogletree, "I don't suppose we have much choice."

"How soon? And how much from each?" quibbled Mr. Boyd.

"I figure we need a few weeks to find and hire the men. We might need to supply some of the guns and shot. We split it four ways. More if we can convince the other smaller plantations to take part," said Mr. Crumb.

"All right, then, we strike in the next few weeks!" said Mr. McGrath.

Nora held her breath. She'd heard talk about catching runaways all her life, and she hadn't thought too much of it. *Rose, Homer, and Ada, they were different, weren't they?* But something in Nora's father's words made her blood run cold. It didn't match the father who tucked her in at night.

She slipped out of the room, crept down the stairs and out the back door. Book in hand, she ran across the lawn toward the quarters. No sound came when she put her ear against the cabin wall. The smell of sweat and dried blood wafted out as she opened the door. There was no movement from the small body on the pallet. Rose was asleep. Nora pulled the book from her dress and left it beside Rose's hand, then she crept out.

The kitchen wasn't the same without Rose. Mrs. Petunia did what she could, but her food certainly didn't taste as good. Unsure where else to go, Nora sat there each day waiting for Rose to come back. Surely, her gifted book would help make that happen.

That evening, Anna came to the kitchen. When Petunia's back was turned, Anna pulled the same green book from her apron and set it before Nora.

Protest spread across Nora's face. Anna's face hardened and her voice was flat but sure.

"If Master Crumb or Stokes catch her with that book, she'll get the lash again."

Nora kept her eyes to the wooden table. Anna's words sent a chill down her spine. To hear her father connected to the idea of hurting Rose turned something in Nora. Yes, Stokes was mean. He was cruel and feared. But her father? Anna's words were like a first small crack setting into a sheet of lake ice.

33

Homer

"WE CAN'T GO BACK, HOMER," MAMA TOLD ME, and I didn't listen.

If I'd done as she'd asked, maybe the three of us would be up North. I said we needed to get Anna. Instead of me, Mama went back. Now nothing felt right—not the swamp, not Freewater, not freedom. The thought made my body heavy like a lead weight.

Or maybe it was the blanket of wet leaves on my chest, or the heavy rag wrapped around my head.

Eyes still closed, I lay there, letting Mama's voice fade away.

Forest, river...tree boat. What came before tree boat? I needed to remember it so Mama could know it. *Green water, secret water door.* Then the *tree people, right? Zigzag, sky bridge.* There were so many steps. Had I remembered enough? I lay there pulling at memories in my brain, praying I knew the right ones for Mama to find her way. She always found us. This time would be the same.

I peeked my eyes open. Morning had come and bits of light poked through the bark roof.

I was alone. The room was square, big, and open, with

mats of leaves and corn husks on the floor. Over me, the ceiling was raining plants and flowers. Bunches were tied with string and left to dry, making the room smell of herbs. Small wooden bowls lined the walls.

Ada. Where was Ada?

Then, clear as a morning blue jay's song, came a voice from outside.

"What's this? What you call that?"

Ada.

"Two Shoes!" she called. "Hey, Two Shoes."

Like cold water poured over me, everything from the night before came back. We were in this new world and Two Shoes was here. How?

I peeled away the wet leaves and rag, got to my feet, left the cabin, and followed Ada's voice. Sunlight splashed my face like a warm cloth as I stood outside and looked around. There was no tangle nor swamp brush, only thin trees dotting the dry ground. I let my toes curl into the dirt.

"Homer!" Ada's voice was a piece of home come to life. I wasn't one for folks touching me. It broke my rule of being invisible. But Ada never paid any mind to my rules. She jumped into my arms and wrapped her little legs around my waist.

"You woke up! I was there, waiting for you, but then Mrs. Light told me to go with Juna. Is your head still hurting?" she asked.

I pulled back and gave her face a good look. She was all happiness. Pieces of pollen and leaves had already caught her cloud of hair. We'd been here not even a day and she already had the look of Freewater.

"My head's all right," I said. "Who's Juna?" I asked.

"Over there." Ada pointed.

Tall with a long face, Juna was cut from dark polished mahogany. Her hair was braided atop her head with small flowers strung through it. Animal skin made a sort of shirt and skirt, and strands of wooden beads circled around her neck, waist, and arms. She had big cinnamon eyes and a sad mouth. She was beautiful.

"Maybe she's an angel?" asked Ada.

"There ain't no such thing as swamp angels." Even as I said it, I wondered.

"Why not? If there are monsters in the swamp, seems only right that there would also be swamp angels," insisted Ada.

I didn't have time to argue. Juna was walking right up to me without a second thought, like she had been knowing and seeing me every day of her life.

"So, you're up!" said Juna.

My eyes went to my feet, and embarrassment oozed like sweat from my skin. Ada pulled my arm and saved me.

"Look!" she said. "Two Shoes!"

There he was. I couldn't help but glance around for more

pieces of Southerland. Master Crumb could be behind the next tree.

"You mean Turner?" asked Juna.

Ada scrunched her nose up. "His name is Two Shoes," she corrected.

"I guess he chose Turner for his Freewater name," Juna said. "Many folks change names when they come here."

He was bent down working at a big pile of wood or string, or something I couldn't make out. Even with Ada's loud call, Two Shoes was slow to look up.

"Let's leave him be," I said, but Ada was already off and dragging me behind her.

"Everybody was wondering what happened to you," said Ada.

Head down, Two Shoes was set on sorting through the rope pieces in front of him. Without answering, he kept working—big ones here, smaller ones over there. But that was no matter for Ada.

"You like it here?" she persisted.

"It's all right," Two Shoes said slowly. He was quiet for a time then asked, "Y'all run off?"

"Yeah," I said.

"We thought we were going North," said Ada.

"Your mama know you here?" asked Two Shoes.

Both Ada and I got quiet. But we shook our heads.

"Little Minnie started walking," said Ada. "Old Joe

made her a new wooden doll and she walks all around the quarters with it."

Hearing his daughter's name made Two Shoes wince, like someone poked him in the eye. He kept working on that rope.

"I see your new friends are waiting for you. You best be on your way," he said into the rope.

My belly made a tight knot and I pulled Ada back toward Juna.

"What's wrong with Two Shoes?" asked Ada.

"Don't know, but let him be," I said.

"I want to tell him about Minnie and everything else since he's been gone," complained Ada.

"I said, keep clear of him!" It came out louder and harder than I'd wanted. Still, something about Two Shoes didn't feel right to me.

34

Homer

"COME ON," JUNA CALLED TO ADA AND ME. "AS long as you're up, you may as well come down to the river for a drink." I nodded a yes. I was thirsty, and the idea of getting away from Two Shoes and going anywhere with Juna felt right.

The quarters, the Big House at Southerland, and the outhouses around it were what I knew of the world. Once a year, I went with Master Crumb and Old Joe into town to help fetch supplies for crop planting. Freewater wasn't anything like those places.

Slave quarters were made of wood, save for a brick hearth in each cabin. These houses were made of...swamp, like the dirt under my feet had risen up attached to long pieces of tree bark and dried into the walls of a four-sided cabin. The roof was made of more gray bark. Their floors were raised and built on sawed-off tree trunks. A flap of animal skin hung down as a door for each. A few even had a hole or two in the walls for window openings.

Then there were the people. Each person was dressed different. Some had shirts and pants and dresses like me and Ada. But then there were others, like Juna, with animal skin and fur, sewn together with vine or leather, to make all sorts of clothing.

Ada and I took it all in as we followed Juna through the village. People were everywhere. Two women waved to Juna as they stood over a small fire with a clay pot of something boiling.

"It'll be finished this afternoon, come by and try. We are set to know who makes the better turtle stew," one called.

The other woman laughed.

"They are the best cooks in Freewater. But I don't like turtle stew," whispered Juna to me and Ada.

Another man and woman were arms deep in mud as they filled in a hole in their cabin's wall. Pieces of wooden sticks and bark showed through.

"Almost finished?" Juna called.

"We'd have been done a long time ago if he'd listened to doing it my way," the woman teased. The man shook his head and packed the mud onto the wood before smoothing and blending it into the surrounding cabin wall and placing on more bark.

There was a pen with two small and skinny cows.

Four little children went running around us, one pretending to sling a rock at the others. Each one laughed with a different pitch, like notes from a harmonica.

Two men stood with a pile of animal skins laid between

them, one shaking his head and frowning while the other spoke.

"They can't ever agree on anything," said Juna.

Everyone was moving—moving in different ways than I'd ever seen—this way and the other without looking back to see who might be watching or checking for permission. Ada had the same thought because we both stopped to watch everyone around us.

"You got a Big House here?" Ada asked Juna. She was looking in the distance for the center of things.

"We've got cabins," said Juna. "My mama and papa have the biggest one, so Mama can help people with her medicines."

"That ain't big, I mean a Master house." Ada opened her arms wide. "The kind that lights up like a monster at night."

Juna frowned, a little confused. "No, we don't have any monster houses here, and no masters. I've heard talk of them, but no white people have ever been to Freewater."

"You've never even been on a plantation," I said. It wasn't a question; it was me realizing things.

She might as well have said she was dropped straight down from the moon. I'd never met anyone who didn't know a plantation. If she didn't know plantations, what did she know?

"I was born here. I am the first child of Freewater," said Juna.

154

"The first child of Freewater," I repeated to myself. "What about everyone else?"

"Apart from the children, most everyone else came from a plantation. I suppose if you ask them, they'd know about the Big Monster House," said Juna.

"What about Two Shoes?" I asked.

"Who?" asked Juna.

"Two Shoes. I mean, Turner," I said.

"Oh, him, he's new, sort of. You know him?"

"Yeah," I said.

"He's real quiet, but he's always around trying to help, so he fit in fast. Helping is our way," said Juna.

People gave me and Ada quick glances as we walked by. There was knowing in their eyes, like they'd already spoken to us about things.

"Come this way," said Juna.

We walked a small path. Leaves and vines brushed my arms. The path went downward, not steep, but enough for the dry ground to turn damp, and before long we were at still water.

Two women were already there, skirts upturned and filled with thin damp leaves and small flowers.

"Juna!" they said together.

"Hello! For Daria's wedding clothes?" Juna asked, pointing to their leaves and flowers.

"Yes, they'll knot nice once they're clean and dried. She

won't care for much, but that doesn't matter. We'll dress her still." They all laughed.

"You gonna use leaves in a wedding?" asked Ada.

The ladies laughed again. "Yes," they said.

"And who is this?" one asked, bending down to smile at Ada.

"I'm Ada, and that's my brother, Homer," said Ada.

"Yes, we heard of you. The brave children who escaped on their own." She smiled.

Ada glanced up at me. We both didn't say anything.

"We'll use these, but I think we have a spare one, for brave girls." The lady took a flower and leaned forward to Ada.

"Mistress say you could touch those flowers?" asked Ada, rubbing her arm. We both knew the consequences for doing that. The women flashed knowing eyes on Ada.

"Why don't you put this in her hair," she said to me, and placed the flower in my hand.

"I'm taking these two for a drink. They'll be so thirsty." Juna waved goodbye, took my arm and Ada's, and started walking toward the water.

Empty wooden bowls sat neat and clean along the water's edge.

Juna filled two and handed them to us. The water was cool and tasted of wood. That was fine by me.

Juna watched us.

156

"You hungry?" she asked Ada and me.

Ada and I looked at each other and then at the swamp around us.

We both shook our heads no.

"You eat these vines or something?" asked Ada.

"No." Juna laughed again.

We knew there was no use in being hungry when there was no food to be had.

"You sure you're not hungry?" Juna asked again.

"I don't see any food," said Ada.

Juna smiled big. "Come," she said.

35

Billy

AS JUNA, HOMER, AND ADA PASSED BILLY, HE ducked into his familiar spot between the bushes near the water. He watched. For Billy, seeing Juna walk through the swamp made him feel like swamps were meant to be lived in, loved, and enjoyed. In the midst of mud, bugs, tangle, and vine, she seemed to glide.

Billy did any number of things to make this true. He sprinkled dry dirt on muddy pathways where he knew she'd travel, cut back vines that would impede her way, and even chased off snakes slithering nearby. That Juna never knew of Billy's actions satisfied and even pleased him. It made it all the more true that Juna did float through the swamp.

Today, by the time Homer, Ada, and Juna passed the water, he'd already done what he could to clear the tumbled pathway and to clean the bowls left at the water's edge. He sat back behind the brush and watched them fill their bellies with water.

Today, it was easy to know where Juna would travel. There were things she liked to do for newcomers. First she'd take them for water, then to the place with the broom head bushes.

He knew because she'd done the same for him, years ago, before he'd grown tall and gangly and she'd grown beautiful.

That first day, he was seven and she was eight.

"Come on," she'd said to him, as if he'd been in Freewater a lifetime. He was seated on the damp ground in the village, dizzy with exhaustion. She leaned down and offered him her hand. His hand shook as he took hers, but she didn't say anything as she led him down the path to the water.

Just as with Homer and Ada, people smiled and welcomed him to his newfound freedom. By the time he got to the water and drank from Juna's bowl, he thought his chest would crack from the weight of all that freedom. Instead, he started to cry. Tears of fear and despair for all he'd left behind and for the uncertainty that lay ahead. Tears streamed down his face, wetting his shirt and clouding his vision.

Juna sat still beside him, quiet for a long time. Then she turned to him and asked, "Do you like fishing?"

Billy dried his eyes. "I d-d-don't know. I n-n-never d-d-did it b-b-before," he stuttered. His words came out like hailstones hitting the ground. But that didn't bother her any. From beside the water she picked up a long stick with a knotted net on the end.

"You have to be quick," she said. She caught one fish, then another. When it was his turn, his nervous hands dropped the net, and the wooden handle broke. "I-I-I'm s-s-sorry," he said.

Juna just shrugged. "There's lots of sticks," she said.

He'd gone right away to find the very best stick. She was first to find one, but he did find a piece of wood rounded all around with a hole through the middle. He'd handed it to Juna. A peace offering for having broken her stick.

"Look!" Juna said, and smiled as she put her hand through it. It was her first wooden bracelet. Billy smiled for the first time in freedom.

Much had changed since that day. The older and taller Billy got, the more self-conscious he became of his stutter and of his clumsy ways. Juna grew more beautiful and became the keeper of her mother's knowledge and expectations. Everyone knew he liked her. They always assumed it was because she was pretty. Everyone liked Juna. But Billy knew it was because of how she'd treated him that first day. Never once had she laughed or frowned or pitied him when he spoke to her.

Today, he raced ahead of Juna and her new arrivals, clearing a path to the half circle of broom head bushes. The path was so perfectly cleared and the day seemed so perfectly right, Billy even considered giving her the bracelet he'd made. Once she came to the broom head bushes he'd be there. He felt confident until he heard Ferdinand's laugh come from above in the trees. No, today was definitely not the day. Instead, he shrank behind a tree.

36

Homer

JUNA TURNED AWAY FROM THE WATER AND headed toward the trees with Ada and me following close behind. Ada squeezed my hand, or maybe I squeezed hers. Before long we came to a clearing. In the middle was a half circle of bushes, each with shaggy green leaves shaped like big, upside-down broom heads.

Ada and I stopped; our breath caught at the sight. The clearing was filled with children, just like us. The four children who we'd seen on the village road ran past us. A boy and a girl, a little bigger than me, were sword fighting with branches. Another boy was sitting in the shadow of a tree with wood shavings at his feet. Three girls just a little younger than Ada sat with a pile of vines, braiding and twisting them into crowns that they put on each of their heads. Two were running around the bushes, giggling as if nothing sad had ever happened in the world. The air was buzzing with talk and laughter.

"This is where the kids come," Juna said.

Ada and I stared at the children around us.

"Is this okay?" my sister asked. Her eyes were almost

afraid. I understood, it felt strange. Like seeing the last rose in a garden when summer ends. It's pretty, but it doesn't seem right that it's there.

"Yes," said Juna, with enough strength in her voice to make me exhale.

"Juna!" a voice yelled from up in the trees. There were two boys in them. One was hanging upside down from a limb, with a long shiny knife in his hand.

"You need some help?" he called to her again.

Swinging his legs around, he let go of the tree and sliced off a thin branch as he landed on the ground. He had a big smile on his face.

"A walking stick for you," he said, flipping his knife in the air and handing the stick to Juna. Everyone stopped and watched. Juna shook her head.

"Ferdinand, keep your stick. You best be careful with that knife," she said and turned her attention back to Ada and me. "You're hungry," she stated to Ada and smiled. "The swamp almost always has food if you know how to find it." Juna put her hand into one of the broom head bushes and lifted up its leaves. Underneath were bunches of small round green, red, and purple fruits.

"These are ready," Juna said, pulling the two deepest purple fruits and putting one in each of our hands. The skin was smooth and thick.

"Watch," said Juna, picking another. Using her thumbs,

162

she broke the skin and juice squirted out. Pale green meat showed on the inside. Juna put the whole thing into her mouth. The two little kids stopped running and came over. They grabbed hold of the small fruit and popped them into their mouths, too.

Ada and I did the same. Juice filled my mouth. Grapes. I once tried grapes on Southerland, but these were the biggest and sweetest I'd ever had. A smile broke out on Ada's face as she chewed. The fruit hit our bellies and our hunger woke up.

Juna picked more. We ate, our faces fat like squirrels with grapes.

"It's okay, there's more." Juna laughed, walking away. "Watch this."

Ada and I grabbed for as much fruit as our hands could hold and followed. "You think she's trying to find more grapes?" Ada gurgled, dribbling juice.

Juna walked outside the clearing and stopped under some trees. Small white blossoms clustered together along each branch. She undid a strap around her waist and put it about a tree's trunk and climbed up some fifteen feet. As she went, her steps shook the branches and tiny white blossoms fell from above.

Ada spun around in them.

"Look, Homer, it's raining flowers," she said.

A hive with sleepy bees buzzed in the tree. Quiet and

easy, Juna pulled off a piece of honeycomb. She took a leaf and wrapped it.

Juna dripped the honey onto the grapes in Ada's hand.

"Try it," she said.

Ada chewed her honey grape. No words, but laughter was all that came. I tried it. The warm, sweet, flowery honey hit my tongue and I understood. It tasted like happiness. For a moment, I forgot about Southerland and Anna and Mama being left behind, and I laughed, too.

Until a hawk-like screech came from overhead.

"RAH, RAHHHHHH!"

Ada grabbed my hand and I ducked down to cover her. Who knew what dangers Freewater had? But Juna didn't seem a bit worried. She rolled her eyes and shook her head. "It's okay," she said and pointed up.

Sure enough, like a flailing bird swooping down from a tree came the Bow and Arrow Girl. She howled as she let go of the rope and landed in front of us. She pulled a bow from her back and fired an arrow, hitting one of the juicy grapes in the bush.

"Sanzi!" yelled Juna.

Sanzi didn't pay Juna any mind. She strolled over to her arrow, pulled it from the grape, wiped the juice onto her pant leg, and placed it in her quiver.

With a grin like a cat that's caught a mouse, she looked at me then Ada and asked, "You think that was like Suleman?"

I knew there was only one right answer, "I guess so," I said.

Ada wasn't having any of it.

"But Suleman didn't have ropes," she pointed out. "And he didn't go yelling like that," said Ada, looking overhead. She still hadn't learned to say what people wanted to hear.

Sanzi ignored the critique. "I thought so," she said to me.

"You were so busy being Suleman, you scared them," said Juna, shaking her head at her sister.

"I heard he can shoot off six fire arrows before you can blink your eye," said Sanzi. She pulled her bow and pretended to fire arrows. "Did Suleman use his fire arrows?" she asked me.

My face grew hot. "He shot two," I said, hoping that would satisfy her curiosity.

"You saw him?" Sanzi bit her lip, like she would've traded places with me. I'd never met anyone who'd want to trade places with me. "Did you attack a plantation with him?" she asked.

"Not exactly," I said, hoping to not have to share more. More meant sharing that we'd left Mama behind, and that it was my fault.

"We were running, and he helped us," I explained.

"Leave them be," said Juna. I could tell she knew Sanzi would just keep pressing for more.

"I saw Suleman, and I know he didn't have a sad bow

like that." The Knife Boy laughed from across the clearing. He held his knife in the air.

"Ferdinand, you don't know anything about my bow!" Sanzi snapped back.

"I know his doesn't look like that. You can't shoot nothing but grapes with that ol' thing," said Ferdinand, balancing the handle of his knife on his fingertip.

I watched a swirl of anger rise in Sanzi's eyes.

"I'm gonna shoot that knife right out of his hand," she whispered. Then, quick as a whip, she pulled an arrow from her quiver, loaded her bow, and fired.

Sanzi might have been intent on proving she could shoot, but I guess she wasn't too good. Or maybe her bow really was sad because, instead of hitting the knife, her bow veered left and sliced a cut across Ferdinand's hand.

37

Anna

ANNA STARED AT THE CHICKEN FRYING IN Mrs. Petunia's pan and waited for it to darken. Burned chicken was the first step in her plan. Mrs. Petunia's near blindness meant her cooking always teetered on the edge of disaster. Most times, Anna was there as Mrs. Petunia's eyes and would alert her to a starting fire or a boiling-over pot, but today, she gave no warning. As Mrs. Petunia turned one way then another, struggling to get potatoes roasted, gravy thickened, and a cake baked, the chicken started smoking and slowly burned to a crisp.

"I'll have to figure something else for dinner," the weary woman said, rubbing her eyes and willing them to see.

"I could run down to the river and fish something for dinner," said Anna, feigning innocence.

"Master Crumb does like a good piece of fried fish. All right, go on down there and bring back what you can for ..."

Before Mrs. Petunia could finish her sentence Anna had a fishing rod in one hand and an empty jar in the other, and she was out the kitchen door. There wasn't much time. As she raced to the river, she hoped the jar would be big enough, but it was the best she could find without its disappearance being noted. Plus, this one could tuck into her apron pocket.

At the river's edge she baited her fishing line and cast it into the water. Then she dug a narrow hole about a foot deep and stuck the rod into it. That would have to do.

With that done, she could finally turn her attention to the next step in her plan. Sunlight shone on a thick bed of maypop flowers on the bank of the river. The purple, feathery, striped petals with a ring of gold made the flower so striking and ornate it seemed hard to believe it was known for its power to sedate.

Anna looked left, then right, making sure she would not be seen, then trudged knee deep in river water to the bed of maypop. She plucked the fancy flowers one by one until her apron was full and nothing but green leaves remained. With a few stones and a flat piece of fallen wood, she began. It seemed a pity to crush such beautiful little flowers. Each one set off a fragrant sweet aroma as it turned to pulp. She only paused when she saw the tremble of her rod. The fish could probably smell the maypop on her as she pulled them from the water.

Her jar was almost full once she carefully put every bit of pulp into it. Old Joe hadn't mentioned how many flowers he'd used for his maypop water. Would it be enough? It would have to be.

With her fish in one hand and the bottle tucked in her apron, Anna returned to the kitchen. By the time the fish was fried to a burn, the roasted potatoes dried out, and the cake deflated, Anna was sweaty, exhausted, and hungry herself. She balanced the food on a serving tray and carried it to the dining room, stopping right before entering to place her jar of precious pulp just outside the door.

Nora took a few polite spoonfuls but everyone else pushed their plates away.

Viola pouted. "Mama, this a disaster. We can't have everyone eat this for my wedding. We need to have Rose back cooking."

"Whiskey, sir?" Anna asked of Master Crumb.

"Bring the bottle from my study," said Crumb.

Like a key turning in a keyhole, the next step of Anna's plan clicked into place.

"Yes, Master," she said, and left the room with a water pitcher in hand.

In the office, Anna found the bottle kept beside Mr. Crumb's desk. Before returning to the dining room she poured whiskey to fill her jar just far enough to cover the pulp.

Thump. Thump. Anna's heartbeat filled her ears as she re-entered the dining room and poured whiskey into Mr. Crumb's glass, and began walking back toward the door to return the bottle.

"Leave it here," Crumb said. The whiskey bottle turned hot as red coal in her hand. *Would he note that too much was missing from the bottle?*

"Yes, sir," she said and placed it beside him on the table. He stared at it.

"Girl, clear these plates. Have Petunia send us some smoked meat, bread, and cheese. I imagine she can't mess that up," sighed Mrs. Crumb.

"Don't worry yourself one bit, Sweet Pea. Rose will be there to do what she's told," Mrs. Crumb continued, reassuring her daughter. "You've got your dress. You're gonna look like a princess. The wedding tent is here and we'll have it up in a couple of weeks. Your new in-laws will be sending over their darkies to help with serving at the reception. Never mind we'll be missing the Homer boy who ran off. But maybe he'll even be caught by then. Almost the whole county is coming. Sweet Pea, this wedding is gonna be like nothing this county has ever seen!"

With that, Mr. Crumb's ears perked up and his attention was called away from his whiskey.

"Speaking of runaways, I received good news this evening," said Mr. Crumb. "We've heard from some militiamen who work the swamp in North Carolina. Good ones, too. They're expected in two or three weeks. I tell you this will work. Heck, maybe I'll even ride out with them."

Hearing their plans for Homer and Ada, Anna looked

up, and in a flash she imagined all of the table's wasted food turned over on each of their heads. Potatoes, gravy, fish, and cake ran down their faces. *Yes, that's about right,* thought Anna.

"Take those dishes out," said Mrs. Crumb, frowning as she watched Anna. Then, she hissed to her husband, "How could you go to the market and bring back this wicked-eyed girl?"

Annoyed, Mrs. Crumb turned her attention back to the issue at hand. "Mr. Crumb, must I remind you that a few weeks from now is your daughter's wedding? Did you ever stop to think about that? I'm not having you and militia-men running about the swamp when you need to be here tending to the most important day of your daughter's life," said Mrs. Crumb.

Anna stacked the plates a little higher and turned to leave.

"Girl," Mrs. Crumb called, "take that food out to the dogs. I imagine they're right hungry from all this chasing after runaways."

"Yes, Mistress." Anna left the room. She picked up the jar outside the door as she went.

Out in the yard, a fight over the food ensued between the dogs. As Anna watched, ideas tumbled in her head. Where would she hide her jar?

Nearby was a large bush with a patch of soft dirt under

it. Anna took her jar, filled the remainder with water, and sealed it shut. Using her hand as a shovel, she dug into the moist earth and buried it.

She was still hungry, but as she patted the ground that now held her plan, she felt full of satisfaction.

38

Sanzi

IT WAS EARLY MORNING.

Behind the wooden divide of their cabin, Sanzi listened to her father move about, preparing to leave with the patrollers.

Sanzi preferred the quiet of the morning. It contrasted with the yells and screams of the day before. First Ferdinand's scream as blood poured from the cut on his hand. A slash right across his palm.

"I'm gonna break that bow into pieces!"

There was Juna's yelling as she wrapped his hand in a soft leaf and tied it with a bit of vine from one of the girl's crowns.

"We have to get him to Mama!"

Most of all, there was her mother's yelling.

"You could have really hurt him! There is enough hurting out there—we can't have it here in Freewater!"

Her mother had gone on and on. Glaring at her with one disappointed frown after another. Sanzi tried to explain that it was an accident, but that didn't matter.

Mrs. Light had taken Sanzi's bow, quiver, and all of her arrows. Sanzi awakened early with that thought in mind.

Thankfully, this morning was quiet and only her father was awake. Sanzi liked to mix the mud for him. Among the bowls that lined the walls of the cabin, she moved the largest to the hearth. The water in the bowl shimmered orange from the fire. In another smaller bowl was mud from the day before, caked and hard. With a bit of warm water and a whip of her wooden spoon, the mud went soft and smooth. She dabbed a small bit on the back of her hand and let it dry. The color and feel were perfect.

David emerged from behind the wooden divider, inspected the mud, and nodded in approval.

Arms, legs, and chest bare, her father sat down with the bowl before him. He scooped small amounts of mud into his hand, and with even strokes, applied it to his skin. Sanzi watched him, moving in mirroring motions on her own legs and arms. When his face had almost disappeared behind the mud mask, she pulled the bowl close and dabbed her hand in the mud and began applying it to his back. The crisscrossing scars stretched from his neck to his waist and across his shoulders, like a nest of snakes frozen under the skin.

Her fingers trembled slightly as she smoothed the mud onto the ridges of his back. In the firelight, her father turned and smiled, his reminder for her that the scars no longer hurt.

"What happened with Ferdinand?" asked David. His words didn't have the sting Sanzi had heard from her mother the day before.

"It was an accident, and he's always saying things," said Sanzi.

David nodded and pulled his daughter close into his muddied arms.

"I have the scars on my back, you can touch those. But most of the scars we get from out there aren't ones you can see. Be patient with Ferdinand. You're my brave girl, and nothing Ferdinand can say will change that." He hugged her tighter.

Be patient? Sanzi thought. Ferdinand was awful! It was like he wanted to make her miserable.

"Now let's fix this mud before it dries," he said. And they did. Once done, Sanzi pulled over bowls of vines and leaves. Rubbing the leafy vines with a little mud, her father applied each one, spiraling them upward from his legs to his chest and arms and finally his neck. He was ready.

"This is good work," her father said as he pecked a kiss onto her head.

"I want to go with you," she told him. He sighed.

"No, you're coming with me today," said Mrs. Light, who stepped around the divider, arms folded.

Sanzi groaned inside. Most days she could avoid her mother's work, but today would not be one of them.

"No long face, I'll see you soon," said David before he hugged Sanzi and a sleeping Juna and left the cabin.

"We leave early," said Mrs. Light to Sanzi. "Go get ready."

"We are going into deep muck. Remember, bend your knees," said Mrs. Light. Her pensive stare prickled the hairs on Sanzi's neck.

"I know what to do, Mama," said Sanzi. Morning mist clung to the leaves and created shadows of gray between the trees.

Sanzi bent her knees, picked up her heels, and balanced on the balls of her feet to keep up with her mother's swift pace through the darkness. Mrs. Light glanced back at her daughter, ignored her sour expression, and sniffed her approval.

"Ginger. We'll need plenty," said Mrs. Light. Knees sunken into the soft earth, Mrs. Light bent low, allowing her hands to sink into the mud under a bed of heart-shaped leaves. Each little heart came up easy, as if they knew they'd be treated well.

"The swamp knows to give and to take away," she said. "Mrs. Sanzi, the oldest woman on the plantation taught me just that. A fool we called 'master' had us go into the swamp, just on the edge, for plants and herbs and every other thing, because he had a sick child who nobody knew how to make better. Mrs. Sanzi had come from people who knew the swamp, and she taught me."

Up came the ginger root. She rubbed the reddish skin, raised it to her mouth, and bit down. With two fingers, she pinched off a piece and handed it to Sanzi.

"I named you for her."

"I know," said Sanzi, taking the root. *I've heard this story a hundred times!*

"You *know*," Mrs. Light said, shaking her head wearily. "Go on, eat," she ordered her daughter.

Sanzi bit down, letting the heat of the root take hold. She clenched her jaws, willing her mouth to accept it. Finally, her eyes watered and she coughed.

"It's strong, it's ready," Mrs. Light said, reaching down to pull more. Sanzi knew to help her. "Remember, don't—"

"I know, I know," sniffed Sanzi, fingering the plant, pulling off the firm red knobs, and leaving behind the buttery-yellow delicate baby roots. Each heart was put back in its place and the bed was left looking untouched.

"Don't take all. Only what the plant can give," finished Sanzi.

"Out there—" Mrs. Light's voice grew stronger. She pointed to the place beyond the fog, beyond all that Sanzi had ever known. "Out there, they take and take from the land. They use us to do it. Only ugly comes from that land."

Mrs. Light suddenly stood, waiting for Sanzi to join her.

"We'll need a bit of wood for rope." Sanzi turned about, eyeing each tree and walking a bit farther until she saw the smooth trunk of a poplar tree. Lying at the foot of the tree were fallen branches big and small. Sanzi chose a large one.

"Use this." Her mother handed her a sharp stone. Angling the stone, Sanzi scraped back the smooth bark to reveal the fleshiness underneath. She pulled off long pieces of creamy wood.

"Let me see," said Mrs. Light, taking several pieces and tying them together in a tight, long strand. She pulled hard on each end of the strand. It held.

"This is good," she said, satisfied. "We'll need to fill this." She pulled out a large net.

That will take forever, Sanzi thought but did not say. Instead, she sighed and found another large branch.

They worked for much of the morning. Once the net was full, Mrs. Light stood up, tied it to her back, and began walking among the trees, touching one plant to see if it was ready for picking or smelling another.

She'd hand each leaf or root to Sanzi and wait for a response. "Elderberry," said Sanzi. Sanzi followed.

"This one?" said Mrs. Light. Sanzi drew a blank.

"Pink swamp rose," said Mrs. Light, waving the plant in front of Sanzi.

"Now we go home. West. Show me," said Mrs. Light with an expectant look at her daughter.

Sanzi scanned the swamp around her.

"You'll need to look for—" started Mrs. Light.

"I know!" said Sanzi, exasperated, as she touched the damp moss of a tree and pointed left. Her mother had shown her a million times. It was the most important thing Mrs. Light had taught her in the swamp: being able to find her way home.

"This direction is west." Sanzi scowled and began walking.

"It's good you know them. You may need them one day to find your way back to Freewater," said Mrs. Light.

"I'll never need them because you'll never let me leave," said Sanzi. Her eyes blazed. "I know all of these things!"

Mrs. Light looked at Sanzi for a long while, contemplating her daughter's words. She took Sanzi's angry face in her hands.

"*You know, you know, you know* so much, but you still don't see," said Mrs. Light, as she picked a handful of wild white azaleas and wrapped them with a thin vine.

"Come," said Mrs. Light.

They headed west on familiar paths until Mrs. Light made a sudden turn. They walked to the edge of Freewater, and to Sanzi's shock, they crossed over its boundaries. Mrs. Light made no mention of it.

They walked on a short distance, until they came to a hulking cypress tree.

Sanzi's mother pulled back the brambles and uncovered bouquets of dried flowers at its base, and on the tree's wide trunk, a carving of a crescent moon. Years had turned the crescent a deep brown. Mrs. Light kissed her fingertips, touched the crescent, and placed her azaleas at the foot of the tree.

"It's time you knew the story about how we ran away," said Mrs. Light.

Sanzi sighed. "Yes, you were on the plantation and there was man who tied up the master, and you ran until you found Big Tree." Sanzi knew the tale by heart; all of the children of Freewater did.

"Well, there was more," said Mrs. Light, gently touching the tree as if it might break.

"His name was Moonlight, because that's all he ever saw," she said.

"When we ran, he was only one day old. He was born in the moonlight, we ran in the moonlight, and after days of walking in the dark swamp—hungry, hot, with no place for sleeping, he died in the moonlight."

"I couldn't save my Moonlight. He died the day before we found Big Tree and came to the place that would be our home. He was my first child and I couldn't save him." Tears flowed from Mrs. Light's eyes.

"I had a brother?" was all Sanzi could think to say. A

brother. It felt strange even thinking it. Mrs. Light nodded and touched the ground under the tree.

"Yes, he was the reason I found the courage to run with your papa. Most who ran were caught and whipped, and I didn't want that. But when I saw Moonlight, I knew he must be free. Must be free."

She touched her face to the tree and let tears fall.

"When you and your sister and the other children were born, you knew so little of pain. There was no need to pass this pain on to you. We told Juna when she was thirteen, and we planned to do the same for you, but this can't wait. It's time for you to know that the world out there can take the things you hold most dear. It took my Moonlight. I swore I would never let slavery take another child of mine." And she hugged Sanzi.

"You only see the gifts that Suleman brings, you don't see the ugly world he fights in," said Mrs. Light. "We have done all of this so that you wouldn't need to fight in that world."

Sanzi listened and thought of the brother she'd never know.

39

Homer

YOUR WHOLE WORLD CAN CHANGE IN TWENTY-one days.

We'd been in Freewater for that long, and sometimes life at Southerland felt like a distant dream. Mrs. Light's salves and bandages had healed my head wound and ankle. Now Ada almost never asked about the Big House, Mistress, Master Crumb, nor Stokes. We no longer peeked around corners and trees, looking for them.

Even the steps to get Mama to Freewater were jumbled and disappearing from my memory, but I still tried. *Forest, river, tree boat, lily pads . . . sky people?* I wasn't sure anymore.

Mama and Anna were still there, but for a time I tucked them away in my mind—where I wouldn't mix what I was seeing and becoming in Freewater with what I'd been and done in Southerland. Still, my mind failed me at night as I slept. They both came to see me in my dreams.

After our first few nights in Freewater, Mrs. Light had Ada and me move into Billy's cabin with his father, Ibra, and the oldest woman in the village, Mrs. Faith.

"Welcome! It's good that you are with us. You will be

happy here." Ibra said this confidently and with a big smile, as if happiness hung from trees. That was his way. At first, his happy-for-no-good-reason way made us nervous.

Of course, Ada asked, "Why are you always so smiley?"

For the first time, Ibra spoke with a face as serious as death. "Every day in Freewater is a day my Billy ain't out there. That's enough to make me smile."

Today, we were in the fields. Most of Freewater had come. Ada, Sanzi, Billy, and I had our "piece" to clear for the day. We hadn't finished much of it. Ada was being Ada, and Sanzi…in the past twenty-one days I'd learned that Sanzi had a way of finding trouble.

"Watch this," Sanzi said.

She whipped her sling in the air.

Whiss, whiss, whiss, it went. Then she released. The ear of corn didn't see the stone coming and it fell off the tall stalk without a fight.

"We should go hunting—that would be a heap better than picking boring ol' corn!" said Sanzi.

"Sanzi, we need to do our p-p-piece," said Billy.

"Now you're starting to sound like my mama," she replied. "I'm going!" And with that, Sanzi was gone.

Billy, Ada, and I worked in silence for a long while.

"You think they got any flowers around here?" asked

Ada, brushing aside the corn stalks, half expecting to see blooms hidden behind them.

"Don't worry with the flowers right now," I said.

Juna had braided Ada's hair and taught her how to twist flowers into garlands and to weave them through her braids. Ever since, Ada walked about in search of flowers, determined that she would be Juna's twin. It was her way of missing Mama. Like Juna, Mama loved flowers. Mama couldn't be here, so Ada loved Juna.

We continued pulling corn ears off and tossing them into nets on the ground. It was early morning, but plenty folks were there. We couldn't see them, but their talking, laughing, arguing, and crying came pouring through the stalks. It mixed with the clatter of the swamp, animal chirping, and tweeting. Everything felt...alive.

"It feels d-d-different, don't it? The work," said Billy.

As soon as he asked the question, I understood the answer.

There was no one there directing us, whipping us, threatening us. The swamp gave us our directions. When the rain came and the fields went wet, we knew to leave. When it was dry and the fog cleared, we knew to work.

Sweat poured down our necks and backs. Free and Hope ran through the stalks with water in bowls for us to drink. Today, Billy drank and pulled off his shirt to wipe the sweat from his brow. A raised *C* mark shone on his shoulder like a curved serpent slithering under his deep brown skin.

"You remember?" I asked Billy, pointing at the mark.

"C-C-Copperwood," said Billy, rubbing his serpent. "You?" he asked.

"Southerland," I said.

"Field?" I asked.

"M-m-most times," Billy said. "My father worked for the o-o-overseer. Sometimes I was w-w-with him."

"We weren't branded on Southerland," I said.

I'd seen that Copperwood *C* a few times at Souther-land. I didn't know a thing about reading, but I knew that mark.

"Yeah, m-m-mostly it's for runaways, but Ogletree liked to h-h-hire us out and he didn't want any m-m-mistaking where we belonged."

"Does it hurt?" Ada asked as she reached up and traced the shiny mark with her fingertip.

"Ada, don't," I said. She didn't know a thing about boundaries.

But Billy let her.

"I-i-it's okay," he said, bending down for her. "No, it d-d-doesn't hurt."

"Mine doesn't hurt anymore, either," said Ada, pulling up her sleeve and showing the crumpled-up stiff skin on her arm, brown lace frozen forever. "I picked some flowers in Mistress's garden. She was mad."

Billy ran his finger over the curves of Ada's lace.

"It h-h-hurt?" asked Billy.

Ada nodded.

"You remember when they did it?" I asked Billy, hoping Ada wouldn't go back to remembering Mistress Crumb and her mean ways. Billy picked fallen ears of corn and pushed them into the net bags.

"Yeah, I was maybe s-s-seven," Billy said.

"That's like me. Mama says I'm seven," said Ada.

"It felt so h-h-hot, it was cold," said Billy, rubbing his arm.

"I cried a whole lot. That kettle water was hot," said Ada. "You cry?"

"I got d-d-dizzy. I suppose I c-c-cried," Billy replied while staring into the corn nets.

"What did Ibra say?" I asked.

Billy was quiet a long while.

"He was the one who d-d-did it," he said. Then he started pulling ears of corn from the stalks quick as lightning.

Ada's forehead wrinkled. "Ibra did that to you? But he's so nice. He's not a thing like Mistress."

"It w-w-was his job. He did it when the overseer told him to. He didn't h-h-have no choice," said Billy into the stalks. "I r-r-remember Papa's eyes. They looked s-s-so... s-s-scared, that's when I knew something b-b-bad was about t-t-to h-h-happen. Mama wrapped it in a p-p-poultice to h-h-help it heal. It hurt a long time." Billy rubbed his arm.

"Your papa ever say anything about it?" I asked. My mind was still trying to make the Ibra I knew match the one who'd made the mark on Billy.

"N-n-no," said Billy.

More quiet.

"That's when I s-s-started t-t-talking like this," whispered Billy.

"You mean like chopping wood?" asked Ada. "I don't mind."

"Wasn't long after that P-P-Papa and me l-l-left," said Billy.

"We were scared when we ran away," said Ada. "Were you scared?"

Billy shook his head. "I d-d-didn't even know we were r-r-running away. I thought I was g-g-going to w-w-work with Papa. The o-o-overseer would send him to t-t-town s-s-sometimes with a p-p-pass to get things for the c-c-crops. He'd g-g-go walking. This time he asked if I could go with him for h-h-help. W-w-we walked off the p-p-plantation, like any other d-d-day."

"How'd you get here?" I asked. "To Freewater?"

"Papa was set to have us live in the swamp. We w-w-walked a lot and I got s-s-so t-t-tired I thought I would crumble into the g-g-ground, then Papa picked me up and we kept walking. Then David c-c-came along and he b-b-brought us here," said Billy.

I started pulling ears of corn. My mind was swirling.

Ada watched me. We both had the same question, but I didn't want to ask it, and Ada didn't know how not to ask it.

"What about your mama? The one with the poultice?" asked Ada.

"Hush up about that!" My neck felt stiff as iron as I tried reaching for even higher ears of corn. Billy wouldn't want to go talking about his mama, so why did Ada need to pry?

"Later Papa told me they decided on things t-t-together. He'd r-r-run w-w-with me. If she c-c-came we'd have b-b-been c-c-caught. Master would have n-n-never thought we'd r-r-run off w-w-without M-M-Mama, that's why h-h-he let us g-g-go. Mama had her m-m-mind set on m-m-me being f-f-free," said Billy.

"You say goodbye?" asked Ada.

Billy's face melted with sadness. "How I was gonna say g-g-goodbye when I didn't even know w-w-we were l-l-leaving?"

Billy picked up an ear of corn and threw it high over the stalks.

"She tried to h-h-hug me, but I was busy trying to r-r-run off and catch up to P-P-Papa," he said.

"What happened to her?" asked Ada.

"Don't know f-f-for sure. Suleman s-s-sent word that she w-w-was sold. Don't know that w-w-we could e-e-ever f-f-find where to," said Billy.

I knew it was coming and I wasn't ready to hear it.

"Me and Homer didn't get a chance to say bye to Mama," started Ada.

"Ada, he doesn't need to worry about all that now. Why don't you go on and find some flowers? I think I might have seen some near the front of the field," I said.

Ada's eyes went bright and everything else was almost forgotten.

"You did?" she said.

"That's right, go on," I said. And off she ran.

For a long time, Billy and I worked without saying a word. Only the songs and talking of the other folks in the field filled the space between us. We were both only half there. He was thinking through his story and I was thinking through mine.

A light rain came down and the ground got soft under our feet. Folks started to leave. Juna came up to us.

"You're learning Freewater work," Juna said to me. "They say the sweat is the same as back in the old place, but it smells sweeter."

"Hi, Billy," said Juna, turning toward him.

"H-h-hi, J-J-Juna," said Billy, keeping his eyes on the corn.

"Where's Ada?" Juna asked.

"Off picking flowers," I said.

"That girl. I finally found someone who likes them more than me," Juna said, touching her flowery crown. "Let's go get her before we head back."

189

Juna, Billy, and I went to fetch Ada at the field's edge, but she wasn't there. We went farther into the swamp. Nothing but the sound of swamp clatter.

"ADA! ADA!" we called through the corn stalks and into the bush, but she didn't call back.

It was my fault. I'd sent her away and then I'd lost her. My fault, all over again.

She needed a finder. Ada needed Mama. *I* needed Mama.

If I could guide Mama to me, she could get me to Ada.

River, sinkhole, lily pads . . . tree hideout . . . tree people, I huffed to myself as I ran through the corn stalks. That wasn't right.

Forest, river, tree hideout, lily pad . . . zigzag, tree people, sky bridge. No, No, No.

As I tore down the path to the river and up the dirt way through Freewater's cabins, everything came clear. Mama wouldn't know those steps. Mama wasn't coming. If there was finding that needed doing, I'd have to be the one to do it.

Where was Ada?

40

Nora

"STAND UP STRAIGHT, NORA," CHIDED HER mother.

They were in Viola's bedroom. It was six days before the wedding and Nora stood, covered in muslin and silk. She was fidgety and impatient about the whole affair. Rose was back. At first, Nora expected that things might finally return to normal. But they hadn't. Most of the family didn't notice much difference. Apart from moving a bit slower, Rose's meals were made on time and tasted so good that Viola's worries about her wedding banquet dinner dissolved.

But for Nora, there wasn't anything normal about Rose. Although her body had come back, Rose's mind and spirit were elsewhere. Her eyes were so empty and dark, to look in them was like peering into one of the kitchen's empty cast iron pots.

Nora had also heard Rose whispering in despair to Mrs. Petunia.

"My Homer and Ada, they've been gone so long, they

could be dead in that swamp. I don't know if there's any living if my babies are gone."

As time passed and it didn't seem likely Homer and Ada would be found, Nora had made it her singular purpose to fill Rose's eyes. A flower left on the kitchen table, a ribbon placed on her bed. Anything to make Rose as she was before everything had gone wrong. Today, Nora was hopeful. Peaches had arrived, and making preserves was Nora's favorite activity. And unfortunately, for this dress fitting, Rose and Nora had been pulled away from a bubbling pot of peach preserves.

"Rose, you be sure to get that hem straight as a rod," ordered Mrs. Crumb.

"Yessum, Mistress," said Rose. She was on her knees, pinning the hem.

Nora could feel Rose's warm breath tickle the skin on her leg. She giggled and Rose glanced up, serious-eyed.

"Please, child, stand still so we can get this done," scolded her mother. "I can't believe the time and work you take out of me, Nora."

Nora squirmed. The peach jam was almost finished, and she was determined to be there. Peach jam meant she could get the sugary sweet syrup left over at the bottom of the large black pot. Rose always saved it for her. Nora could almost taste the sticky goodness on her fingers.

Once the hem was pinned, Rose sat back on her

haunches. It was perfectly straight. She bent down on her hands and knees and began collecting her needles and thread.

Mrs. Crumb and Viola stood examining Nora.

"Nora, why do I always have to remind you to wear your hair down?" Mrs. Crumb uncinched Nora's hair and tried pulling bangs over her left eye, in an attempt to conceal her strawberry mark. Nora swerved right then left.

"Stand still!" said Mrs. Crumb.

But Nora continued.

"If you won't stand still, you'll have to sit," said an exasperated Mrs. Crumb, and in one quick movement she held tight to her daughter's shoulders and sat her right down onto Rose's bent back.

It all happened so fast Nora wasn't quite sure what to do.

The most imperceptible exhale of air escaped Rose's nostrils.

For an instant Rose glanced up at Mrs. Crumb. Then she averted her eyes solidly to the floor.

Nora tried standing up and her mother pushed her back down.

"You heard me, sit." And with that, she pulled Nora's hair over her octopus mark.

Through Rose's threadbare dress, Nora could feel Braille-like scabs across her back, marks thick as the cord Papa used to tie up their porch swing.

Viola and Mrs. Crumb prattled on.

"Look at that, you see, her mark will be well hidden for your day. You can hardly tell it's there!" said Mrs. Crumb to Viola. Nora peered down. Silent tears spilled from Rose's face and dripped into the rug beneath her. As if struck by lightning, Nora jumped off and ran. Once in her room, she slammed the door behind her.

"Nora! We aren't finished," yelled her mother.

Nora put her back against the door. What had she done? She tugged the dress over her head and threw it to the floor. By the time she made it downstairs to the kitchen, Rose had already poured the peach jam into their glass mason jars and was closing each one.

Rose didn't look up.

Instead, she placed the jars neatly along the counter and stood at the kitchen window. Nora stepped closer to the stove and peeked into the large black cast-iron pot, expecting a taste of the jam. However, it was wiped clean. While staring at the forest and swampland in the distance, Rose spoke.

"You know, when she was small, your sister would come visit this kitchen. She'd come and sit in that seat, where you are now. She wasn't like you, staying here all the time. Mistress and your father wouldn't have liked that. But she'd sneak away. Come right on in here, begging for milk and peeking in my pots for food. Boy, did that child love milk. If she could've had it right from the cow she would have.

I always kept back extra for her. She'd sit there, talking on about one thing or another. Most times, I couldn't understand a word she said. But she'd talk to me. And I'd give her milk and any small cookies I had. Of course, in time, she stopped coming."

Nora had sat in that wooden chair most of her life, but for the first time it felt hot, burning her backside. She stood up. Viola had sat in that chair, *her* chair. She used to visit Rose, but she never spoke to Rose now. Never. To her, Rose didn't exist, except to cook. Nora was nothing like Viola. Was she?

Nora could never be like her. Then a flash of Rose's tears when Nora sat atop her back came to mind. Her face flushed with shame and something else that caught her by surprise.

She was filled with fear. Fear that if she didn't do something, she would become like her sister.

41

Sanzi

FREEWATER WAS QUIET BUT SANZI'S MIND WAS not. It had been twenty-one days since her incident with Ferdinand. Twenty-one days without her bow. For twenty-one days, thoughts of Moonlight had haunted her, and she was close to rethinking her dream of becoming Suleman.

Then Suleman brought three new souls to Freewater along with precious gifts—salt, real rope, and a cooking pot. No tools, but still all of Freewater had come to see and praise Suleman's offering. Sanzi had touched each one. Like a changing season, slowly, her dreams returned along with her itch for exploration and adventure. Along with it came her yearning to reclaim her bow. It was time. Mrs. Light didn't agree.

Sanzi left the work of the cornfields, climbed a high limb of Big Tree, and peered down.

There were circles of people at work in the shade. Each circle was piled high with wood in the center. Each person moved intently, pulling the wood meat from the bark and braiding the pieces together into rope. Her mother was there, the hardest working of them all.

Gauging by the pile of work before her mother, Sanzi judged that she could take her bow for the afternoon and have it back in the cabin before her mother even knew it was gone.

She came down the tree and snuck around the back of her cabin. Inside, she went directly to her parents' divider. Against the wall lay her bow and quiver. To Sanzi, they looked forlorn and neglected. She'd fix that. She strapped on the bow and left.

Sanzi already had her destination in mind. Her place. Today Suleman was sure to be there. She would show him her bow, he'd show her how to shoot, and they'd go on adventures together.

Sanzi went to the river, walked along the edge, found her boat, and rowed toward her place. She docked at the bottom of the small, inclined slope and listened as sounds of thumping and breathing came from her hill. Perhaps Sanzi's fantasy had come true! Excited, she scrambled up the embankment.

Someone was there. *It must be Suleman.*

"I knew you'd come," she said as she climbed up.

"What do you mean?"

Sanzi's heart sank as she recognized that voice.

"What are *you* doing here?" she demanded from the top of the hill, trying to shade her disappointment with anger.

"What are *you* doing here?" asked Ferdinand. "Why are you sneaking up on me?"

Like nothing had gone wrong, like he wasn't trespassing, Ferdinand sauntered over to the tree target and pulled out his knife.

"This is *my* spot!" said Sanzi. The slower he strolled, the angrier she became.

Ferdinand glanced around. "What do you mean *your* spot? Who says?" he asked, throwing his knife.

Chop! Again, dead center.

Burning heat sprang up in Sanzi's belly.

He couldn't be here. What if Suleman came back and instead of her, he found this horrible person? Maybe he'd never come back again.

"You see all the marks on those trees? I'm the one who made 'em." In a flash, Sanzi loaded her sling and swung. It hit the handle of Ferdinand's knife and knocked it from the trunk to the ground.

"Hey!" Ferdinand's face grew serious and instead of sauntering, he ran to the tree and recovered his weapon. "Don't hit my knife," he said, brushing the mud from the blade.

"Don't throw your knife at my tree!" Sanzi yelled back. "I don't care a thing about your ol' knife. Besides, my papa says you shouldn't throw knives into trees. It makes the blade go bad faster. My papa showed me you need to get a good hard stone to keep the blade sharp."

"Your papa said this and your papa said that. I'm about

tired of hearing all the things your papa says," said Ferdi-nand, spitting on the hill. On *her* hill!

"Well, go, then!" said Sanzi.

Undeterred, Ferdinand narrowed his eyes, and he brought his face to Sanzi's.

"This swamp doesn't belong to you," said Ferdinand.

"This place does," said Sanzi.

"You're angry because you have to stay right here. Stuck. Ain't no sense in being mad at me about it. You don't know up from down after you leave Freewater. You're not even supposed to have that bow! I swear I'll break that bow to pieces before you get to use it again," said Ferdinand.

Sanzi felt her stomach knot from the stone of truth Ferdinand had thrown. *Show no weakness.*

"You best go," said Sanzi in the strongest voice she could muster.

The two stood face-to-face. A standoff to see who would leave first.

The solution to that quandary was decided by some-thing beyond them.

It was decided by a scream. Ada's scream.

42

Sanzi

AS THE SCREAM ECHOED THROUGH THE SWAMP, Sanzi knew one thing for certain: She wanted to beat Ferdinand to it.

Ferdinand took off on foot, but Sanzi ran for her tall tree, certain her rope bridges could get her there faster. She climbed up, took the belt from around her waist, and slung it over the nearest tree rope.

Ziiiiiip! Sanzi teetered and swung as she careened toward the scream. When she hit the ground, she saw Ferdinand was just behind her.

The two encountered three wild pigs snorting and squealing around Ada, who in terror had rolled herself into a ball. The horn of one pig was caught in Ada's dress, making it shriek even louder and causing Ada to do the same.

Sanzi let out a howl and charged. The boars, apart for the one entangled in Ada's dress, scattered into the thick of the swamp. The last beast was too close for her bow. Instead, with a quick wind-up she swung her sling. It struck the pig in its right temple, causing it to heave to one side. Ada's dress tore free. Angry, the pig swung around. Grunting deeply, it charged at Sanzi and Ferdinand. But Sanzi stood her ground, loaded her sling, and swung again. Not to be outdone, Ferdinand aimed and threw his knife at the pig. The blade flashed through the air but Sanzi's stone hit first, straight to the head, knocking the animal sideways toward the forbidden edge where the dry land dropped off. The hilt of Ferdinand's knife hit the pig's leg, knocking it off-balance, and sent it tumbling over the edge and out of sight.

43

Homer

I ONLY ARRIVED IN TIME TO SEE SANZI'S SLING shot, Ferdinand's knife throw, and a pig tumble over the edge. I've seen some courageous things before but nothing like that. It was bravery for all the world to see. For a moment, I wanted to be like them.

Ada ran over and squeezed me. I hugged her right back, one worthy of me and Mama put together.

"They came after me," Ada said into my shirt. "I didn't even know pigs could be angry. I thought they were gonna eat me."

"I'm sorry, Ada, I should have never sent you running off," I said. "But I found you." I hugged her once more.

"It's the acorns," Juna said and walked over to a nearby tree. "They fall from these oaks. That's what they wanted, not you."

Ada looked at the acorns as if they'd attacked her.

Shuddering and heavy grunts echoed up from the ditch below, loud at first then quieter until there was silence.

"You think it's dead?" Ada asked.

"Well, it sure ain't sleeping down there," sassed back

Ferdinand. Ada, Billy, Juna, Sanzi, and I stared over the edge. Down the slope maybe ten feet lay the pig, a spear of wood cut clear through its belly.

"We gotta get it up from there," said Sanzi.

"Your brain must have gone over the edge with that pig," said Juna. "You know going down there would be leaving Freewater. Mama would hang you by the feet right alongside her herbs and flowers when we got home."

"Let's just leave it. That ol' pig ain't worth all of that," said Ferdinand, picking up his knife from the edge of the cliff.

"We shouldn't leave it down th-th-there," whispered Billy. "N-n-nothing deserves to be l-l-left like that."

His words hung in the air like a fog cloud.

"I don't see how we could get it up from there," I said. More white-pointed spears were all around the pig, making it almost unreachable.

Sanzi was already unwrapping vines from around her waist and knotting a harness.

"Give me some of your rope," she said to Billy and Juna.

Before we knew it, Sanzi had a harness strapped on and she threw us a long tether rope to hold.

Juna sucked her teeth in disapproval and resignation. "Right, so I see we're all gonna be tied up there with Mama's herbs." She turned to the group. "We'll line up, hold the rope, and put her down there real slow," she instructed, then she looked back at her sister. "Just don't do anything crazy."

"I don't know what you mean—I don't ever do anything crazy," Sanzi said with a frown.

Ada tugged at Sanzi's arm. "Hey, do you know how to fly?" she asked, serious as sin.

Sanzi rolled her eyes and shook her head. "I don't need to fly, that's why I've got this," Sanzi said, tugging on the rope.

"Those spikes hurt so bad. It would be better if you knew how to fly," Ada counseled.

"Ada, you have the most important job," said Juna. She took Ada's hand and walked her to the drop's edge. "Lay down here, look over the edge, and keep your eyes on Sanzi, while we set her down there. That way we can make sure she gets down right up close to that pig. You'll be our eyes."

Ada smiled, pleased to be given an important job by her swamp angel.

As for me, I wasn't sure about any of it. I silently wished I was back in the village tucked under a mat in Billy and Ibra's cabin. But watching Ada lie at the edge made me nervous so I set myself closest to her at the front of the rope. After me was Juna, Billy, then Ferdinand with the end of the rope wrapped around his waist. I couldn't believe it. I was the leader.

"Y'all ready?" said Juna. There wasn't a bit of me that felt ready.

"I'm always ready to help you, Juna!" called Ferdinand, with a little bow and fresh smile.

Juna rolled her eyes.

"Y'all ready?" she asked again.

"Yes!" they called out. So, I said it, too. When we said it together it sounded true. Sanzi took off her bow and arrow and let the rope hold her as she slid herself off the edge. The rope went tight and heavy.

"Send me down," she called back to us.

I looked back and Juna had the rope wound around each hand. I tried to do the same except my hands were slick with sweat.

"You've gotta tell us when to let out the rope," Juna said to me.

"Okay." I said it fast, before my mind was clear that I had broken one of my rules for invisibility. *Never be the one telling anybody what to do.* But Juna seemed certain that this was right.

"Okay," I said again, trying to sound strong. "Give some rope."

"What?" Ferdinand yelled.

"Give some rope!" I said louder. My voice felt like a thunderclap in my chest. But the trees didn't fall and the sky didn't part. The only change was that more rope came down and Sanzi's face disappeared over the drop-off edge.

I tried it again. "Give some rope!" Another thunderclap. Again, more rope came.

I let the rope loose, a small bit at a time.

"Y'all planning on getting me to the bottom sometime today?" called Sanzi.

"You let us do this!" Juna yelled back.

In that moment, I was ready to break another rule. I could've hugged Juna.

"That girl is crazy. Nothing is exciting enough or fast enough for her. Don't pay her a bit of mind. You're doing right," said Juna.

"She's almost down there," said Ada back to me.

Ada lay directing us, making sure Sanzi went where she needed. Then the rope went light again.

"I made it!" Sanzi called from below. We all ran to the edge.

She was down there waving and smiling.

"Girl, stop all that showing out and put the rope around that pig," yelled Ferdinand.

"You shut your face, Ferdinand!" Sanzi yelled up.

"Would y-y-you b-b-both stop," said Billy. "If w-w-we don't get b-b-back soon, they're g-g-gonna come looking f-f-for us."

That set everyone quiet. Sanzi took the harness rope off and tied it around the stiff body of the pig.

The pig stretched maybe three feet long, not too big, but as soon as we started pulling up rope, you could feel it was heavy. Mud came up around my feet where they started sinking in as I pulled.

"Go on," said Juna to me.

"Pull!" I called out, and up came a bit of rope.

"Pull!" I called again. Sure enough they all pulled and more rope came up.

"It's coming!" called Ada. "That pig is flying!" she squealed.

Up we pulled. Quiet this time. Seemed right to be quiet pulling up the dead.

"Pull!" I called. But the rope held still.

"Ada, what do you see?" asked Juna.

Ada looked over the edge.

"The pig's about to get out, but the leg's caught," she called.

"Maybe we should let it down again?" said Juna.

"I can get it!" yelled Ada, and up she ran to the rope.

"Ada!" I called. I could almost see her tumbling over.

"Don't worry," she said.

"Don't!" I wanted to run to her, but the rope was tight around my hands.

She bent over the edge, tugged and pulled until the leg gave way. Up the pig came, until finally it landed on the bank with a dead thud. We dropped the rope and came around it.

"Sure is heavier than it looks," said Ferdinand.

"Hey!" called Sanzi from the ditch below. "Don't y'all do anything with that pig until I get up there!"

"What do you think we're gonna do, cook it?" Ferdinand shot back.

"I'll cook you, if you touch it," yelled Sanzi.

"Hush up, the both of you. I don't know which of you is worse!" Juna said.

"Hurry up!" called Sanzi.

Billy pulled the rope from around the pig and threw it down for Sanzi. Quick as anything Sanzi had herself back in the harness.

"Come on!" she yelled.

We all lined up again, and this time we moved quicker. That's where we made our mistake. Perhaps Sanzi forgot to tie the rope tight, or we pulled too quick? Either way, the rope broke and Sanzi screamed. I went falling and sliding to the edge, then looked over and saw Sanzi was clinging to the hillside.

"It's too wet!" she yelled. Slowly, she was sliding down the drop's side toward the wooden spikes below.

I put myself over the edge and reached down.

Sanzi grabbed my hand but her legs slipped, and she came loose.

"AHH!" she yelled.

I leaned down farther and reached again.

"Sanzi, get my hand!" I shouted. This time when she grabbed it I heaved up with all my might.

Then I felt my legs being pulled back. Juna had one leg,

Billy and Ferdinand had the other, and they were all dragging me and Sanzi up.

When Sanzi finally reached the top, she lay there, covered in mud from head to foot. It may as well have been the dead of winter, because my hands were rattling. I clapped them together, not believing they'd helped save Sanzi. We all sat there with the pig between us, panting and breathing. It was quiet for a long while.

Then there was Ada.

"I told you it's better if you know how to fly," said Ada.

Sanzi was the first to laugh, then Juna and then all of us. The laugh turned into whoops, dancing, and jumping up and down for what we had done, and for the bad that could have happened but didn't.

We were masters of the swamp.

Then came the swish of the trees, and the hiss of the snake, and there in the middle of our whooping landed Daria.

44

Homer

"STOP," SAID DARIA, LOW AND CALM. "WHAT IS this?" She shot a cold stare at each of us.

No one said a word. I did all I could not to catch her eye. Juna had sorry written all over her face. If Billy slumped any lower, he'd have sunken into the mud. Ferdinand's face looked tough, but even he dipped his eyes when Daria stared at him.

Ada was unfazed. "You just come from those trees?" she asked, peering up like more people would rain down.

"We caught a pig, same as you grown folks," said Sanzi, pointing at the dead catch.

"I see it," said Daria. She pulled the wooden stake from it and held its bloodred point to our faces. "You think you've done something here?"

We did! I could see the words in Sanzi's eyes, but she didn't dare say them.

"You crossed outside the boundaries to get that pig you're so proud of. When you leave Freewater and break the rules, you put us all in danger," said Daria.

We squirmed.

"Since you're so grown, you'll carry that pig back to the village yourselves," Daria said, turning to walk back to the village.

Ada bent down close to the pig. "You think this pig can still fly?" she asked.

We all groaned and wished it were true.

The pig was heavy.

Sanzi, Juna, and Billy each took a leg, then tied a sling to it. I didn't know much about tying ropes and slings, and from the way it kept slipping off our leg, I could tell Ferdinand knew as much as me.

"It's better if you tie it like this." Sanzi showed him. "Papa says it's a tighter knot, see."

"I told you, I'm tired of hearing about your papa. I don't care what your ol' papa said," spat Ferdinand.

Sanzi raised her head, offended. "I was trying to help you. Looks like your papa didn't ever show you the right way to tie knots!" Sanzi shot back.

Ferdinand's chest heaved in anger.

"Don't you never say one word about my papa! Forget this!" said Ferdinand, and he took off into the swamp.

"Y-y-you shouldn't h-h-have said that, Sanzi," said Billy.

"But he was talking about Papa, so I said it right back!" said Sanzi.

"Sanzi, sometimes you don't understand anything," Juna said, shaking her head.

"Come on, we best start pulling," I said. "Ada, you come over here with me."

After Daria's scolding, I was all nerves as we walked into Freewater. But everything was quiet. Daria was standing at the end of the dirt path waiting.

Ibra was the first person to see us. He lifted the pig onto his big shoulders and smiled, and a bit of relief washed over all of us.

"You helped do this?" Ibra asked his son.

"W-w-we all did," said Billy.

"It's a good pig. We haven't caught one like this for a long time. What do you think, Billy? Is it time?"

Billy smiled, looked at Ibra and then Daria, and said, "I th-th-think so." Daria almost smiled.

As he walked through the village, Ibra put his face to the sky and let out his call, the hoot of the owl, *"Hoot! Hoot! Hoot!"*

People came out of their cabins, smiled up at the pig, and set off their own sounds—the calls of the blue jay, the eagle, the egret, the bear, and the bobcat—until Ibra rested the pig by the fire pit in the meeting space.

"See," said Sanzi, "they're happy. We're like heroes!"

"They sure seem to like the pig," said Ada, marveling at the celebration around her.

Mrs. Light hushed the village.

"Again, our swamp has been good to us. We thank you," she said, touching the earth at her feet.

An uproarious swamp howl erupted from everyone as they also touched the ground in appreciation. Us kids did the same.

Mrs. Light quieted everyone again. "And we give thanks to you, Ibra, for this catch."

Cheers began. Yet Ibra was quick to shake his head and wave his strapping arms.

"It's not my catch! It was the children!" reported Ibra.

Murmurs went through the gathering. Worry swept across everyone's faces as they looked at us kids. Mrs. Light kept her gaze on the bloodied wooden stake. A shiver went down my back.

"Yup," Juna whispered to us, "we're gonna be in so much trouble."

Not wanting the happy moment to be spoiled, David laid a hand on Mrs. Light's shoulder and called for quiet.

"Today, we finished Ibra and Daria's new home. We have a pig. Perhaps it's time for a wedding! Let us see if the couple agrees." His voice was all encouragement.

Ibra smiled hopeful at Daria, along with everyone else. It seemed it was for Daria to say. With a small tilt of her head, she nodded her reply to Ibra. He let out a big howl and the whole village joined him. Ibra opened his great arms and hugged Daria and Billy together.

David waved his hand. "From the looks of this pig, it'll take about two days for smoking, so we will have a wedding in two days and feast on what the swamp has brought to us!"

A wedding? Any wedding I'd ever known meant trouble.

45

Nora

ASHAMED BY WHAT SHE'D DONE TO HURT ROSE, Nora kept her distance from the kitchen for the first time. That meant avoiding her mother and spending more time finding new refuges and hideouts around Southerland. After a lifetime of hearing the soulful songs coming from the fields, Nora ventured out to see their origin. She hid among the rows of tobacco and listened to the crack of Stokes's whip and saw that the eyes of field hands looked much like Rose's. The pain she saw frightened her and sent her running back to the house, and back to being within her mother's reach. Suddenly, the tobacco leaf fields she'd seen in the distance every day didn't look beautiful. Nora knew they were pain-filled. Her home wasn't what she'd thought. Maybe this was why Rose had run off in the first place.

On this particular morning, feeling unable to eat in the kitchen with Rose, Nora joined her mother and sister in the dining room for breakfast. As their meal ended, Old Joe came and stood just outside of the door and waited. Nora wondered why, but Mrs. Crumb knew.

"Nora, fetch some paper and my ink pen from my chest. Take this." Mrs. Crumb removed a string necklace that hung from her neck. It held one key, which she gave to Nora.

Then Nora remembered. It was Thursday, the one day each week Old Joe was allowed to leave Southerland and walk to town to sell his wooden whistles and playthings for children.

The key turned easily in the lock of Mrs. Crumb's top bureau drawer and slid open to reveal a small stack of stiff paper and a tiny glass jar of ink, both of which Nora delivered to her mother. Mrs. Crumb dipped her pen into the tiny black ink pool, tapped it on the edge of the jar, and with a smooth, sweeping hand she wrote:

> *On this, the 13th day of August, I, Mrs. Sherline Crumb, owner of slave Old Joe, grant him permission to leave Southerland Plantation for purposes of selling goods in the common marketplace in town. Old Joe will return to Southerland Plantation by 3 o'clock this same afternoon.*
>
> *Signed, Sherline Crumb*

She waved the parchment in the still morning air. Satisfied that it was dry, she handed it to Nora.

"Give this to Old Joe," she ordered.

Nora studied her mother's swirly print as she walked out of the room and found Old Joe outside the door.

"Thank you kindly," said Old Joe. He folded the note and deposited it into his front shirt pocket and started out the door.

Nora had never given much thought to Old Joe's trips to town, but today she circled around to the house's back door and followed him. Old Joe, bent over with a burlap bag of woodenwares on his shoulder, headed down the drive toward the road.

Nora trailed him at a distance, watching his slow and steady progress. He tipped his hat to each person he passed. Nora would have remained inconspicuous had one of Old Joe's wooden dolls not fallen from his bag.

Unknowing, Old Joe walked on. Nora picked up the baby doll and ran down the lane to him.

"Miss Nora, what are you doing out this way on your own?" said Old Joe as he took the doll and placed it in his bag. "You and me both know Master Crumb and Mistress wouldn't abide by you leaving Southerland—now go on back."

Obstinance spread over Nora's face.

Old Joe coaxed again, "Go on, there ain't—"

"Boy! Boy!" a loud voice interrupted.

Old Joe stopped cold. His eyes, once contemplative, now clouded.

He said nothing, but he was different. His shoulders hunched so low he looked shrunken by a few inches, and his face hung with a tired expression that made him appear even older. Nora could hardly believe it.

A man, pale with ragged clothes and missing teeth, approached the two.

"Boy! Where you think you going with that white child?" The smell of whiskey touched Nora's nose hairs.

"You bothering that child?" the man slurred. Without awaiting a response, the man raised his hand and struck Old Joe across the face, causing him to fall atop his bag. Nora stood stunned.

Unmoved, the man raised his foot, to follow his strike with a kick. Old Joe said nothing, but he reached into his shirt pocket, pulled out the stiff white parchment, and held it up to the stranger. The man paused, then took the note, as if to read it.

"Oh, you got one of them fancy passes. I guess you one of them fancy darkies." The man spat and threw the paper back at Old Joe. "You need to git, little girl. Go on! I know ya papa wouldn't think kindly of you walking the road with one of his darkies."

He turned to Old Joe. "Take your pass—don't let me catch you out here without it. I'll make you sorry," said the man, and he stumbled down the road.

Old Joe calmly picked up the note, dusted it off, refolded

it, and placed it in his pocket. He didn't say a word to Nora as he collected his sack and headed down the lane toward town.

Nora watched him, trying to understand what had happened. That man had hurt Old Joe for no reason, and she'd stood there frozen. Embarrassment heated her face. As she slowly walked back home, one thing stuck with her. The power of that piece of paper. She hadn't helped Old Joe, but maybe there was something she could do. She had a plan.

46

Sanzi

FERDINAND HAD TAKEN HER BOW AND ARROW, Sanzi was sure. She'd left them at the forbidden edge where they'd pulled up the pig, and when she returned to the very same spot, both items were gone.

She'd accused him right to his face when she noticed their disappearance.

"What would I want with your stinky old bow?" he'd said, flashing his knife before her.

His refusal to confess only further infuriated Sanzi. Something needed to be done.

Quiet as a cat, she rolled from her mat, pulled back the door flap, crawled out of the cabin and into the morning dark. Not much was needed to awaken Billy. From where he slept, Billy's long foot always ended near the door of his cabin. Sanzi pushed her hand under the flap, felt for his toe, and squeezed. At first, he rolled over. Another squeeze.

"Ouch!" he said and crawled out of the cabin.

"Sanzi, what are you d-d-doing?" said Billy, rubbing his eyes.

"Ferdinand took my bow and I'm gonna get it," Sanzi said.

"Maybe he doesn't even h-h-have your b-b-bow," said Billy.

"I went back to the edge where we got the pig and it wasn't where I left it. No one else would even think about taking it but him," said Sanzi.

"Even if h-h-he did t-t-take it. How are you supposing to g-g-get it?" asked Billy.

"He's sleeping. I'll be quiet, go in his cabin, find it, and be gone before he knows a thing. I just need you to keep watch," said Sanzi.

Billy shook his head. "Ain't nothing good gonna come f-f-from you sneaking in Ferdinand's c-c-cabin. What if he w-w-wakes up? What if one of the other two in his cabin wake up? Then what are you g-g-gonna do?"

"The other two are on patrol and won't come back until sunup. For now, Ferdinand is all alone. He ain't gonna wake up. Watch in case anyone comes by. The last thing I need is for Mama or somebody to see me going in or out of there. They'll just say I'm causing trouble."

"But you are c-c-causing t-t-trouble," said Billy.

"Ferdinand started it when he took my bow!" Sanzi said.

"But this a-a-ain't gonna d-d-do nothing but make things worse," said Billy.

"Stay close by and whistle if you see anyone coming. Are you gonna do it or what?" she asked.

Billy sighed.

Once they were near Ferdinand's cabin, Billy set himself in the shadows beside it.

"Whistle if I need to get out," Sanzi said.

She put her ear to the cabin flap. A soft snore hummed, growing louder once she pulled back the flap and slipped inside. Ink-black darkness enveloped her. Sanzi stood still, waiting for her eyes to adjust. Near the flap were two empty mats, one on each side of the door. Soon she could make out Ferdinand's body across the cabin.

Sanzi crept closer. The curve of a slender wooden bow caught her eye. *He hadn't even bothered to hide it*, she thought. Instead, the bow was leaning against the cabin wall behind Ferdinand. The precarious spot would mean climbing around or over Ferdinand to collect it. Sanzi went down on her hands and knees in a slow, quiet crawl. Inches from his body, cool metal passed across her hand. She stopped, letting her fingers travel down the blade to the smooth wood handle of Ferdinand's knife. She picked it up. As if Ferdinand sensed that his most prized possession had been touched, he moaned and tossed on his mat.

"No!" he said.

Sanzi stiffened and clenched her teeth. She was ready to protest, to tell Ferdinand what a terrible person he was and why she had every right to be there to claim what was hers.

"No, Papa!" he groaned and tossed. He was asleep. "No, Papa don't let them take me. Don't, Papa, please don't let them take me." His voice grew louder, and he started punching and kicking his legs at the air.

Panicked, Sanzi pressed her back to the wall as his limbs sailed past. "No. No. No. Please, no!" Ferdinand yelled. Then he got quiet, tucked himself in a tight ball, and began weeping. "Please, no. Please, no," he whispered over and over.

Only then did Sanzi hear Billy's clear and loud whistle. Distant voices of the two patrollers were coming toward the cabin. Sanzi grabbed her bow, backed away from Ferdinand, and ran. Whether she meant to take the knife or was so afraid that she forgot to leave it, she wasn't sure. But she ran with the knife out of the cabin and into the dimly lit early morning.

She nearly crashed into Billy.

"You g-g-got it?" Billy asked.

But Sanzi didn't hear him. Instead, she ran right past him, as fast as her legs could carry her away from the weeping cry of Ferdinand.

Unsure where to go or what to do, Sanzi went to the cornfields where they'd last picked, dug a shallow hole, and buried the knife.

Then she returned to her cabin, waited until her mother was out of sight, and returned her bow.

47

Homer

I DON'T MUCH CARE FOR WEDDINGS.

The Big House wedding had taken over everything at Southerland. For us who had to see that all was done just right for the big day—it brought nothing but worry.

That worrisome feeling woke me up before sunrise the day before the wedding. Night still hung over everything and the sky was turning from black to dark blue. Billy, Ibra, and Ada were asleep. Then I realized that I had to go pretty bad. Quiet as I could, I left the cabin and crept to the outhouse, a dug hole with a mud wall around it.

Walking back, I felt the comfort of having darkness all around me. Darkness took eyes off me and gave me a chance to...to...breathe. Right before I got back to the cabin, I stopped and sat down beside one of its walls, where not even the night could see me.

I heard his steps before I saw him. The hard sole of Master Crumb's old shoes, hitting the soft dry ground and going right past Ibra's cabin, down the center of the village, alone. Without making a sound, I followed Two Shoes. He walked into the thicket behind the meeting place. Dark gray clouds puffed from the covered pit where our pig lay smoking. Two Shoes got to his knees and pulled the grass cover from the pig. Tiny orange sparks sprang up. He dug his hands in the heap of cooled wood ashes piled on the side of the pit and shoveled it into his pockets.

Once he couldn't carry anymore, he covered the pit back over, stood up, and headed my way. I ducked behind one of the arms of Big Tree and watched his shoes move past. He pulled back the flap to his cabin and went inside. *Why did Two Shoes want coal ash? Why hide getting it?*

The sun was making its way into the sky, which told me I needed to hurry before light gave me away. I pulled the door flap back a small bit and peered into Two Shoes's cabin. It was all darkness.

Then a match was struck and there was Two Shoes sitting cross-legged on the floor, his mat beside him, and a packet of matches resting in a small hole dug into the dirt floor. He put the lit match into another shallower but bigger hole of wood and brush. It caught and the flames cast shadows all over the cabin.

Two Shoes had matches? As best I knew, there were no matches in Freewater. Two bowls were at his feet. Careful as could be, he put ashes in one of the bowls, then he poured water from the next over the ash and stirred it with a bushy wood stick. The water turned black and heavy. From his pant pocket he pulled out another stick, this one short and pointed at the end. He set it next to the black water bowl.

Then he went for his shoes, untying the laces as if about to take them off.

"Homer!" I jumped at Ada calling my name.

Two Shoes listened and, swift as the wind, he pulled the mat over his matches.

"Homer! What you doing? You going to see Two Shoes?" *Ada. Oh, Ada.*

Two Shoes looked toward the flap door and there I was for him to see.

48

Homer

ADA'S VOICE WAS LIKE A BOLT OF LIGHTNING cracking in the night sky. Everything was illuminated. Through the small opening in the cabin flap, Two Shoes saw me and I saw that he didn't want to be seen.

There was nothing wrong with making black water or whatever it was he was doing. There was no crime in having your own matches. But Two Shoes's eyes said there was. Then just as quick, the wrongness dissolved from his face and a smile appeared in its place. I wasn't sure what to do, so I did what I'd learned. I copied him. I smiled back. He put one bowl atop the other to cover his black water and moved it aside.

"Homer! Is that you?" he said, nice as ever.

I pretended right along with him.

"Hi, Two Shoes!" I tried for my happiest voice, but instead the words came out choked and whispered.

"Come in!" he said.

Ada rushed in right around me.

"Hi, Two Shoes! You're up with Homer? What are y'all doing?" she asked.

"I was here getting things together in my cabin," said Two Shoes, looking this way and that at the five items in his cabin. "Homer, what ya doing up this early, and...and..." It was like his words lost him. "...and walking around this way?" he finished.

I wasn't one for having words to say, but funny thing was that plenty started pouring out.

"I...I...I was coming to see you. Wanted to see how you were. We were about to go to the fields to do some corn picking and I was wondering if you had a knife or something I could use out there," I yammered on.

"Oh, right then," said Two Shoes. "I don't have anything in the way of tools. You need to see David or Ibra for that. They keep track of those. You're staying with Ibra, right?"

"Oh yes, that's right," I echoed.

"I don't have tools, but I can offer you both a bit of breakfast before you go," said Two Shoes.

"Um, there's no need—" I started.

"All right, that sounds good!" Ada said, settling onto the floor.

I wished I could have pulled her up, but instead, I sat down beside her. Two Shoes grabbed for a pouch behind him and unwrapped a small loaf of corn bread.

"It don't taste much like what we had in the quarters, not much salt here, but we did get some good honey." He pulled two big pieces from his loaf, handed one to Ada then to me, and set his water bowl before us. "Go on, then," he said. "You'll be wanting something in your stomachs for when you get out there."

If Ada was uncomfortable, she didn't show it. Instead, she bit into the corn bread and got right to what was on her mind.

"You know, little Minnie started walking just after you went away." She said it as if he'd been off on a trip. "I was there to see it. In the middle of the morning when I was playing with her while Mrs. Two Shoes was washing sheets. I tried showing Mrs. Two Shoes, but her mind was somewhere else. Like she didn't even see me. Mrs. Two Shoes didn't seem good, but everybody kept saying she was all right," said Ada.

That corn bread stuck like a lump in my throat. Maybe the same thing happened to Two Shoes because he didn't say a word. He sat there chewing his corn bread slow, as if it was the last piece of food left on earth.

"This corn bread is good," I coughed. "Thank you kindly for sharing it, but we must be going. Mrs. Light said she wanted us gone to the fields first thing."

"All right," said Two Shoes.

I got up to leave. Truth is, Two Shoes looked even more relieved than me to see us go. "Thank you" was all I could say, and finally Ada and I were both out in the open air.

49

Homer

IT TURNED OUT THERE WOULDN'T BE ANY WORK in the fields that day, nor anytime soon. We'd gone out there—Billy, me, Ada, and Sanzi—but right after arriving the warning horn sounded. We all ran.

All of us followed the rules and took only what was in our hands. Our hearts pounded at the thought of outsiders invading Freewater. Freewater was *ours*, mine included. I wasn't sure the swamp would hear our calls for protection, but in the hideout I touched ground like everyone else as Mrs. Light chanted to the swamp.

Ada and I smiled and hugged like everyone else when the all-clear horn sounded, then gathered with everyone else at the meeting space when we got back to the village.

The talk was all about the tree cutters. It was Master Crumb's business that did some of that tree cutting. They were his tree cutters.

"They keep coming," said Wisdom. "Coming like they mean to claim all the swamp."

"Wisdom is right, we can't wait much longer to get that bridge down," said David. "If they're a half day from it now, won't be long before they start clearing trees right around it." Crumb was getting closer. My twenty-one days of change felt washed away.

"What about the new bridge? We shouldn't take one down without having another. The same plan remains. If one bridge is found out, we cut it and we escape on the next," said Mrs. Light.

"Do we have enough rope for a new bridge to the swamp lake?" asked Wisdom.

"I counted it yesterday. It's short, but it should make it. There won't be room for mistakes. No tangles, no knots," said Ibra.

"Best we wait until we have more rope. Another week or so should do it," said Wisdom. *No,* I thought, biting my nails. I suppose Wisdom didn't understand that Crumb was coming closer.

"How many more times can we sound the horn before it's too late? I say we go now. We have enough rope," said Daria.

"She's right. We wait and it'll be harder to get that bridge down," said Ibra.

"There isn't any need for waiting," said Mrs. Light, standing to the front of the gathering. Everyone listened. "We hang the new bridge now. It will take us to the swamp lake and give us an escape. We can make it there."

Heads nodded in agreement.

"Daria, we should call for Suleman. There's no knowing how far he is, but if he hears us, he could be much needed help," said Mrs. Light.

Daria nodded.

"We need people, all we can spare with good climbing legs," said Ibra. "Daria and I have already marked the trees. It's a wet and hard stretch of land. We'll need to work fast," said David.

A few hands went up to volunteer.

"Daria, Ibra, Turner, David," called out Mrs. Light.

"All those who can climb," again requested Mrs. Light, looking through the crowd. She continued picking.

Two Shoes was going. Before my mind could consider the many reasons why I shouldn't go, I put up my hand.

"Bird, Ferdinand, Gabe, Wisdom, Billy, we could use your long legs, and—" Mrs. Light's big, sad eyes rested on me. My raised hand turned cold. *What was I doing?!*

"It's not our way to take newcomers out so soon." She paused. Maybe she could see that I wasn't worthy and that it was my fault Mama was caught. Mrs. Light folded her arms, thinking, then continued, "but we need hands, and your bravery brought you freedom. I imagine it can help us hang a bridge. Yes, you go, too. That will do for now." She thought I was brave.

From the corner of my eye, I saw Sanzi's raised hand. Mrs. Light gave no clue that she'd seen it.

"You'll leave tomorrow. Prepare tonight," she said. "Also, I've gotten word that we have a missing knife. It's the one kept by Ferdinand. Has anyone seen it?" Everyone murmured and looked around, but no one raised a hand. I glanced back and saw Ferdinand, arms folded and eyes blazing with anger. Mrs. Light peered around. "We've never lost a precious tool," she said. "I'm sure we'll find it. For now, we'll hang the bridge, and when it's all done, we'll come together for a wedding."

50

Sanzi

MRS. LIGHT HAD REQUESTED THE KNIFE'S whereabouts, and her stare around the room drilled a hole in Sanzi's chest. Guilt surged from Sanzi's belly and burned a trail up to her ears. Still, her hand felt like lead, stuck in its place. To raise it would mean confessing, in front of everyone, that she'd taken the knife. A mortifying and unacceptable outcome. She couldn't give Ferdinand that satisfaction; he'd never let her live it down. Instead, she'd return the knife, and no one would be the wiser. But how? When?

She'd tried. Earlier that day, while they were working in the cornfields and all eyes were turned elsewhere, she'd attempted to retrieve the knife from where she'd hidden it in the corn. However, at that moment, the horn sounded and everyone had run for the hideout. Then she planned to sneak off during the meeting, but just as she was leaving, her mother began picking people to do the sky bridge hanging. Sure, there was a rule that the children of Freewater couldn't leave, but Sanzi was one of the best tree climbers. Her mother would have to let her go. She'd stay and volunteer, then go get the knife afterward.

But Mrs. Light had not chosen her—she hadn't even looked her way. Even Billy had been picked. *He doesn't even want to go!* Sanzi thought. Ferdinand, the bow thief, was going! Homer, the newcomer, who didn't know anything about anything, was going. Flames of hot anger raged inside of her. This was her state when Mrs. Light called her name right after the meeting.

"Sanzi," she said. Sanzi turned to Mrs. Light, who stood right beside Ferdinand. "Sanzi, come."

"Yes, Mama," she said with all the calm she could muster.

"Ferdinand thinks you might have seen his knife. Is he right?" asked Mrs. Light.

Her eyes were so serious and hard Sanzi bit down on her lip.

"I know you took it!" barked Ferdinand.

"Where's my bow?" Sanzi shot back.

"Sanzi, your bow should be in our cabin! And your bow is for games. That's not like missing a knife for Freewater!" said Mrs. Light.

Games! she thought, enraged by the insult. "You don't even care he took my bow," said Sanzi, and before tears could come, she turned and ran.

235

51

Billy

BILLY HAD HEARD MRS. LIGHT'S WORDS, BUT THEY didn't sink in at first. There would be a group leaving Freewater and he would be part of it. The whole thing had happened so fast. After months of avoiding the woodcutters, just like that, he was set to leave Freewater the next morning.

Dizziness and nausea overcame him as he stood and began moving toward the entrance of the meeting space. Ibra saw him and understood. By the time Billy had exited, Ibra was there beside him. Billy, who was almost frozen with fear, allowed his father to guide him to the base of Big Tree.

Ibra watched the piqued expression on his son's face and he touched his hand to the markings on Big Tree.

"Each one of these markings shows the days Freewater has been here. They are only here because our people did so many things to make sure we survived. Each of us is as different as these ax strokes. We all have different things to contribute, and you don't have to hang a sky bridge to help," said Ibra. Billy silently nodded.

"Do you understand?" asked Ibra. Billy nodded again, but his stomach said otherwise. It tumbled and squeezed and threatened.

Billy wanted to say something brave, but all that could come was, "I n-n-need to get some w-w-water." And off he ran, through the village and down the path to the water's edge. He didn't drink, but he did splash his face with cool water and placed his head between his knees. He imagined his runaway hunter crouched at the border of Freewater, gun drawn, waiting for him. They'd be caught for sure. *He'd* be caught and life as he knew it would end.

Billy's mind spun. He'd say he was sick, maybe he could even make himself sick. What if he broke his leg? As he began imagining the million ways he'd explain why he couldn't go, he heard—

WHACK! WHACK! Then a pause and again, *WHACK! WHACK!* coming from a short distance up the water's edge. Someone was there.

He peeked around a tree and saw Juna, standing at the water's edge filling her sling with a stone, then with all her might flinging it at a tree across the water. *WHACK!* She stopped, brushed tears from her eyes, and loaded her sling again. *WHACK! WHACK!* Splinters of wood flew and plopped into the water. She sniffled and wiped tears away.

What should he do? If he ran, she'd be there crying all

alone. If he stayed, he'd have to talk to her. But all of that was decided for him when Juna saw him.

"Billy," she said. To Billy's surprise, *she* was the one who looked embarrassed as she rubbed tears from her large eyes.

"Are y-y-you all right?" asked Billy, silently cursing that he had not gotten the sentence out smoothly. He joined her at the water.

Juna nodded, looking into the coffee-brown water. "I don't want Papa to go again," she said. "I don't want any of you to go."

Billy exhaled. There was only one thing to say. "It's g-g-going to be o-o-okay," said Billy.

"Sometimes I wish I was like Sanzi. All she ever wants to do is go running out there saving something or someone," said Juna. "If it was up to me, Papa would never leave to go patrolling, but instead he's always the first one to go." More tears. She loaded the sling, and *WHACK!*

"It's a-a-all right." He searched for something to say that could help. "That p-p-part of the swamp is s-s-so far in, I d-d-don't suspect w-w-we'll run into anyone out there." The words helped to convince himself as much as her.

Juna wiped her tears. "I thought you didn't like going out there, either. You're going?" she asked.

"Y-y-yes, they n-n-need long legs," Billy said, pointing to his spaghetti limbs and smiling with more confidence than he felt.

For a brief moment Juna's eyebrow raised, then settled back into place. "Yes, you're right, they need you," she said.

"R-r-right," said Billy, reassuring himself again. They both stood there a long while looking at the water.

"Do y-y-you remember when you sh-sh-showed me how to f-f-fish?" asked Billy. He remembered every last moment of that day, but they'd never spoken of it.

"Yeah, you broke my pole." Juna smiled.

Billy could feel the bracelet he'd made burning a hole in his pouch. Now would be the perfect time to give it to her. He'd say something smart like, *Here's another bracelet for breaking your pole.* He'd say it clear and smooth, perfectly.

He started, "H-h-here's—" *Oh dear, that didn't sound smooth at all.*

He stopped, his hand frozen in his pouch.

Then, clear as day, Mrs. Light called from a distance. "Juna!"

Juna turned to him. "I'd better go."

Billy nodded, not wanting to try any more words.

"I don't know what I'm going to do when you're gone. Who'll clear all the paths for me?" She smiled mischievously.

Billy melted. He opened his mouth to deny it but nothing came out. Juna headed up the path toward the village.

Just before she was out of sight, Juna turned back and said, "Hey, since you're going, maybe you could look out for my papa? It'll feel good knowing you're there," she said.

"O-o-okay," said Billy, who could hardly deny any request from Juna, even one he didn't dare imagine fulfilling. Then Juna ran up the path toward her mother's call.

Billy's heart swelled with surprise and a hint of pride. Maybe she thought he was brave. Maybe he could be. He'd do it.

52

Homer

EVERY HAIR ON MY BODY SAID THAT TWO SHOES needed watching. Nobody else knew that, so it was up to me to keep an eye on him. My hand went up during that meeting without even remembering that I don't know a thing about tree climbing and I don't care for walking across sky bridges. That's not how I do things. I'm careful. I don't lead. But my old rules didn't have a good place in Freewater.

Not a second after the meeting, I was swept up with the other sky bridge builders. David took us behind Big Tree and gave us each a thick rope about eight feet long with a loop at the end.

"Most of you were part of the last bridge hanging—you know what to do. Check your rope, and you'll want to have a long sling and a bow with you. No need for many arrows, but a strong bow," said David.

I stole a peek at the others, trying not to look out of place. *How exactly do I "check" my rope?*

Daria came over and watched me clumsily pull at my rope. Disapproval spread over her face.

"Check the rope to be sure it will hold. This is what will keep you to the tree as you climb," she said, with an impatience that said maybe I'd never learn.

"All right," I said. But it didn't come out like I knew what she was talking about.

She shook her head and pulled me to a nearby tree.

"Find thin trees with little or no branches. Tupelo and cypress are good. Put the rope around your waist, then bring it around the tree trunk. Then pull it through the loop. Hold the end steady."

With that, she leaned back on the rope and worked her way up the tree like a racoon.

"Your turn," Daria said.

Later that night, I lay realizing that I'd made it up some twenty feet on a tupelo tree. Never mind that I'd slid and scraped my knees as I came down like a clumsy squirrel. It felt terrible. But it must have been good enough because Daria nodded and walked away.

David smiled and passed me a sling and an old bow. "You might be needing these," he said.

We met at the foot of Big Tree before sunrise, ropes in hand. Each of us had a pouch with a piece of bread and smoked meat. We were all shapes and shadows in the darkness at Big Tree that morning, but the spit-shined leather of Two

Shoes's shoes stood out. I counted that as a blessing as I tried to keep my eyes on him.

My neck was still warm with Ada's hug.

"You keep to Juna," I had told her before I left. "Take care to mind her."

"You think after you put up that sky bridge, I could use it to fly to the water? I want to see the water," said Ada.

"I don't know. But maybe," I said. That seemed to be enough for her. After that, I took my bow, my new sling, rope, and pouch and left the cabin with Ibra and Billy.

Now, a cloud of quiet hung around Billy. His hands rubbed the leather of the sling tied like a pendant across his chest.

A tall pile of thick, twisted rope lay coiled like a huge serpent at the base of Big Tree. Daria went to the pile and started looping the rope around her shoulders ten times each. Then they let some ten feet of rope lag. Next, Wisdom came forward and he wrapped the rope around his shoulders like Daria, then more lag. Each climber stood in line to do the same. I put myself right after Two Shoes. Billy put himself by David. We wrapped the rope until the serpent was gone and we were all connected by it.

David eyed our line. "When we string up the bridge, we'll do it by two," said David. "Daria and Wisdom, Turner and Homer, Ibra with Gabe, Ferdinand and Bird. Billy you're with me."

What that even meant, I wasn't sure.

"We climb up together. If you need to stop, send the signal." David whistled into the air. "We must move as one."

What am I doing? My mind screamed, and I rubbed the rope with my slick wet hands.

"Together," repeated Daria as she grabbed the pegs on Big Tree. She climbed up two pegs and sucked in air, *"Sip,"* then up she climbed one step. *"Sip."* She moved up steady and calm to another peg. *"Sip,"* up, *"Sip,"* up. The rest of us followed behind. Each foot and arm moving together like a flock of birds making our way to the sky.

By the time I made it to the flat wood base in the treetop it was a foggy morning. Misty white hung about us. I glimpsed the other sky bridges hanging as if the clouds themselves held them up. Each reached in a different direction of fog and haze. Daria, with the rest of us following in step, walked onto a westward pointing bridge. The fear from my last bridge walk came back, but the ropes on my shoulders were heavy, and Daria's *"Sip"* call was so insistent, I stayed steady and moved forward in time with everyone else.

Not long before the bridge's end, we saw our way was blocked up ahead and we stopped. Enveloped in the morning fog and pink light, as if he were floating on the clouds themselves, stood Suleman, still and calm, with a long bow showing over his wide shoulders.

53

Homer

SULEMAN'S EYES FELL ON OUR LONG SNAKING rope and he nodded his approval. For me, being seen was almost never a good idea, but in this one moment, I hoped Suleman would see me. It meant he'd know that I'd made it to Freewater and back out again. Somehow that mattered. I'm pretty certain Ferdinand had the same thought as me because he stood extra tall and kept bobbing his head around the others in line.

Suleman walked to the bridge's end where it connected to a small platform and another tree. No one went down the tree. Instead, we waited.

"What's wrong?" I whispered to Two Shoes, who hadn't said a word the whole morning.

"We can't do it in the fog, we wait," he said, watching the ground below. Slowly, the morning sun burned the fog from the trees. Then Suleman put a match into Daria's hand. She nodded her answer. She and Wisdom unwound the rope from their bodies. Down the tree they went.

We all stood waiting and watching the bed of trees before us. For what, I wasn't sure. Then, from atop a low tree some fifty feet away, a flame waved back and forth. Suleman watched the light, took out his bow and a long strong arrow. He tied the end of the bridge rope to the arrow's tail and aimed at the flickering flame. He let out a call, then fired. As the arrow passed over the waving flame, a sling came up and caught it.

Everyone on the sky bridge did a quiet clap. Ibra and Gabe were next. They stepped forward and unwound their rope.

"You'll do fine," Ibra whispered to Billy before he went down. Billy did a nervous nod.

Again, Suleman placed a match in Ibra's hands and down they went. We all pulled the rope forward and let it swing over the bridge's end. This time it took longer, much longer. We waited, and about one hundred feet away a flame blinked in the treetops. Suleman tied more rope to another arrow, then sounded another call and fired toward Daria and Wisdom's tree. In unison, a sling came up and caught the rope as Daria fired rope toward Ibra and Gabe's flame. It flew in a rainbow curve into the sky and went over the flame. Again, a sling came up and grabbed the rope from the sky.

David unwrapped himself from the ropes and embraced Suleman in hello. The expression on David's face went serious after Suleman said something quietly in his ear. David looked at him and nodded.

"Follow me," David said to Billy as he went down the tree.

Billy stood stone-still watching the place where David had descended.

"You can do it," said Bird with encouragement.

"Go on," huffed Ferdinand, impatient. But Billy didn't move. His hands were clutching the bridge for dear life.

"Billy, you'll be needing to stay close. David needs you," said Suleman.

That seemed to awaken Billy and he started walking to the bridge's end. His mind found courage, but I don't know if his body did, because his long legs wobbled. He tripped, lost his balance, and tumbled over the side of the bridge.

We all silently screamed.

Even with his body over the bridge's side, Billy's long arm had hooked the bridge rope and he was swinging from its side. It was my nightmare come to life. His weight began tipping the bridge sideways with him. We all leaned the other way.

Suleman acted. He walked onto the bridge, bent over the edge, and with both hands pulled Billy back onto it. The bridge steadied. Fear and shock smothered our voices. No one said anything.

Suleman pulled Billy onto the platform. "Your partner needs you to hang this bridge. We need you. Do you understand?" Suleman declared again.

Sweaty and panting, Billy looked in Suleman's eyes and inhaled. "Yes," he said. Then Suleman placed a match in Billy's hand and sent him down the tree.

We stood there quiet as mice. Then Bird went with Ferdinand. My heart started pounding: Two Shoes and I would be next. I stood next to Suleman and we pulled more rope and watched it move from one tree to the next.

Firelight appeared like a tiny dot in the trees. Another arrow flew and a sling caught it, like a dance. Billy had done it.

Our turn. As Two Shoes descended, Suleman turned to me.

"Old Joe asked me to pass on that your mama is okay. She's not sold. She's back in the kitchen preparing for the wedding in three days," he said.

My heart heard the words before my head. Mama. I didn't feel the tears come, but I know my cheeks went wet. Without my body waiting a moment for my head to think, I hugged Suleman, tight. Shock went across his face.

"Thank you," I said into the collar of Master Crumb's stolen shirt. Suleman nodded.

"I make it my business to know plantations. Weddings, in particular, and from what I hear, this will be a big one." As he spoke, I'd swear he was glowing in the sun, his black eyes sparkling.

"You really do know Old Joe," I said.

"Yes," Suleman.

"Do you know Mama?"

Suleman shook his head. "Only what Old Joe told me, and now I've told you," he said.

"Is Mama mad at me?" I asked. I knew he didn't have an answer, but he was the only person I could ask.

Suleman blinked, confused. "You should go—your partner needs you for the next arrow. We can't slow the bridge," said Suleman.

I felt desperate. My mind was full of things to say, but all I could get out was "Please have Old Joe tell Mama I'm sorry."

I'm not sure Suleman even heard me.

"Go down and keep learning what it means to be free," said Suleman. He put a match in my hand. "Light it when you reach the treetop," he said, and with that he pushed me down the tree pegs.

Down I went. My head was still thick with Mama. I was halfway there when I wished that I'd told him to tell Mama that I loved her. Before I could think hard on it, I heard a "*Sip, sip*" call coming from below. It was Two Shoes.

54

Anna

A FEW WEEKS HAD PASSED SINCE ANNA HAD crushed the maypop flowers and stolen the whiskey. Each day she snuck behind the kitchen, pulled her jar from the dirt hole, and shook it. Each day the liquid grew a little darker, until on its final day, it had turned a deep brown. Anna raised it to the sun and nodded at the promise it held.

She'd spent those past weeks waiting for the next step in her plan to be ready. The wedding was only a few days away and signs were all around Southerland. The tent was being erected beside the Big House. Everyone watched in amazement as the large cloth structure filled the space on the lawn. Neither Anna nor any other enslaved soul on Southerland had ever seen anything like it. Chairs, dishes, food, gifts, and more arrived each day.

Finally, on this morning, Anna's ears perked up as she heard the wagon from the whiskey distillery roll up the lane to the Big House. Onboard was a local tradesman who Crumb came out to meet, with Old Joe right behind him.

"Well, my wife got her flowers and plates and things for the wedding, and I'll have my whiskey," chuckled Crumb.

"Only the best, sir," said the tradesman.

"Well, I'll let you know if it is," said Crumb. The trades-man hopped down, went to a twenty-liter cask on the wagon bed, undid the cork, and ladled out a small glass full. Crumb held it up to the light to see the amber, then swallowed it down.

"My, my, that's fine," he said. "We'll need the whole cask," he said. "We won't have one dry glass all night!"

"It'll be one whopper of a wedding!" said the tradesman.

"Go on," said Crumb to Old Joe.

Prepared for this moment, Anna rushed over and stood beside Old Joe.

"I'll help you," she whispered into his ear.

Old Joe nodded, only a flash of surprise crossing his face.

The two carried the cask into the house and headed toward the study, where the whiskey was usually kept. Anna could feel the heavy jar in her apron pocket. She held her breath as they walked. She was so very close to finishing her last step.

"Oh no you don't!" said Mrs. Crumb. Anna's jaw clenched. *Did Mistress know?*

Old Joe and Anna stopped.

"We can't have that whiskey in the study; there won't be a drop left by the time we get to the reception. Take that to the cupboard, where I'll lock it with all the gifts and china for the big day," she said.

As they turned from the office, which had been a crucial next step in Anna's plan, Anna's heart sank.

With a turn of her key, Mistress unlocked the cupboard and waited while Old Joe and Anna rested the whiskey cask among the many gifts and wares. Old Joe went walking down the hall, but Anna lingered. In order for her plan to work, she needed a moment alone with the whiskey. Her mind raced.

"Come on out of that cupboard so I can lock it," said Mrs. Crumb.

Anna thought fast.

"Mistress, I think Miss Viola had a few more things she wanted put into the cupboard for safekeeping," said Anna in her sweetest voice.

"That girl would lose her head if it wasn't sewn on." Mrs. Crumb sniffed as she walked away from the cupboard and toward the stairs.

"Viola!" she yelled.

There was little time. Anna backed into the closet, uncorked the whiskey, opened her jar, and poured the whole contents inside.

"That child is not answering," Mrs. Crumb said as she walked back toward the cupboard.

Just as Mrs. Crumb's heels clicked toward her, Anna moved away from the cupboard and hurried down the hall. Had she made enough maypop water? She didn't know, couldn't know until the wedding reception.

Most nights before closing her eyes to sleep, Anna saw a vision plain as day. Her walking among guests pouring out whiskey and watching as each person—plantation owners and overseers and slave hunters—grew drowsy and, by the night's end, fell into a deep slumber. Some of them might be so overcome, they'd sleep soundly where they sat. Anna envisioned puffy clouds floating and sheep leaping in the air over their heads until they dozed past morning. It had worked for Rose, and yes, it could work for Anna.

With everyone asleep, she'd walk right off Southerland Plantation and run toward her new home and mother in the North.

Little did Anna know that although her maypop water was very strong, its effect, at least initially, wouldn't be sleep. Yes, her maypop water recipe had been right. Steep the maypop pulp in a little whiskey and it releases the sedative sleep effect that Anna had seen work on Rose.

However, drinking that maypop water by the tumbler glass in whiskey changes its effect. Instead of putting the drinker to sleep, the first feeling becomes a kind of dizzy, boisterous delirium that would make the wedding reception anything but the quiet slumber of Anna's imaginings.

55

Homer

"WE NEED TO FIND THE NEXT TREE MARKING," said Two Shoes as we made our way through the deep, thick swamp muck. At a few places, Two Shoes stopped to put his shoes over his head. He helped pull me from the mud a few times and I did the same for him. We worked so well together, I almost forgot all my distrust. We were partners.

"There it is!" I pointed.

A freshly carved cross was on one of the trees. Two Shoes pulled the climbing rope from his waist and tied it about the trunk. Muck and water were all around the tree. My feet sank to my shins.

"You come behind me," ordered Two Shoes as he went up.

My eyes followed him. Two Shoes knew how to climb— even in his shoes! I put my strap around the tree and went on up. I was slow, much slower than Two Shoes, but I made it to the top.

The breeze in the treetops cooled my wet back. In the distance I saw water. I'm not certain it was the sea, but it was so big it could have been. It was swamp brown with fog hung over it, but on some parts, where the sun came through, the water shone and even sparkled.

"It's a lake," said Two Shoes, watching my stare. "Now, tie off the rope so it'll hold you." Two Shoes showed me how. At the loop end, I tied the rope so I could rest my hind side on it while I used the tree trunk to brace myself. "Go on, he gave you the match," said Two Shoes, handing me an arrow.

A piece of my old shirtsleeve came off easy. I wrapped it about the arrow's point. My hand shook as I struck the match to the tree's trunk. Careful, I brought my wobbly flame to the arrowhead. It caught fast.

"Don't just sit there, hold it up!" said Two Shoes.

With the end of the arrow in one hand, I held it up as high in the air as my arm would take it.

Two Shoes let up a call, and we heard a call in return. Two Shoes readied his sling and watched the sky. The sky bridge rope flew overhead. Two Shoes swung his sling high and it caught the flying rope.

"Yes!" we both said with relief.

He patted my back and I patted his. One last tree was left. Suleman would go to it and tie the final knot. Before long, Suleman waved his fire in the air from the tall tree. Two Shoes tied the rope's end onto his arrow, pulled his bow, and shot the arrow into the air. Suleman swung his sling out and caught it, pulling it up until the bridge swung in the sky. Then he unwound the twisted rope to let loose a three-sided bridge. He pulled the bridge until it hung tight and tied it to the last tree. It swung there, free as a bird. Overhead, Suleman stepped into the middle of our new bridge and let up a call that filled the air, and the swamp set off howling, chirping, and clattering in return.

I went down the tree fast, slipping and skinning my knees all over again. Two Shoes came behind me. His shoes proved slippery on the trunk and both came off and fell from the tree. I went running to get them for him.

"Leave them!" Two Shoes shouted.

"I'll get them!" I called. The mud and muck would surely take them if I didn't.

I found the first shoe right away. The second had fallen behind a bush. I caught it right before it fell into water.

"I'm coming!" Two Shoes shouted as he hurried down the tree.

I picked up the second shoe and something plain and yellow caught my eye on the inside. From the shoe's sole, I pulled a neatly folded piece of paper. It was worn and unfolded easily in my hand. Words written with fancy lettering were on one side. I turned it over and in black ink I saw a drawing. A big house, a river, a secret gate, spikes, and then sky bridges connecting to Big Tree. It was a map. A map of all the steps from Southerland to Freewater.

"Leave my shoes," Two Shoes barked as he made his way down. I stuffed the paper into my pants pocket and tossed Two Shoes's shoes into the water right before he came down.

Watery muck and mud were no matter: Two Shoes dove in, searching for his shoes like an ant searching for food, serious and intent.

You'd think the paper was made of fire itself the way it burned my pocket. My whole body was trembling as I looked down and around, avoiding his eyes, sure if he caught sight of mine, he'd be able to see what I'd done. I swiped my hands around in the river and watched the water swish as I pretended to help.

"I think they both fell in the water," I said to the mud.

Two Shoes grunted.

I felt the hard sole of one shoe under my foot.

"I've got one!" I called, pulling it up.

Impatient, Two Shoes grabbed it from me. Wet and mud poured out as he tipped the shoe down and felt the sole inside. He stared at me hard. I swear he saw the map straight through my clothes.

"Maybe the other is over that way." I pointed, trying to turn his gaze on something else.

The water had carried the other farther away, but Two Shoes found it, tipped it over, and watched as only mud spilled out.

"You found the other one!" I said, trying to make my voice happy.

"What?" Two Shoes said, looking up at me like he only now had remembered I was there.

"Your shoes," I said.

"Yes, right," he said, trying to make his anger sound like relief.

Without saying more, Two Shoes dove down into the water.

"*Toooot, toooot,*" blew Daria's horn.

Two Shoes raised his muddy face. His eyes were wide and worried like a deer caught unaware.

"We best be going," I said. "I think that's them calling us back."

"I'm coming," said Two Shoes. But even as we walked away, he let his eyes wander back to the water.

"Right, coming," he said to the water.

56

Homer

BACK AT FREEWATER, IT WAS SUNSET AND everyone was out preparing for the wedding. Mrs. Faith and Ada were gone helping the others with final touches on Daria's dress. Ibra was already in the meeting place.

Billy and I were the only ones left in the cabin. Pieces of corn husk were scattered at his feet as he wove a few last bits into his green sash. He knotted each strand until it was perfect. Still, the sash's rough edges caught Billy's mass of kinky hair as he tried to pull it over his head. I got up to help him and we put the sash over his shoulder and chest, making sure it was neat. Billy looked down at himself.

"I w-w-wish Mama c-c-could be here," he whispered. "That's s-s-strange, huh?" He smiled one of his sad smiles at me.

I shook my head. I wished for Mama almost every day.

"Mama's s-s-sold off. It's g-g-good Papa's m-m-marry-ing D-D-Daria," said Billy. "He's s-s-so happy. And she's s-s-strong like Mama," explained Billy. "But w-w-when special things h-h-happen I s-s-still wish Mama back, even for this," he said. He went to his mat and pulled out a wooden bracelet. It matched the one he'd made for Juna, but it was thinner and smaller. He slipped it on his wrist.

"Are you gonna give the other one to Juna today?" I asked. He pulled his pouch over his shoulder and touched the bracelet within as if it might have moved from the spot it had been in for weeks.

"I think I-I-I will," he promised to the pouch. "I best g-g-go," he said. Then he left to join Ibra.

I was finally alone with Two Shoes's map. *Forest, river, vines and bush, watch for the sinkhole, more vines and bush, green water, tree boat, lily pads, secret water door, tree hideout, tree people, zigzag, sky bridge.* It was all there. But the map had more to it: markings and signs to help with each part. I traced my finger from Freewater back to Southerland. Mama couldn't find us, but I realized maybe I could find Mama. Was there a way? Even the thought scared me. I folded the map and went searching for Ada.

It was dusk, and Hope and Free were busy digging holes in the dirt along each side of the path coming from Daria and Ibra's new house to the meeting space. In the middle of the space, across from the fire pit, they made a circle of holes then put small bits of tree sap into each. Behind them came Sky, who touched the sap with torch light. It ignited a flame in each hole and made a path of dancing firelight from the cabin to the circle. Hope and Free squealed with happiness. It was spooky beautiful.

I followed the light path right to the cabin and stood near the door wondering what to do. Laughter and talking spilled out.

"All right now, Daria, it's time. You ain't gonna walk down that path with your horn in one hand and a bow in the other," Juna said.

"I don't see why not. That's what I had in my hands when Ibra asked me to marry him," said Daria.

"Listen to her. Stubborn as ever," another woman said.

"Run and get the beads, Juna. We've got all the flowers, but we need the beads for the walk," said someone else.

I backed away from the door as Juna opened it. There she was with Ada at her side.

"Homer!" Ada said. Her hair was braided exactly like Juna's. She pulled me close. "You can't go in there," she said, smiling.

"Oh no?" I said.

"Uh-uh, you can't see a thing till Daria comes walking down that path," Ada explained.

"What about you? Why do you get to see her?" I asked.

" 'Cuz I was helping," she said, resting comfortable in my arms. Those fire holes may as well have been light in her eyes, they were so bright. She was happy, and I forgot all about what had happened and about Two Shoes's map in my pocket.

"I get to help in the wedding," she said proudly.

"You're in the wedding?" I asked.

"Uh-huh," she said. That was Ada, coming in and making herself part of it all. She didn't pay any mind to eyes being on her. "I'm the flower holder."

"Flower holder?" I asked.

"That's right. We need to go up near the front so I can do it," she said, pulling me down the path, into the meeting space, right by the circle of light. Everyone had come. There was laughing, talking, and waiting.

In the middle of the circle was Ibra, smiling and pulling at his clothes. He wore a pale green sash of weaved corn husk like Billy, except his was woven with tiny white flowers.

"I put those flowers in there," Ada said. "We found them down by the river and I didn't even see one bit of monsters."

Then there was another blow of the horn and everybody stood. Women came out of Daria's cabin with beads in their hands and positioned themselves on each side of the path. Finally, out of the house at the top of the lighted path came Daria.

Everyone started howling and the swamp came alive.

Neither I nor Ada had ever seen anything like Daria. Soft sage-green leaves were woven to create the knotty cloth of her billowy blouse. The sleeves opened wide around her arms and wrists. Where the blouse stopped, a cascading skirt started. It was a pattern of copper-colored leaves and lined with more of the sage green that made her blouse. The skirt touched the ground and formed a train of copper and green behind her.

Daria wore a round woven hat, piled atop with flowers of sunshine yellow, silky white, and orange. Spilling from her headdress and shading her eyes were strands of delicate, small white-and-orange flowers, dotted with a red crimson center. As she walked down the light path, the shadow of flames danced on the copper color of her dress. She looked as if she'd risen from firelight.

"She's a swamp queen," whispered Ada, like she'd always suspected it, and finally she could show the rest of us, swamp queens walk the earth.

As Daria passed the women on the path, each hugged her close and put necklaces and bracelets of wooden beads on her neck and wrists. Soon, the jewelry piled high, almost covering her chest and arms.

"It's time!" said Ada, and quick as a fire ant, she was working her way through the people, getting to the front where Daria had stopped.

Daria saw Ada there smiling. She pulled off the flower veil and handed it to Ada, then she bent down and kissed her forehead. Ada froze. Her smile disappeared and she dropped the flowers to her side and ran over to me. She sank into my lap.

"Ada, what's wrong?" I asked.

She picked up her head, and tears wet her eyes and face.

"She kissed my head like Mama," said Ada.

Mama, the map, Two Shoes, and Suleman came back to me. Each one took a seat on my shoulders. I bent down and hugged Ada, tight. Part of me felt relieved to see her also miss Mama. There was no freedom without Mama. We sat there, Ada crying, and me thinking. The crinkle of the map in my pocket sent shivers down my spine.

With all that thinking, I didn't hear much of the wedding. David spoke, then Mrs. Light came into the circle of light and took hold of Daria's and Ibra's right hands and held them together.

Daria and Ibra faced each other.

"I am with you," said Ibra.

"And I am with you," said Daria.

Then Ibra smiled, bent down, and threw his arms around Daria.

She hugged him back, and everyone set out whooping and hollering.

57

Homer

EVERYONE SPILLED INTO FREEWATER'S CENTER. Some played Ibra's drums and other instruments, which had been brought out for the special day.

"Take! It's you who caught it," said Ibra. He tore three pieces of meat from the pig and put each in a large leaf and handed one to me, then to Ada and Billy. He smiled and hugged us in happiness and went off dancing.

I tasted the warm meat. The savory juice ran down my hand. It was like nothing I'd ever eaten.

A whistle came from overhead.

"Sanzi," I said, trying to find her. She was sitting on a high branch of Big Tree, away from us all, dressed in her Suleman clothes. I realized I hadn't seen her since coming back from the sky bridge. She'd taken to hiding. She whistled again down to Billy.

"C-c-come on," said Billy, pulling my arm.

Up the tree we went—me, Billy, and Ada. We all sat there quiet, watching Freewater below. They moved without a care for who was there watching or coming or running or hurting or being hurt. They moved free.

"You saw him?" asked Sanzi.

"Who?" I asked, feeling her eyes on me.

"Suleman," she said.

I nodded.

"He helped put up the bridge?" she asked.

I nodded again, unsure what more I could say without everything spilling out.

"He told you all sorts about him fighting masters and taking all their tools and animals, huh," she said.

"It wasn't like that. I didn't hardly have a chance to talk to him," I said.

"I bet they know him," she said, looking up into Big Tree. I followed her eyes but didn't see anyone.

Billy said, "Look r-r-real close and y-y-you'll see them."

Ada and I both strained our eyes in the dark and sure enough I saw a leg, then an arm.

"Tree people!" said Ada.

There were two. They were wrapped in leaves and vines and almost disappeared into the foliage.

"They're the f-f-far p-p-patrol," said Billy.

"They are the best patrollers in Freewater. They say they can sit in a tree one week straight without moving," said Sanzi.

"They've gotta move to eat, don't they?" asked Ada.

"Nope," said Sanzi. "I heard catchers could be two feet from them, but they'll be so good at tree hiding, the catchers walk right past."

Ada waved at them.

"Don't," said Sanzi.

"Why are they staying up there?" I asked.

"L-l-long p-p-patrol k-k-keep to themselves," said Billy.

"They don't like coming in here with everybody. They like the trees," said Sanzi.

"They've gotta be hungry," said Ada, waving again.

"You're not supposed to do that!" said Sanzi. But, up above, a tree-covered hand returned Ada's wave.

"Did you see that?!" said Ada, excited. She was almost back to her old self after her memory of Mama. She went scooting past us and down the trunk of Big Tree.

From our branch spot, we watched her head weave through the people toward the pig. She came back with two leaves full of meat in her hands.

She climbed back to our branch and held her offering up to the far patrollers.

"I told you they don't even eat," said Sanzi.

Nothing happened at first, but then one of them moved. Down the tree the far patroller came, and when the patrol was right over us, Ada reached up her little hand.

"Thank you," said the patrol, taking the meat. Small black eyes showed through layers of leaves.

"You're welcome," said Ada. "Hey, is it true you can go a whole week with no food?" asked Ada. I'm not sure if the patroller smiled or what, but she shook her head.

"We stay quiet. We become the swamp, no different than a tree or a vine," she said, proud like.

"Why don't you come down and eat?" asked Sanzi. You could tell even Sanzi was happy for Ada's questions.

"Our minds need to stay out there, watching and hearing. We can't have Freewater in here," she said, pointing to her head. "But we know that what we do makes this be," she said, looking below. "And this is what matters."

Now I needed to know. "But why'd you come back today?" I asked.

Her dark eyes watched me.

"For weddings, everything changes. All of us, for a short time, we leave our posts to come. We must all be here or it's bad luck. So, for a short while, Freewater only has our traps, the thick of the swamp, and what's up above to watch over her," said the far patroller. She turned to Ada once more. "Thank you." And then, as fast as she came down, up the tree she went.

Like a thunderclap, her words rang in my head. *For weddings, everything changes.* Everything would change at Southerland for Miss Viola's wedding. All the old ways would be new for the wedding. Could a person get lost in the new and disappear? Maybe. My mind considered the idea. The wedding was in a few days, and that might be my one chance.

Mama couldn't get to us, but maybe I could get to her.

Maybe Anna, as well. I had a plan. I hugged Ada and her face went bright like moonlight in the dark.

"You hugged me first," she said, then she threw her arms around me.

"Come on, let's go down," I said, jumping from the branch.

"You go," said Sanzi, looking around. "I'll stay up here."

58

Billy

THUMP, PUMP, PUMP, THUMP, PUMP.

The thumping of the drums gave Billy courage, or so he thought.

It was partly why he'd taught himself to play the drum. The pulse of the sound made his heart feel stronger than it ever did those mornings when the woodcutters came in search of him.

Since the trip to hang the sky bridge, no one had mentioned his near fall. Satisfaction and relief from the bridge having been hung made the wedding party even more jubilant. Billy had tried to forget his misstep and concentrate on the fact that he'd helped David, and they'd both returned safely. In some ways he'd fulfilled Juna's request. He'd watched over David. Sort of.

Billy was contemplating these things as he danced across the village circle, his head hovering over most in the crowd. He passed Homer, who was twirling Ada to the drumbeat. Juna was there with younger girls all about her, dancing in a circle.

A tap on the shoulder should do it, he thought.

"Hi, Billy," said Juna. She broke from her circle, spun about, and started dancing with him.

Billy's heart soared. He'd do it. He reached for his pouch. But he was so determined, he failed to see Ferdinand approach.

"Where is she?" Ferdinand demanded.

"Huh?" asked Billy. "Who a-a-are y-y-you t-t-talking about?"

"Y-y-you know who I-I-I mean: S-S-Sanzi! She has my knife!" Ferdinand imitated.

"Hey! Don't do that!" said Juna, who stopped dancing. The moment was broken.

Ferdinand turned on her. "I don't even know why you bother with him! He's so afraid of his own shadow he almost pulled us all off the sky bridge. Suleman had to save him. He could've killed us all!" Ferdinand walked off, continuing his hunt.

"What?" Juna's brow furrowed and she looked at him. "What happened?"

Billy felt the ground rumble beneath him. "I'm s-s-sorry" was all he could say as he backed away from her.

Meanwhile, Ferdinand had finally spotted Sanzi in Big Tree.

"You heard Mrs. Light—you need to stop with your games!" he yelled up at her.

59

Sanzi

THE WEDDING FESTIVITIES HAD ENDED HOURS earlier. Everyone had floated off to bed with full bellies and happy memories—but that wasn't true for Sanzi.

Games! The insult screamed in Sanzi's head as she rowed her boat into the darkness toward her place. Clouds moved in from the east, blotting out the moon and threatening rain. She'd taken a small flame torch to help her navigate the ink-black night. The flames shone on her and illuminated the outline of her bow. Yes, she'd taken it, and now she didn't care who knew.

With her torch in her mouth, Sanzi unfurled her belt and climbed up her tree past the platform where her ropes were tied and continued up to the high perch.

Games! That's what her mother thought, what they all thought. Would they call what Suleman did games? Never. He was a hero. She could be like him. She knew it, even if no one else did.

Frustrated, she pulled her bow from her back and fired two arrows, one after the next. Even if she couldn't show the others her bravery, she'd show the swamp. But both arrows disappeared soundlessly in the darkness. Dissatisfied, Sanzi looked to her torch flame and an idea ignited. Tonight she really could be like Suleman. She needed cloth. She didn't have much. What could be better than using the piece of cloth given to her by Suleman? It tore easily from the animal-skin tapestry in her shirt. She wrapped pieces around the points of two of her arrows and touched one to her torch flame. A tingle and zing went down her spine at the sight. It was just like Suleman's. It was just as she'd dreamt.

She fired one arrow. *Swoosh!* The flame cut the air, arched high over the trees, then fell like a falling star in the night sky and landed in the waters below her. The fire went out as the water swallowed it. *That had to be like him,* she thought.

She lit the second arrow and aimed the same way. Like the last, it arched high over the trees. However, a sudden gust of air took hold and pushed the arrow west. The flame roared, leaving a comet's tail in its wake before it hit the ground with a burst.

In a sea of darkness a small light flashed, dancing back and forth. Sanzi watched as the flame grew from a whisper to a murmur, changing from yellow to orange and lighting what lay around it—corn. The cornfields!

Sanzi's heart froze. Her anger turned to fear. Fast as a

squirrel she made her way down the tree and into her canoe. Frantic, she rowed toward the village.

Freewater was quiet. Everyone was asleep, drunk with joy and bellies full from the wedding. The quiet felt wrong to disturb. For a long moment Sanzi stood in the middle of the cabins, unable to believe what she'd done. *Maybe it hadn't happened. Maybe she'd imagined it.* Then she turned and saw a thin line of smoke in the distance.

"Fire in the corn!" she yelled. "Fire in the corn!"

Her mother, Mrs. Light, was one of the first ones to emerge from her cabin and looked toward the cloudy sky.

"Oh Lord, it must have been lightning!" she said, and headed right for the smoke already coming from the fields.

Nearby, cabin flaps opened. Ibra and Daria emerged.

"It's in the cornfield" was all Sanzi could say.

The fire had taken no time spreading. Plumes of smoke came up from the center of the fields.

Daria raised her horn and sent out a wail that made the hairs on everyone's necks stand up. It told everyone, near and far, that there was real trouble. Each person came out of their cabins with a wooden plank in hand and ran toward the cornfields. Gabriel, Ibra, Wisdom, Daria, and more went straight to the smoke.

David handed planks to Sanzi, Homer, Billy, Juna, Ada, and Ferdinand, then took them to cornfield's edge.

"Stay here on the outside. We'll go to the center. When you see the small flames catch the stalks, beat them back with the planks! Be careful, swamp fires are tricky. They can move underground and come up, so keep out of the cornfield," David instructed.

Like fiery orange jewels, embers from the fire floated through the air and landed on the silky stalks around them. The touch of the embers set stalks aflame.

"Beat it down!" shouted Juna, as they each raised their plank and began swinging until the flames died out. Then another shower of embers arrived and they started swinging anew. They were left panting, coughing up smoke, when another shower of embers rained down on them, burning their arms and legs.

Ada screamed. "It's raining fire!" she said, placing the plank over her head.

"Go back!" shouted Homer.

By now more had started to arrive with water in bowls. They took animal pelts, soaked them, and used them to beat back the flames. Children were running to fetch water. Ada joined them.

"If I had my knife, I could cut this down!" coughed Ferdinand.

His words struck Sanzi. The fire was spreading and it wouldn't be long before it burned where she'd buried the knife. Once caught in the flames, it would be destroyed.

"I'll be right back!" Sanzi yelled, and she took off running into the cornfields.

"Sanzi! Come back!" Juna called after her. "She's crazy!"

"I'll g-g-get her!" shouted Billy, and with plank in hand, he ran into the fiery cornfields after her.

Sanzi

SMOKE CLOUDED THE WAY OF SANZI'S QUEST for the knife. In the ash and showers of embers, one patch of corn quickly resembled another. When she thought she'd found the spot, she dropped to her knees and began clawing at the ground with her hands.

"What a-a-are y-y-you doing?!" yelled Billy.

Sanzi hardly glanced up, frustrated that her hands hadn't found the metal blade nor the wooden handle.

"The knife," she said. "I need to find Ferdinand's knife!" Sanzi gave up on one spot, then searched in another.

"His *knife*?" coughed Billy.

"I know it's here!" In a new spot, again, Sanzi dropped to her knees and dug.

"We c-c-can't stay!" said Billy, ducking bright orange ember showers and beating them back with his plank.

"I buried it!" said Sanzi, her arms already deep in dirt. Nothing.

"What?" yelled Billy.

Sanzi tried another spot, raking her nails through the dirt, willing her hand to touch it. Before she could answer, a breeze swept through the stalks and carried with it a shower of embers.

"Sanzi! We have to g-g-go!" shouted Billy.

The stalks of corn around them burst into flames. Finally, Sanzi felt the smooth wood of Ferdinand's knife. She pulled it out of the dirt.

"Look!" cried Sanzi. She held up the knife.

"You took h-h-his knife!" said Billy. Before Sanzi could explain, they heard it. *CRACK!* Orange flames whipped the cornstalks, lashed out, and surrounded Billy and Sanzi. They stood back-to-back striking at the flames, Billy with his plank, Sanzi with the knife. There was nowhere to run.

"Oh no," said Billy as the flames roared.

"I'll cut through," said Sanzi, chopping at the stalks. But it proved too little: A gust of flame shot out of the stalks and licked a burn across her hand. In pain, Sanzi dropped the knife and the fire swallowed the precious metal and wood.

Then, through the smoke, they heard a call.

"Billy! Sanzi!"

The corn stalks shook, and bursting through the smoke came Ferdinand and Homer, one with a plank, the other with wet pelts. Homer parted the corn stalks and shouted, "This way!"

Billy ran through the opening.

"No!" said Sanzi, clawing at the smoldering ground, trying to find the knife.

"Sanzi!" yelled Ferdinand.

"NO!" she screamed, on her knees. Ferdinand picked her up, threw the wet fur over her head, and ran as Sanzi grabbed at the corn fire.

They came to the cornfield's end and Ferdinand set Sanzi down.

"Are you okay?" he asked. There was no teasing nor irony in his voice.

"I'm sorry," whispered Sanzi.

Ferdinand pulled back, surprised, wondering what smart thing she'd say next.

"What?" he asked, unsure he'd heard right.

"I'm sorry. Your knife. I lost your knife in the fire. I was trying to get it," said Sanzi.

"My knife." Ferdinand's eyes went wide with confusion. He stood up and watched the flames that had taken his precious knife.

"I'm sorry," Sanzi cried.

Much of the cornfields had become a graveyard of scorched smoking stalks. Plumes of smoke billowed into the air and hung like soup fog over Freewater. Five cabins, with roofs or walls burned through, lined the path. A gaping, smoldering hole shone through the roof of Ibra and Daria's new cabin. Deep, smoke-filled coughs echoed through the village as people rushed about dousing what was left of the fire with water. Only rain had stopped the flames.

Sanzi walked through the village dazed as the droplets fell on her. But even in misery there were hugs and pats of thanks for Sanzi by almost everyone. "You warned us—it could have taken the whole village, but you warned us," each said in some form. She was the heroine she'd always hoped to be. Yet, with each thanks, Sanzi felt lower and lower.

Juna, who'd stayed at the fire's edge as instructed by their father, watched Sanzi receive everyone's praise. Sanzi saw a pang of envy in Juna's eyes—she thought Sanzi had been brave.

"Are you all right?" asked Juna.

Sanzi could only nod with her face set to the ground, unable to raise her head from the weight of shame.

"Let me see that hand," said Juna. She looked it over. "It's not bad," she said, hoping that would help cheer her sister. She ran to their cabin and brought out a bit of balm her mother kept for such things.

Sanzi watched her sister deftly clean and salve her hand. She did it perfectly, as she did most everything, thought Sanzi. *Juna would never have set that fire.*

"Come on, we better get to the meeting," said Juna.

I wish it had taken me, Sanzi thought as she and Juna walked past the village center and saw the destruction. She'd done this. Her bow was still on her back, but now, instead of light and powerful, it felt heavy as an anvil on her shoulders. She wasn't Suleman. She was the opposite of a hero. No one knew. But she did.

61

Homer

THE FIRE HAD ENDED, AND AS I WALKED TO the meeting space, it rained, but I didn't feel one drop. A tingling was running all over my skin. I'd helped save Sanzi and Billy from that fire. I felt different, like I had new arms and legs and everything else. Maybe I could help save Mama.

The meeting had already started when I got there. I sat down in the back by Ada, Sanzi, and Billy. Mrs. Light waved her hands.

"We had another warning. This one came from Suleman. He told David as they hung the sky bridge, the white men are set to send militia into the swamp. They've never found Freewater before. But it's all the more need to stop this fire," said Mrs. Light. Everyone nodded weary heads. She may as well have said that Mr. Crumb himself was coming into the swamp. Some of my tingling turned to sweat.

"Let's not trust that the fire is done," said Mrs. Light. "Swamp fires burn down into the moss. We need to keep watch for it to come back."

Tired heads nodded. We were covered black in soot. Some had burns, others had lost clothes.

"She's right. Even with these rains, fire could start up again," said Ibra. "We need every soul we've got to keep beating the fields. All patrols need calling in, until we know the village is safe from it."

Two people pushed past me.

"We went looking. He's not in the village," said Wisdom.

"That poor man," said Juna.

"He was there, beating the fire with the rest of us," said another.

"It must have taken him," said a woman, crying.

"Anyone see him after that?" asked Mrs. Light of everyone.

Tired heads were shaking.

"Who?" I asked.

Sanzi's hand was wrapped, and her clothes were marked with burns. The look of mischief was gone from her eyes. She didn't say a word.

"Turner. He's m-m-missing," said Billy, full of worry.

Two Shoes was gone. Even in the heat of the day, my body went cold all over.

"Swamp fires can draw you in, then catch you. Next thing you know . . ." Ibra's voice went quiet.

"Let's stop with that talk. We won't know until we walk

283

those fields. He mighta gotten burned and is laid out some-where," said David.

Mrs. Light went to the middle of the room and clapped her hands. "We give thanks that every other soul in Free-water is here and safe," said Mrs. Light.

Freewater let out a weak swamp cry that joined the puffs of smoke swirling into the air.

62

Homer

TWO SHOES WAS GONE. WAS IT THE FIRE THAT took him? Or had he run? I peered around the room. No one even suspected that he might run, but I knew better. There was one way to find the answer.

"Stay here," I said to Ada.

I backed out of the meeting.

"H-H-Homer," Billy called from behind me. But there was no time. I headed straight down the path to the end of the cabin row and pulled the flap back on Two Shoes's cabin. Not one leaf or wooden stick had even been touched by the fire. It sat there as if nothing had happened at all. Against the wall, remnants of dried black ash were still in the bowl. I pushed aside his sleeping mat. No matches. The small dug hole was empty. He'd run off.

"What are y-y-you looking for?" asked Billy. I turned around.

Ada, Billy, Sanzi, and Juna had followed me. What could I even tell them?

"Um, I was thinking maybe…Two Shoes forgot

something," I said without looking their way, hoping that would be enough.

"Homer, it sounded like the fire took that poor man," said Juna.

Someone needed to know what I knew, and they were the closest thing I had to friends in Freewater.

"What if he didn't get burned in the fire? What if he ran off?" I said.

"Ran off?" Sanzi asked. "People don't run from Freewater, they run *to* Freewater," she sassed.

Billy bit down hard on his lip. He understood.

"I found this in his shoe; he doesn't know I have it," I said, pulling the map from my pocket and opening it.

Billy's hands shook as he touched it.

"It's a map. That's Southerland, our old plantation, and this is Freewater. It's showing how to get here," I said, moving my finger over the drawings.

"Two Shoes is going back to Southerland?" asked Ada. "Do you think he's gonna see Mama?"

"I don't think so," I said, unsure how to explain.

"He m-m-made this?" asked Billy.

"Look, the ink's right over there," I said, pointing to the blackened bowls.

Juna went over and touched her finger to the bowl's dried ink and nodded.

"You mean to tell me you have a map to get to your old

plantation?" said Sanzi, slipping it out of Billy's hands and poring over the drawings. "That's the sky bridge!" She pointed. "What's that?"

"It's a river near Southerland. It's how Ada and I escaped," I said.

"Is this part of the map, too?" asked Sanzi, looking at the scribbled writing on the other side. I shrugged. The five of us gazed at the lettering, willing it to make sense. I turned the paper back over. Sanzi touched it and her mischievous eyes returned.

"We could use this to get to that plantation!" she exclaimed.

"Someone could use this to h-h-help white men find Freewater," Billy said. "You think T-T-Turner would do th-th-that?"

"We never had anybody do that. Why would he even want to do that?" said Juna, shaking her head.

I didn't know how to explain the feeling I had about Two Shoes, but something wasn't right.

"I don't know," I said. "I know he's been keeping secrets. He had matches hidden right here." I pointed to the empty hole under the mat. "He kept this map secret. He was one for keeping secrets for Crumb, the master at Southerland."

Billy studied the map. "We n-n-need to tell s-s-someone," he said.

"He's right," said Juna.

"We can't!" Sanzi and I both said in unison. That would be the end of everything.

"We have t-t-to!" said Billy.

I had to say something, or they'd ruin my plan before it even started. "Listen, I need the map to go back and get Mama and my friend Anna. I know how to get them out of there. While I'm there, I'll see if Two Shoes has run back to Southerland. If I see him, I promise to come back and warn everyone," I said.

"You'd really g-g-go back there?" asked Billy. I turned away so I wouldn't see the shock in his eyes.

"You get to go back on the sky bridge," Ada pointed out.

"I suppose," I said.

"I want to go get Mama, too. Besides I'm the best at flying on the sky bridge," Ada said.

"No, you stay here. I'll be back before you know it." And I hugged her to show my promise.

"I don't know anything about his mama and this Anna person, but I know that map can help us," Sanzi chimed in. "You heard everybody out there. We lost cabins and the corn. What if we don't have enough food for winter? I lost Ferdinand's knife. We need tools. That plantation has them, and we have a map to get there. We could save Freewater. We could be heroes! If we tell, there's no way they'd let us go."

"You're both crazy!" said Juna, shaking her head in misery.

"He's crazy if he thinks he's going all the way to some

plantation somewhere without me!" said Sanzi. "He wants to save his mama, and we need to save Freewater!"

"What if you g-g-get c-c-caught?" asked Billy. "We n-n-need to tell."

"Please don't," I begged, feeling my plan begin to crumble. "It's not that crazy." There didn't seem anything left to do but say everything. "There's a wedding coming. It's the one time I could get to Mama and Anna without anybody seeing me. There'll be all kinds of company about, and everything'll be different enough for Mama and Anna to go missing. When we were hanging the sky bridge, Suleman told me the wedding was in three days. That gives me two days to get there. I'm gonna listen for a chance to sneak away, and I'll go." Saying it sounded more certain than I actually felt.

"Suleman," repeated Sanzi. "If he told you, it must be true. I bet it'll be different enough for us to get in there and have some tools go missing, too!"

Sanzi didn't understand.

"Don't even think about it! What would Mama say!" said Juna to Sanzi.

"That's all you ever think about. Do this for Mama, do that for Mama. That's all you ever do! You're never gonna see anything but Mama's plants and herbs!"

"Don't say that!" said Juna. It was the first time I ever saw real sadness in her big sad eyes.

"Why not? You don't understand anything. I need to do this because..." Sanzi's voice trailed off like she was talking to herself as much as us.

"No, no," I said. I could feel my plan flying out of my hands. "Just me," I said, trying to catch it. "Just me!"

"You know what happens if you get c-c-caught?" Billy warned me. "There ain't no c-c-coming back to Freewater after that. She doesn't know a thing about out there."

"I can do it," I said. *Couldn't I?*

Billy was right, the whole plan was crazy, but I couldn't bear to hear him say it again, so I grabbed my map and left.

63

Homer

AS MRS. LIGHT PROPHESIED, ONCE THE RAINS subsided, the fire came back. What little remained of the cornfields was set aflame again. When Daria's horn moaned the next morning, Ibra, Mrs. Light, David, and most all the adults ran to the fields.

The cabin was quiet. Next to the far wall, Billy lay asleep, along with Mrs. Faith. I leaned over and kissed a sleeping Ada on the forehead and said a silent prayer that I'd get back to her and bring Mama with me. I couldn't wake her; she'd tell if I did. Mrs. Faith and Ibra and all the others would take care of her. I knew that.

I pulled out my sack and checked the corn bread and smoked meat I'd stored inside. Instead of my mantra of what Mama needed to do to get to me, I'd created a new chant of all the steps I needed to get Mama and Anna out of Southerland.

Be invisible at Southerland.
Get my wedding clothes from my cabin in the quarters.
Sneak up to Southerland house.

Keep clear of the dinner tent.
Find Mama and Anna in the kitchen.
Tell them to run with me.
Get back to the swamp.

Done.

I went to the cabin flap and watched the dirt path, straining to see its end at Big Tree. All seemed quiet, so I went running for it. A whistle came from the brush.

"Hey! You know how to swim?" I heard Sanzi ask from behind. *Oh no.* There she was, all done up in her Suleman clothes with bow and arrows strapped on. She was ready in the only way she knew. I didn't have the heart to tell her there was no need for all that in Southerland. I said nothing, shook my head, and waved Sanzi back. Maybe she'd go away.

"I saw all that water on your map. I don't suppose you'll be able to swim through it," she said. "You'll drown for sure. You need my boat, so you might as well let me come," said Sanzi.

"Why do you even want to come anyway? You don't have to run anywhere. You got both your mama and papa here." Nothing would make me go back to Southerland if Mama and Anna weren't there. Sanzi was quiet a long while, like she wanted to say something but didn't know how.

"I just need to go, all right. Besides, I'm right and you know it. You can't swim," said Sanzi.

"Maybe," I admitted, coming down from the tree. *Maybe* was as good as a "yes" for Sanzi.

"Come on and help me with this," she said. From behind a patch of thicket Sanzi uncovered a long and slender canoe. I didn't have any argument left in me.

"All right," I said.

"I can help, too," said a low voice. We both turned to see Juna step out from the smoky shadows.

"Where do you think you're going?" asked Sanzi.

"I'm coming," said Juna. It was the first time I'd ever seen her look anything but certain and steady. She wasn't dressed like Sanzi, but she did have a sling tied about her shoulder and a pouch of stones at her waist.

"No way! What about Mama? And getting in trouble?" said Sanzi.

"You're not the only one who can help save Freewater," said Juna as she bent down to pick up the boat.

"Good, help me strap this on so we can get it up to the sky bridge," Sanzi agreed with a smile. *Oh no, Sanzi was one thing, but sensible Juna. How could I stop her from coming?*

"We can't carry this whole boat on our own," I muttered.

"Y'all won't h-h-have to do it a-a-alone." Billy walked over and grabbed hold of the boat.

"Go on back, Billy. You don't even want to do this," I said. *This was not in the plan!*

"That might be so, but I c-c-can't stay behind if you all g-g-go," said Billy, glancing over at Juna.

"No, Billy," I protested. *What was wrong with these people?*

"If you don't let m-m-me go, I'll have to stay here and t-t-tell," said Billy. His expression was nervous but full of determination. There was little changing his mind.

"How you suppose we'll get that boat up to the sky bridge?" I asked Sanzi.

"We got a dead pig up the side of a drop-off," said Sanzi, "but we need to hurry before anyone comes by."

They put rope through a few slits made in the lip of the boat. Sanzi tied herself to one end, then Billy to the other. After going up a few feet we heard talking and footsteps.

"I think I have another plank in my cabin," said Wisdom. "Let me run back and see."

All of us froze on the tree, listening as the voice and steps came closer. I could see my plan ending before it had even begun.

"Hi, Wisdom!" It was Ada's sweet voice.

"Well, hello there, Mrs. Ada. You'll be wanting to be inside with all this smoke," he said.

"I will. Can you walk me by the river? I was wanting some water," said Ada.

Before long, the two voices faded. I gave the boat a

shove, and Billy and Sanzi made their way up Big Tree. In the morning dark, I watched their shadows disappear into the leaves overhead.

There was a tug on my shirt.

"I told you I could help!" Ada said, smiling up at me. "I'm going," she said. Then in a snap, she was up the tree.

There was no catching her.

I looked around Freewater. Even in the smoke I could see the cabins, the meeting place, everything. I'd only been there a short while, but it felt like a place to be missed. Again, as I went up the tree, I knew that for better or worse, things would never be the same again.

64

Nora

NORA AWOKE THAT MORNING WITH A JUMBLE of thoughts, not clear how each one fit with the next. Lately, she felt lost. She couldn't bear to visit Rose, but she couldn't stand the wedding chaos of her home.

Large serving bowls, flowers, tablecloths, gifts, and more filled most every corner of the downstairs. Viola and her mother walked about, yelling instructions and demands at Anna, who seemed to be doing most of the work for Viola's big day.

Nora, determined to get out of the Big House, went for the front door. Blinking in the sunlight, she jumped back. A large man stood in the doorway. He wore a heavy tattered wool jacket, long boots that were scuffed and opened at the knee, and a large rifle strapped to his shoulder.

"Hey, little lady." The man smiled. Yellowed teeth peeked through his overgrown beard. "I'm looking for the master of the house."

Nora shook her head.

"Me and them men down there," he said, pointing

behind him at three other men, "we're the militia your papa sent for to handle your runaway problem."

Nora frowned a *no* and tried to close the door.

"Whoa, little lady," the man said, placing his foot in the opening.

"Who's down there?" called Mrs. Crumb, descending the stairs. "Oh, my Lord!" she exclaimed when she saw her new arrivals. "I can't believe this! Why are you here right now? You boys aren't doing any slave-catching adventures two days before my daughter's wedding."

"Uh, ma'am, I don't know anything about any wedding. We was sent for and we're here," said the man.

"Oh my. This won't work. This won't work," said Mrs. Crumb. "My husband is not able to meet with you today. No. No. No. You'll need to get yourselves to the toolshed for now. It's just over the hill and has a white door. You'll bed there. I imagine you have some means of accommodating yourselves. I can't have you in the middle of my guests." She swept a disdainful eye over the militiamen's appearance. "We'll send some food down later this evening."

"So long as y'all pay for our time, we'll go wherever you care to send us," said the man with another smirk. He tipped his hat, and his men followed him in the direction of the toolshed.

"Isn't this a mess! I can't believe it," Mrs. Crumb grumbled. "Militiamen roaming the property during the wedding. I won't have it!" Nora's mother walked back upstairs.

"Hey, don't worry, little ma'am. We know how to catch swamp runaways and we're good at it," said the man to Nora as they walked away.

Nora watched. The swamp was going to be a dangerous place. Rose needed something better—they both did.

THE
RETURN

65

Ferdinand

FROM THE PLATFORM ATOP BIG TREE, FERDINAND gazed west. About this time, the ditchdiggers would be up. Mornings were cooler and allowed for longer work hours. The clanging is what Ferdinand most remembered. Chains hitting one another as they swung their shovels.

Titus, Adam, and Ferdinand were chained at the ankle, in that order. Chained together because they were all about the same size and build.

"You've got the same swing," said the gang leader.

They moved in unison. Heave—Ho—Heave—Ho, in time, together. They slept together, defecated together, grew sick together, and starved together. They became so close they were one entity. That the snake only bit one of them was a reminder that this was more an idea than a fact. Adam alone was bitten. He alone gasped for air and went unconscious.

Afraid of the cost of losing a hired slave, the gang leader unchained Ferdinand to help attend to Adam. In that ditch, as Ferdinand watched the life drain from Adam, a thought came to him. *Run.* That's what he did.

The gang leader had set his knife down as he unlocked the chains. The moment Ferdinand took the knife and the moment he ran free as his own person were so intertwined, the knife itself became part of his identity—the symbol of who he was and his freedom.

Without his knife, Ferdinand felt unanchored. So lost, he'd gone up to the top of Big Tree, to the sky bridge, on a mission to go find another knife. It was only once he'd gotten to the bridge, he'd paused. Memories of ditchdigging washed over him—Titus and Adam, and the clang of the chains were fresh in his ears.

He was afraid to leave the safety of Freewater, but unsure who he was if he stayed. In the middle of those thoughts he heard the voices of others coming up the pegs of Big Tree.

66

Ferdinand

WHEN SANZI STEPPED ONTO THE PLATFORM, Ferdinand felt embarrassed and surprised. She wasn't supposed to be there, and his doubts and fears about running hung exposed in the air.

"Homer's letting *you* come?" asked Sanzi.

"What?" asked Ferdinand, confused and unsettled by the unexpected arrival of the knife thief. He hadn't seen her since the fire.

To make things even stranger, Billy and Juna emerged from the pegs next, awkward and weighed down by a canoe.

"Y'all brought a boat all the way up here," Ferdinand said, watching in disbelief as they undid their ropes and pushed it onto the sky bridge.

"F-F-Ferdinand?" said Billy.

Juna looked at him a long while. "You're coming?" she asked, trying to hide the worry in her voice.

"There's no need for you to come," said Sanzi.

No need for me to come? Ferdinand stiffened up. He didn't

302

know where they were going, but he didn't appreciate being told he couldn't go.

"That plantation is bound to have plenty of tools. I'll get your knife back and much more for us to have at Freewater," explained Sanzi. To his surprise, she didn't say it with any sass. Maybe there was even a hint of guilt in her tone. A picture started to come clear for Ferdinand. He considered the boat and Billy.

"All of y'all going?" asked Ferdinand.

"Hey!" Ada called as she got to the platform.

"You too?" said Sanzi.

"She followed me," said Homer, huffing up the ladder. "She wouldn't go back," he said.

"We can all go!" said Ada, as if her word should be the last.

"No, no, no! All she has to do is get one cut, then she'll cry and then we'll be caught. Or she'll be talking so much, asking all her questions, she'll have the whole swamp listening to her," said Sanzi.

"No, I won't. I did get cut last time we came here," Ada started. "It was on some pointy wood that didn't look like wood. I cried, but it wasn't loud. Didn't nobody hear it apart from Homer…and I guess Ibra and maybe David, and maybe Daria. But she was kind of far ahead. You think Daria heard me crying, Homer?"

Sanzi rolled her eyes and pleaded with Homer. "What did I tell you?"

Ferdinand listened to it all, then turned to Homer, as he seemed to be a person with good sense.

"You knew about this?" he asked.

Homer nodded. He took out his map and showed Ferdinand.

"Which plantation you headed to?" asked Ferdinand.

"My old one, Southerland," he said, pointing to the drawing. "I intend to get my mama and my friend and bring them back," Homer said.

"You're bringing all these with you?" asked Ferdinand.

"Yeah, it looks like we're all going," said Juna to Ferdinand.

"I suppose," said Homer.

Ferdinand considered the sky bridge. Morning sun had made it shine a pale pink. Somehow running with all of them seemed better than running on his own.

He bent his head toward Sanzi. "I can get my own knife, thank you." Then he walked onto the bridge, stepped over the canoe, and began pulling it behind him. They all watched him go.

"Well, what are y'all waiting for?" Ferdinand called back to them.

67

Ferdinand

ABOUT THIRTY SECONDS AFTER FERDINAND walked onto the sky bridge, he began to realize the insanity of their plan. Ada, who forgot the prospect of danger once she saw the sky bridge, bounded over the canoe and past him to run across the sky. Arms wide and flapping, she sang, "I'm flying! I'm flying!"

This isn't going to go well, thought Ferdinand. Then he looked behind him.

Juna's legs were quaking as she stepped onto the bridge.

"It's so . . . shaky," said Juna as she put her hand to one of the rails.

Even Sanzi could hardly pretend bravery as she stepped onto the sky bridge for the first time.

"It seems much stronger when you're far away," said Sanzi as she steadied herself. Ferdinand understood what she was saying. It looked so steady from a distance, it may as well have been made of steel. But up close, the rope felt as delicate as a thread, rocking back and forth in the sky. Ada's running steps shook the bridge, causing them to sway from side to side as they dragged and pushed the boat forward.

"That girl is gonna have us all caught!" said Sanzi, shaking her head in disapproval.

"Yeah, we best try to catch up with her," said Juna. Holding tight to the ropes, she and Sanzi climbed over the boat and walked ahead, leaving Ferdinand and Homer pulling it from in front, and Billy pushing from behind.

As Ferdinand glanced back, it was Billy who looked the worst. Stone-still, sweat pouring from his forehead, Billy's hands tightly gripped the bridge ropes and his mouth was clenched shut.

"You all right?" asked Homer, pulling the boat to a stop.

Billy nodded. "I'm fine," he whispered as he rocked from side to side. He kept his eyes up and slowly inched forward.

"You sure you're okay?" asked Ferdinand as a tinge of gray came over Billy's face.

"I'm just—" Mid-sentence, Billy's body told the truth. He put his face over the side of the rope and retched into the canopy below. "Now I'm all right," Billy panted.

"I sure hope nobody was down there to get that," said Ferdinand. He looked at Billy and shook his head, then said to Homer, "You think Ada's the one who'll get us caught? I'd bet on him first."

Ada thought she could fly, Juna and Sanzi knew nothing about anything ahead of them, Billy was afraid of his own shadow, and Homer, well Homer's map might not be enough. This group needed some ways to survive.

"You can't go running off like that," Homer said to Ada when they all finally caught up to her at the end of the bridge. "We have to stay together."

Ferdinand shook his head as Ada kept yammering.

"I was flying, wasn't I?" asked Ada.

"You were flying, but we need to be careful," said Juna.

"Ada, I said don't go running off," Homer repeated.

"But what about if somebody's chasing us, ain't I supposed to run then?" Ada asked.

"When I was doing ditchdigging, we used to have a whistle we'd do when we wanted to call someone or warn each other about things," said Ferdinand.

"Like f-f-for when somebody's coming," said Billy.

"Yeah, that's right," said Ferdinand.

"You hear that?" Homer asked his sister. "You need to listen out for the whistle."

"What's it gonna sound like?" she questioned.

"Try it like this," Ferdinand said, and let out a classic songbird whistle.

Sanzi shook her head. "Why do you get to pick the sound? Besides, we need something different, like a sound only we would know."

"If you have a brain, you'll know my whistle," said Ferdinand.

"I'd know it and so would every other slave catcher for a mile around," argued Sanzi.

"How would you know, anyway? You wouldn't know a slave catcher if he stepped on your toe," said Ferdinand.

"Will you two stop fighting? We just need one sound. I don't care if it sounds like a frog!" exclaimed Juna. "I just want to get off this bridge," she said, looking over the edge.

"Listen, I've been making swamp sounds in Freewater all my life," said Sanzi. She put her head back and let loose a high sweet call. *"Eeeoop, eeoop.* Try it," she commanded.

Nothing came at first, but after trying a few attempts, each of them could make the sound. Finally, they had a warning call.

68

Nora

NORA HAD SPENT THE BETTER PART OF THE night working through a plan.

That morning, she would put it in motion.

To be up earlier than her mother was a feat for Nora. Mrs. Crumb prided herself on rising early to get work done. Rose needed telling what to cook for the evening meal, Anna needed directing in housework, and she'd send word for Old Joe to do this or that. As Viola's wedding was the next day, she'd rise even earlier; everyone would. The house would be abuzz from daybreak. Nora had to be awake before any of them.

Out of bed before dawn, Nora opted to remain barefoot. Craftiness was required for her mission. She could do that. After all, the octopus was known for its stealth. She'd snuck down the hall many days and knew where each creaking floorboard lay to get down to the kitchen. However, today, her mission was different. Instead, she traveled the opposite direction to her parents' room.

Each evening, as part of her sleeping ritual, Mrs. Crumb left her key necklace on the end table beside her bed, only to replace it around her neck the very next morning. Nora's mission required getting that key, opening the chest on the far side of her parents' room, and taking the paper within. Asking for paper would cause suspicion. Her mother was careful to never let even a sheet go astray. Heaven forbid a piece fell into the wrong hands. The need to lock away paper seemed absurd to Nora, until the day she'd walked down the road to town with Old Joe.

Holding the door ajar a few inches, Nora crept into her parents' room, where both Mr. and Mrs. Crumb lay sleeping. Nora surveyed the room and saw the glint of the key on her mother's nightstand. She tiptoed toward the small table, paused as her mother mumbled in her sleep and turned over.

With her fingertips, as nimble as an octopus tentacle, Nora gently lifted the key by its string. The click of the key in the chest lock echoed in the room. Nora stopped. Gently, she pulled open the drawer and found what she'd been after.

Four stiff sheets of paper in hand, Nora closed the chest, replaced the key at her mother's bedside, then inched out of the room.

After a few frustrated hours locked in her room, Nora wished that she'd taken more paper. On the first sheet the imitation swirls and dainty curves of her mother's handwriting were more like pools of ink and wobbly cursive.

The second sheet had the same result. By the third, her hand became more adept, her wobbles steadied, and she'd re-created the pass that her mother had written for Old Joe in an acceptable fashion. At the small desk in her room, Nora examined her work. Though adequate, the pass felt lacking. She inhaled, and with the fourth and last sheet of paper, she tried again. Upon completion, she sat back, satisfied that she'd created something able to suit the journey ahead.

Much would be needed to recover what had been lost with Rose.

From her large bureau closet, she pulled two cloth bags, dusty and unused. She shook them out. They'd do fine, she thought, and she spent what remained of the morning completing the last parts of her plan. Once finished, Nora felt powerful. As if she'd moved heaven and earth.

As it was one day before the wedding, the kitchen was humming with simmering pots. An added table had been brought in to make space. It was piled high with vegetables, eggs, and meat. Drenched in sweat from the large fire, Rose, Anna, and even Mrs. Petunia worked. Nora had spent most of her time away from the kitchen as of late, and it felt strange as she entered. Not to be deterred, she waved to Rose. Preoccupied and weary, Rose shook her head and continued working. Nora waved again, this time signaling that she wanted Rose to come with her.

Rose wiped her hands on her apron and glanced around the kitchen at her pots of food.

"Keep your eye on these pots. I'll be right back," said Rose to Anna. Anna watched as Rose and Nora left the kitchen.

Leaving the kitchen put the two in the hum of other wedding preparations taking place around Southerland. A tent, about the biggest her parents could find, was being filled with tables and chairs, platters and flowers by the field hands and other help that had been loaned by the groom's family. The tent, where the much-anticipated dinner reception was expected to take place, stood beside the Big House and a short distance from the kitchen.

Intermixed with the bustle in the tent was the shrill of Mrs. Crumb's voice as she gave instructions to enslaved souls, both those from Southerland and those from McGrath's plantation, who would serve in the tent. All landowning families in the county had been invited. Even the overseers had received unexpected invitations. The wedding had become the most anticipated event of the year. It needed to be perfect.

"These are your uniforms! Pants, shirt, and hat for the boys. Skirts and bonnets for the girls. The hat must be worn at all times!" Mrs. Crumb instructed.

Nora backed away from the tent and headed for the outbuildings. In the larder is where she'd planned to take Rose.

"Nora, I don't have time for playing today. I've got to get back to my cooking," said Rose as she stood outside the shed. But Nora pressed on and waved Rose inside.

Nora closed the door firmly behind them. She lit a lamp and the dark room illuminated. Smoked meats hung from hooks against the wall. The floor was carpeted with hay and storage barrels.

Determined that her presentation be perfect, Nora pulled Rose to sit in the hay on the floor. When the two faced each other, from her dress pocket Nora pulled out her prepared document and placed it in Rose's hands.

Rose held the paper up to the light. Each scribbled sentence twinkled.

She was quiet and stared at it a long while.

"You know I don't know what this says," Rose said flatly. Nora took the paper and pressed it to Rose's chest, and hand-gestured like a bird.

"Free," she whispered in the quietest of voices.

Rose clutched the paper and looked at Nora.

Crawling over to a thick pile of hay, Nora cleared it back and from underneath she pulled two cloth bags packed with belongings for each of them.

The soft gingham of one of Nora's dresses poked out of one, along with a favorite baby doll. Smoked meat and biscuits, a knife and more spilled from the other.

Nora motioned with her hands. "You, me, free," she said.

Pleased with her plan, Nora sat back down and hugged Rose.

Rose's face fell on the paper's letters, and in barely higher than a whisper Nora read the words.

This slave, called Rose, is of a dark brown complexion with a scar marking her right hand. Rose has served as cook at Southerland Plantation. I hereby certify that she is granted her freedom.

Signed by Sherline Crumb

"You and me," said Rose. "And where, miss, do you suppose we'd go?" asked Rose. "North?"

Relieved that she finally understood, Nora nodded and pressed her head onto Rose's damp chest. Rose could be free of the ugliness of slavery and Nora could be free of a family that didn't see her. They could be together as they always had been.

Rose sat a long while, straight as a peacock, looking down at the paper and at Nora. Then she pulled away, grabbed Nora's arms, and held them tight.

"I ain't running off North with you or anyone else until I have my Homer and Ada. Dead or alive, if they're down there in that swamp then that's where I belong," Rose said.

She leveled her eyes with Nora's. Nora thought she would drown in their never-ending pools of sadness.

"You wrote this free paper for me, Miss Nora?" asked Rose.

Nora nodded. Rose shook her head a long while.

"There's somethin' wrong with the world when a child can free the woman who raised her. Go home, Nora. *Go!*"

Nora ran from the shed, almost knocking over Anna as she went.

Anna peeked in the shed and saw Rose shove the emancipation paper deep into the cloth bag, then hide both bags behind a bale of hay. Just before Rose swung the larder door open, Anna ran back to the kitchen.

69

Sanzi

WHEN SANZI CAME DOWN FROM THE SKY
bridge and set foot for the first time outside of Freewater,
her first thought was, *Same?* A million times before, Sanzi'd
imagined new smells, colors, plants—undeniable difference. Instead, everything was the same. She half expected
to see her mother walking in the shrubs looking for plants
and roots.

"Step back," said Ferdinand to Ada, his voice gruff and
tense as he pulled a large branch from underneath her feet.

"You sound funny," said Ada.

"I don't see you laughing," Ferdinand snapped back.

"I guess, you sound...not funny," Ada corrected.

Crack! Ferdinand snapped the branch on his knee, leaving a pointed tip on the end.

Crack! He broke it again to about the length of his arm.

"You know they're out here searching for runaways,"
said Ferdinand to his fellow travelers.

He swung his branch knife around, cutting the air.

Not wanting to be less prepared than Ferdinand, Sanzi
took a stone from her pouch and loaded her sling, ready to fire.

Juna spied around, as if sure she'd see someone jump from the bushes.

"I don't like it out here—everything looks different," said Juna, certain that danger lurked everywhere.

"It's just like in Freewater," said Sanzi.

"I don't think so," said Juna as she tiptoed frightened around plants and vines she'd known all her life.

"Don't worry, last time we came this way there weren't any monsters," said Ada as she watched Juna's worried expression.

"You s-s-see something?" Billy asked, his head swiveled. He had the boat strapped to his back.

"We need to stay together." As Homer spoke, he tried to read the map again. "We have to go east," he said, turning one direction then another. "It's hard to see the sun under all these trees."

Sanzi didn't know about maps, but she knew about directions.

"That way," she said, pointing.

"How do you know for certain?" Homer asked.

"Mama taught me that from about the time I could run anywhere," Sanzi said.

Find your way back home.

"She's right," said Juna. "She's good with that sort of thing."

Sticky mud tugged at their feet as they made slow progress.

"You're digging your foot. Don't dig, walk on this part," Sanzi said, and tried showing them the ball part of their feet. "Move fast. That way the mud won't suck you. If it gets you, pull up, heel first." Her mother's voice came to her again. Sanzi grew quiet and pushed the image of her mother's face from her mind.

Wet ground turned to dry low brush.

"Finally, some dry land. Come on, Juna," said Ferdinand, heading toward it.

Homer looked ahead. "I think I remember this place. I think, " he said slowly.

Oblivious, Sanzi felt the relief of having her toes out of the muck and started to run behind Ferdinand.

"Stop," Homer commanded. *What now?* thought Sanzi, but she froze along with everyone else.

"Traps," Homer said, bending over and letting one of the spikes prick his finger and draw blood.

"It's the mean grass," said Ada, still bitter about her last encounter with it.

"We gotta keep a close eye for them. When David did it, we all followed in a line," said Homer.

"Go on, then," said Sanzi. They all watched and waited for him to start the line.

Homer looked at Sanzi and paused. He seemed a little shocked that he would have to lead.

"All right. Come on, Ada, you keep behind me," said Homer.

They walked in a zigzag line through the spikes, silent and watching. Billy's pant leg caught one spike, Sanzi's sling caught another, but that was all. When finally they no longer saw the tiny white dots, Homer dropped and cried out, "We made it!"

"You sure sound surprised," said Sanzi. He didn't sound quite like the hero she'd dreamt would accompany her adventures.

They all laughed at his relief.

They trudged on. Hours passed. Weariness set in as they roamed in search of the next marker on the map, a knotted tree.

"It looks like it's supposed to be real big," said Juna.

"I don't even remember a tree like that," said Ada.

"Me neither. Maybe Two Shoes made a mistake when he was drawing," said Homer, studying the map, unsure of their next steps.

Sanzi looked at her friend and asked, "You come this way when you ran away?"

Billy bit so hard on his lip it broke skin. He shrugged. "I'm n-n-not sure."

"He probably had his eyes closed the whole time he was out here," teased Ferdinand.

"You be quiet," ordered Sanzi. "Come on, try to remember," encouraged Sanzi.

"Maybe," said Billy. "I remember we were w-w-walking about for a long time before David saw us. I d-d-didn't think I could w-w-walk another step."

A wave of pride washed over Sanzi. She was treading on the same land as her father.

"Where's the tree?" she asked Billy.

Billy walked ahead.

"Come, I think it's th-th-this way!" he called, and soon after, there it was, massive, knotted, and twisted.

70

Sanzi

"NOW WE GO EAST AGAIN," SAID HOMER. "There should be a river."

The river was stagnant. Massive trees rose from the water, as if they were grown on land. Their leaves shaded and dappled the light on the mirror-still water.

Sanzi raced toward it and smiled.

"We need my boat," she said, looking back at the others. This was her time to shine. The many months it had taken her to carve the stubborn wood from the tree's trunk had been meant for this moment.

Sanzi pushed her canoe through the brush and tangle at the water's edge, and it splashed into the water, rolling clumsily from one side to the next until settling upright.

Troubled by the disturbance, birds set off in a symphony of chatter.

"We're supposed to ride in that thing?" said Ferdinand.

"What? You got your own boat hidden somewhere?" retorted Sanzi.

Of course, Sanzi's boat had been made for one, maybe two people. Like Suleman, Sanzi had planned to travel alone. So, the prospect of fitting six souls in the well was an unanticipated challenge. They all waded into the water.

Sanzi hopped in first. "All right, you next," she said to Ada. Then came Juna and Homer, and just about the time it came for Ferdinand to get in, the craft began to tilt.

"Hold it steady!" called Sanzi. But it was too late. As Ferdinand placed his other leg into the tight well space, the boat toppled over, throwing everyone into the water with a splash and a howl from the tossed passengers.

"There ain't no way we're all gonna get into that boat!" said Ferdinand.

"We could if your head wasn't so big!" said Sanzi. Again they tried, and again, the boat tipped over.

"I don't think this tree boat is like Suleman's," said Ada, wiping her wet face.

"Everyone has to balance," said Juna, coughing up swamp water. "You lean left. You lean right," she instructed the passengers.

After another try, the group found their balance and with branch paddles in hand, they rowed into the watery forest.

Down the river they went. Sanzi carefully traversed the tall trees, and the group ducked from low-hanging brush as they passed through carpet beds of lily pads. They rowed until a wall of vines greeted them and the river became impassable.

"Your map brought us to a dead end," said Sanzi.

"It's not a dead end. There's a door," said Homer, pulling out his map.

"I don't see a door," said Juna. "Maybe we're meant to go another way."

"No, it's, like, a secret door. You have to swim up under there and open it," Homer said.

"Homer doesn't know how to swim," announced Ada.

"I can swim," said Sanzi, sure she could jump in.

Juna held Sanzi's arm. "This ain't Freewater swimming," she said, looking down at the murky, tea-colored water. "Who knows what's down there."

Billy stared at the wall of vines in silence.

"I r-r-remember it," whispered Billy.

"You sure?" said Juna.

"There's a latch if you s-s-swim under to the other s-s-side." He breathed in real slow, then out. "I c-c-could open it," he said. His declaration was met with silence. Could he open it? Before he could think otherwise, Billy stood up, leaned over the boat's edge, and jumped.

A long while passed and nothing. The water was still. They watched it for signs of him.

"You think he forgot how to swim?" asked Ada.

"You can't forget how to swim," said Sanzi.

"That's some dark water," said Ferdinand, trying to hide that he was impressed by Billy's jump.

They waited.

"He's not gonna drown or anything, right?" asked Juna. She touched the water, as if it could tell her.

"He isn't drowning!" shot back Sanzi, but even as she said it, she unwound her sling and cloth bag, and went to the boat's edge, ready to jump.

"That's a long time to hold your breath," said Homer, scanning the water. Nothing.

"Suleman did it," said Ada, "but Billy's not really like Suleman."

"I'm gonna jump in," said Sanzi.

"Wait. Give him a chance," said Juna.

"Besides, the last thing we need is the both of you drowning," said Ferdinand.

"I ain't gonna drown! My papa—" Sanzi started then she looked at Ferdinand and tried again. "I learned how to swim as good as anybody. Better than you!"

"You wanna find out?" said Ferdinand, throwing off his shirt.

Suddenly, the water rippled with a small splash, the wall of vines shook, and sunlight came through as Billy swung the vine door open. Water spilled from his soaking-wet hair and clothes, he was coughing and sputtering, but his face was bright.

"Hey, r-r-row through!" Billy called.

"You did it!" said Ada.

"Are you all right?' Juna asked him. Her eyes shone with admiration.

Billy nodded in disbelief.

They glided through, Billy latched the door closed, jumped from the wall's ledge into the water, and swam back to the canoe. As they rowed away Billy looked back at the wall and sat up a little straighter in the canoe.

The small landing was next. The very same place where Homer and Ada had spent the night with Suleman. It was almost sunset by the time they reached it, and everyone was bone-tired when they pulled the boat up to the landing and crawled out.

"Come look," said Homer. He didn't have to check the map to remember. The tree was still tall and wide. He felt along the cracking trunk until his fingertips caught an opening. With a firm tug, he pulled back the trunk's skin to reveal its hollow center.

"What kind of tree is that?" asked Ferdinand.

"Suleman showed us this place," said Homer.

"This is Suleman's secret room," whispered Sanzi. A tingle ran down her spine.

"I suppose," said Homer.

"Hold on, we need some light," said Juna as her voice echoed into the dark, hollow tree trunk.

With an expert eye, she turned to the nearby swamp floor. Sanzi watched as Juna for the first time stopped looking nervous and started to see what she'd been taught about the swamp. She searched and found kindling, and even pine sap and sticks for torches. *She looks just like Mama*, thought Sanzi. With an expert rub of the kindling, like Mrs. Light, Juna started a fire, then put sap-coated sticks into the flames and made torches. They shone the light into the trunk.

Sanzi was first to enter the dancing torchlight of the hideout. "I bet he stays here during his raids." She touched the bows hanging from the wall. Outside the secret room, Juna swung her sling and caught two squirrels while Billy and Homer hid the boat.

After eating, they all laid around the fire listening to the howls, growls, and squawk sounds outside their borrowed tree hideout. They sounded more menacing than swamp noises in Freewater.

"When we get to Southerland," Homer whispered into the fire, "it should be night, about when they'll all be at the wedding dinner. I'll sneak in, get Mama and Anna and see about Two Shoes, and then I'll come back and take one or two of you to get the tools."

"Where are the tools?" asked Sanzi.

"Down a small hill from the Big House. There's a white shed with farm tools. There's sure to be something we could use in there," said Homer.

"Sounds like I can get those tools as well as anybody," said Sanzi.

"Like I said, I can get my own knife, thank you very much," said Ferdinand.

"I thought so m-m-many times a-a-about what I'd s-s-say to my mama if I saw her again," said Billy. "W-w-what are you gonna say to your mama?"

Homer stayed silent a long while. "Sorry," he whispered.

"What are you gonna say sorry for? You're rescuing her like a hero," said Sanzi.

Homer coughed and watched the flames of the fire. "I'm tired of people saying that. I ain't no hero and I wasn't brave when we ran away. Ada and I weren't alone. Mama was with us, she went back on account of me, she got caught on account of me." Homer's voice choked up in tears.

"Don't say that, Homer. It was Stokes's fault. He got Mama," said Ada.

"You don't understand," said Homer, turning away from the fire.

"I do," whispered Sanzi, tossing a stick into flames. Her heart was full of guilt. "I understand everyone thinking you're a hero, even when you're not," said Sanzi.

"But you saved us," said Juna. "We all complain about your adventuring, but in the end you saved Freewater." Admiration and a hint of envy clung to Juna's words.

"I didn't," said Sanzi. "I was shooting fire arrows from my tree spot and one of them hit the cornfields, by accident. The fire started because of me. I didn't save anything. It was my fault. I'm so sorry," confessed Sanzi, and she steeled herself for Ferdinand's ridicule, Juna's anger, and everyone's disappointment.

Juna did sit up with a start, her mouth hung open in shock. Ferdinand shook his head. Everyone stared at Sanzi. Tears rolled down Sanzi's cheeks and for that moment she felt the courage drain from her body.

Juna sat watching her shame-filled sister a long while.

"I don't like all of your crazy ways, but seeing you this sad is even harder to watch," Juna admitted. "What are you gonna tell Mama and Papa?" was all Juna could muster.

"I don't know, that's why I've got to get those tools. To really help, not just have everybody think I did," said Sanzi. "I have to fix it."

Ada turned to Juna. "I'm thinking Mrs. Light really will tie her up to the roof with the dried flowers," said Ada.

Juna was the first to laugh, then Homer and Billy.

"You really are one wild girl," said Ferdinand, shaking his head.

"Mama's gonna be disappointed for sure, but I guess she'll come around, but you'll be collecting plants and herbs every day until you're old and gray," said Juna.

Sanzi smiled, and her courage started to come back. She felt better for having told her secret.

"Well, at least y'all got mamas and papas to disappoint. Now go to sleep, we've got some fixing and saving to do tomorrow." Ferdinand hugged his stick-knife to his chest and moved closer to the fire.

Sanzi saw Ferdinand's sad eyes as he stared into the fire. She remembered that night in his cabin, him yelling for his own papa. She almost said something smart about him commanding her to go to sleep, but for the first time, instead of arguing with him, she turned over and closed her eyes.

71

Nora

IT WAS NINE IN THE MORNING AND NORA WAS already itchy and hot in her dress.

"Stand still," Mrs. Crumb commanded, dipping a fuzzy puff into a dish of white powder and dabbing Nora's face. "That's much better, isn't it?" Mrs. Crumb asked Viola.

Nora stared at her ghostly white face in the mirror.

"Well, I guess it will have to do," Viola answered.

Mrs. Crumb wagged her finger at Nora. "Now that we've got you all ready, you keep clean, don't touch your face, don't sit down on anything that could crumple your dress, and don't touch your hair." Mrs. Crumb's instructions droned on, but Nora wasn't listening. Her plan had failed—Rose wasn't happy and Nora was still stuck in a family where she didn't fit in.

Loneliness washed over Nora, and she yearned to be seated in the familiarity of Rose's kitchen with a favorite book in hand. She couldn't be in the kitchen on the wedding day, but maybe she could at least have her book.

Nora touched her hair, then the ribbon in her mother's hair.

"Oh my, we've forgotten your ribbon!" said Mrs. Crumb. Nora nodded. It was the only excuse Nora could conjure up that would not lead to criticism nor suspicion.

"Go on and get it," said Mrs. Crumb.

Swishing with frills and taffeta all around, Nora left the Big House and headed for the larder. She hadn't been back there since Rose told her to leave, but she knew her book would still be in one of the cloth bags.

Just before pushing in the door, she heard a scramble of movement. Nora peeked through the door's crack and spotted Anna bent over the hay, the two cloth bags in her hands. Apparently, she'd heard the swishing of Nora's frills, and she was frozen in the half darkness, peering at the door and straining to see who was there.

Nora backed away and hid behind a set of bushes around the far side of the larder. Not long after, Anna emerged, looking all about as she crept out and ran toward the kitchen.

To Nora, Anna was very nosy. Her eyes were always spying whatever Nora did, but for once it was *Nora* who knew something Anna wanted kept secret. A tiny bud of satisfaction began to grow in her heart. Her plan had failed for Rose, but perhaps it could work for Anna. *When will she run?* Nora wondered. She'd be watching.

Nora went to the Big House and upstairs to her room. She stopped in front of her mirror. A little spark of happiness shone in her eyes for the first time that day. Irritated by the white powder caked onto her skin, Nora poured water into her porcelain basin and washed her face clean.

72

Juna

WHEN JUNA AWOKE THAT MORNING, FEAR AND alarm swept over her. Light spilled through the opening in the tree log overhead. She wasn't in the safety of Freewater. But tucked just beneath Juna's fear was a hint of pride.

In Freewater, Juna became known as her mother's student. Most times she was proud of the label. But sometimes, in the moments when Sanzi ran through Freewater seeking adventure, Juna wondered if she could be more than her mother's helper.

Sure, this morning, Juna was scared and part of her wanted to go home, but as she peered around the hideout, she thought, *Yes, this is definitely an adventure.*

Everyone soon came out of the hideout sleepy-eyed.

Sanzi took one last look at the tree cave and put the secret door back in place. Homer examined the map.

"We're not too far, less than a day's journey ahead," he said.

"We are?" Sanzi's eyes got bright as lamp lights.

"Yeah, we're low here on the water edge. I'm guessing

from up high, you could probably see the plantation lands," Homer said, looking at the map. "I ain't sure about this part, it's different than when we came."

Sanzi popped up. "I'm going to see," she said, and up the tree she went.

"S-S-Sanzi! Don't," Billy called up to her. But soon they couldn't see her in the verdant foliage.

"Sanzi, come back down here!" called Juna.

"That girl's wild," said Ferdinand, pointing his stick knife at Homer. "Let me see that map—maybe I can make out the next step."

Homer handed it to him, with the cursive script side facing up. Juna stood next to Ferdinand and ran her fingertips over the strange, curved lines of mystery writing. Ferdinand watched and wondered.

"I can guess what all this writing is," said Ferdinand.

"You know what it says?" asked Juna.

"No, but I'm think—" He stopped, before exclaiming, "Dogs!"

"Dogs?" repeated Juna. Suddenly, from the trees came panting and gnarling noises.

Juna had seen bobcats, bears, and pigs, but never had she seen a dog. Curiosity was her first feeling when she saw the new four-legged creatures. One was black and the other two were brown with white spots. She bent forward for a closer look as they approached. Only then did she realize

the fury in their eyes and that their anger, barking, and vit-
riol was directed at her. She jumped back.

"Stop right there!" came a shout from behind them.
"What are you darkies doing about these parts?"

Homer, Billy, Juna, and Ferdinand froze. It was only Ada
who thought to raise her head and call to the trees, *"Eeeoop!
Eeoop!"*

Billy shrank back. His newfound courage evaporated.
His towering, thin body went limp and he sank to his
knees, tucked his head down, and curled into a ball. All the
while, the dogs barked about him.

"He f-f-found me," said Billy, his eyes wild with fright.

"Who found you?" Juna asked, confused.

"Quiet, all of you!" Ferdinand yelled at his fellow travelers. His voice was completely changed.

"I'm talking to you—what y'all doing in these parts?"
asked the man. Juna watched the man. He was old, with
gray hair down his back, and a long beard. His white skin
was so unusual, Juna wondered if it was real and not a mask
of milk. He had bear fur wrapped about his shoulders and
his chest, and pelts piled high on a makeshift cart.

"We're..." Homer started.

Ferdinand held up the map for the man to see.

"Sir," began Ferdinand.

"What's that you got there?" yelled the man. "Give it
to me!"

"Yes, sir," said Ferdinand, stepping toward the man. "You see, sir, my master wrote a note for me."

The man took the paper, not even looking at the map. Instead he started reading what was on the other side. He read it, scrutinized Ferdinand, then read it again.

"You say this is yours?" he asked Ferdinand.

"Yes, sir," said Ferdinand.

"You're the one who's supposed to be out here catching runaways to bring back to Southerland?" he asked.

"Yes, sir," said Ferdinand. He pointed his stick knife toward Homer, Juna, Billy, and Ada. "You all best sit down and mind what I say!" Ferdinand shouted at them.

The man looked Ferdinand up and down. "Well, where's your shoes?"

"My shoes?" Ferdinand stopped a moment.

"Says here, I'm supposed to be able to tell you by your shoes," he said, looking at Ferdinand's bare feet.

"I lost them trying to chase these four down in the swamp, but I'm bringing 'em back just as Master wanted," he said.

Ada's eyes got wide, but she kept quiet.

"What happened to that one?" asked the man, looking over Juna's animal skin, bracelets, beads, and flowers. Beyond her clothing there was something about Juna that set her apart. Something he hadn't seen before.

"Her?" said Ferdinand, feigning ignorance.

"Yeah, why's she look like that?" asked the man.

"Oh, that one, she's been running for a good long while—she's lost her mind out here," said Ferdinand.

For Juna, it wasn't so much the look of the white man that shocked her. She'd never seen anything like his skin. But what shook her to the core was the feeling she got from the man's stare. It felt like he'd seen right through her. Like the Juna she'd been all of her life didn't exist anymore. She was no longer her mother's protégé, nor beautiful, nor a sister, nor a friend, she was gone. A thunderclap of fear coursed through her veins and turned them ice cold. She thought she'd known that feeling, but in an instant she understood that she'd lived a life with very little fear.

"Hmmm," said the man, looking at Ferdinand hard.

"I got these in good time for Master. I intend to get them there for the big wedding, as a kind of present," said Ferdinand.

"Well, I don't wanna get in the way of Crumb's dealings," he said, considering the note. The man folded the note and tossed it back at Ferdinand, who went to the ground to get it. "If you're supposed to be at Southerland, then you best get yourself there, 'cuz if I catch y'all out here again, I'll take you to auction for myself. I don't care what kind of pass you got. You hear me?"

"Yes, sir," said Ferdinand.

Then the man and his mean dogs were gone.

"Billy?" Juna bent down and spoke to her friend still curled in a ball. For the first time she understood a little about his fears.

"He's gone," she reassured him and herself.

Finally, Billy raised his head. Sweat poured down his forehead and mixed with tears that wet his face. His teeth chattered as if the season had turned to winter.

"You s-s-sure?" he asked.

"Tell me again, what happened!" Sanzi asked Juna and the others.

No one wanted to say much of anything.

"You saw a white man?" asked Sanzi.

"Yeah," whispered Juna.

"What was he like?" asked Sanzi.

"Different," said Juna.

They all silently agreed that the telling of it might bring the man and his dogs back. Instead, they took to the boat again and rowed up the strong river until nightfall when they reached the bank near Southerland.

"This is it," said Homer, trying to keep fear from his voice.

"I don't see any plantation," said Sanzi, looking about.

"You've gotta go up this riverbank, then through a forest that way," he said.

"Y'all stay here. I'm going in to get Mama and Anna and see to Two Shoes. I'll bring them back here. Then, if it looks safe, I'll take one or two of you to get the tools. We'll get as much as we can carry, then we'll all leave here," he said, breathless from his own plan.

"All right, Homer. Go get your mama and friend and those tools fast, so we can get back to Freewater. Hurry up," directed Juna, looking around into the darkness. The encounter with the dog man had been just about enough adventure for her.

Before anyone could say more, Homer was gone. Leaving them all sitting in the boat.

73

Anna

PLATTERS OF MEATS, CREAMED VEGETABLES, AND gravies piled high in the kitchen. Those savory scents mixed with the sweet smell of confections—tea cakes, bread puddings, caramel sauces, and more. Southerland's kitchen had never been so busy.

In the middle of it all was Rose, calm, dispassionate, and focused on completing her assigned task. She stood back and watched as the field hands carried out dishes filled with her food, to serve in the tent. It was done. She sat down.

With Anna's plan now well under way, she felt something needed saying to Rose. Rose had never told Anna that she'd come back for her during her failed runaway plan. There was no need. Still, Anna felt that now was the moment. She suspected that once she started serving in the tent, and her plan was put in motion and she ran North, this would be the last time she'd see Rose.

"You think they'll find Homer and Ada?" Anna whispered to Rose.

Rose was quiet a long while, shaking her head.

"I don't know. They could be free, they could be caught

and sold again, they could be dead. That swamp holds the story. If I can find a way, that's where I should be bound. And where are you bound?" asked Rose.

Anna lowered her head in embarrassment.

"I see you always looking elsewhere, always looking for more," said Rose.

Anna wasn't sure what to share.

"My mama is in the North," said Anna.

Then came a line of field hands looking for dishes to serve, and Anna needed to leave. There was work to be done and a plan to see through.

The cask of whiskey sat untouched until the wedding reception. When the evening came and all of the guests had been shown into the tent, Anna was there clad in her new uniform, with a whiskey pitcher in one hand and a water pitcher in the other. There was Mr. Crumb, then Stokes and the overseers at a table with many of the local runaway hunters. Their glasses would need extra whiskey tonight.

She peeked up at the rafters of the tent and saw sheep and puffy clouds waiting for their moment to descend on the reception. Resolve only grew in her belief that whatever did happen that night would result in her freedom.

She began her duties, walking about filling each whiskey glass.

74

Homer

AIN'T NO SUCH THING AS GETTING NEW EYES. I've seen someone lose an eye. It smashed like a water bug under the heavy strike of Stokes's stick. Crumb was mad as an old dog to see his property marked that way. On the auction block, enslaved souls with eye troubles were the sort of thing that made the buyer pause.

Coming back to Southerland, I swear my own eyes had been pulled out and grown anew while in the swamp. There had been color in the quarters, at least I thought so: the houses, the trees, the little garden plot Mama kept. I'd seen each of them a thousand times. But now, in the moonlight, I couldn't see one single color outside of gray. Daria and Ibra's mud-brown, half-burned home seemed like a brighter spot than our old cabin.

I stood in the doorway, taking in the small room. A hearth, a big pot that sat dry, a few bowls, and spoons. Despite myself, I glanced upward to spy what herbs and plants had been hung to dry. Maybe I just wanted to see something living. There was nothing there. Mama had a few things, a quilt she'd put together from scraps of cloth. But even the most special things felt dead.

With my breath held, I touched Mrs. Petunia's sewing chest, said a prayer, and opened it. Sure enough, as if Mrs. Petunia had suspected my return all along, what I needed was there. New clothes, meant for me to wear while serving at the wedding. My new clothes were now my disguise.

I put on the straw hat, new shirt, and pants. I'd fit right in with the other help, I hoped.

I hadn't been gone long, but I'd changed. All the excitement I used to feel about getting clothes was replaced by how dry and itchy they felt as I put them on. Even the hat was heavy on my head when I pulled it low over my eyes and walked through the quarters.

As I suspected, the place was empty. Most everyone was in the big tent serving. My only thought was to get to the kitchen and call for Mama and Anna. I needed to get them out of this gray, dreary world.

"You ain't supposed to be here."

The words cut through the night air. Sitting on the ground, with his back to his cabin, was Two Shoes. His knees were up and his legs were crossed in front of him. Even if there had been light, I couldn't have seen his face because it hung so low.

"You feel it?" he asked me.

There wasn't much to say. I had only one thought.

"You made that map," I said.

Two Shoes's voice didn't change a speck. "You feel it?" he asked again. "It's like somebody's shoved cotton down my throat. It's like I can't breathe." He looked around. "It wasn't supposed to be this way. I was to go out there and find a few runaways living like savages in the swamp. I was to come back with any I could catch and tell Master Crumb where they were hiding out. For that, he'd buy my son back, and I'd have my wife and family together. That was all it was supposed to be." Regret and wrong filled his voice. "I didn't even know there was such a place to be found." He tilted his head up to the moon. "I couldn't have imagined it. Seeing you, at least now I know it was real. Sitting here, looking at this place, I was thinking I must have dreamt it all. The whole thing. And you, why'd you come back to this place?"

"Mama" was all I could say. He didn't need to know anything of my plans.

He laughed again and shook his head at the moon. "Lord only knows how many of us they keep from running, how many of us stay in these hateful places out of love. I used to think it was from scaring us—beating, cutting, or whipping us that did it. No. They get us best when we love anybody or anything. That's how they keep us."

"You told him about Freewater?" I asked. It was too soon to allow his name back on my tongue.

"I told him there was something out there. Didn't make no sense telling more about that place, he wouldn't have believed it anyway," said Two Shoes. "All he wanted to know was if I could take him and his militia there. They put the militiamen in the toolshed to wait and sleep until tomorrow when we'll go," Two Shoes said.

I swear the world cracked right down the middle and everything in me shook.

"You're gonna take him to Freewater?" I asked.

"I only wanted my son back. There wasn't nothing that was to come from this, apart from getting my son. Now I've been somewhere I wasn't to have been and felt things I wasn't meant to feel," he said.

I was staring at Two Shoes, but all I could see was Mrs. Light and Ibra and all the others dashing out fire, making food, fetching water, not knowing the militia was coming and that it would all be over by the next day.

"What about Freewater?" I asked him.

Two Shoes's voice, full of tears, said, "Please stop saying that name in this place." He rocked back and forth. "I'm so sorry. I'm so sorry. All I ever wanted was to have my son back and to have my wife be happy again. That's all I wanted."

"Run," I said. "You could run again, before he can get to you," I said.

"Run?" He spoke into the night. "And what am I to say to my wife? How am I to ask her to leave her son behind?"

"Seems to me he's already gone. But Freewater is still here and it's real," I said.

Two Shoes shook his head. "You think I can go back to that place after I've done this? I can't be there. It's like dying coming back here. Can't you see I don't have a place to be?"

"You won't know how Freewater will be unless you go back," I said. "Maybe it'll be all right."

For the first time he looked me in my eyes.

"That's enough words outta you. Get. *Get!*" he said.

I turned and ran.

75

Homer

WALK LIKE IT'S ANY OTHER DAY AT SOUTHERLAND,
I said to myself as I headed toward the Big House and
kitchen.

I'd lived on the plantation my whole life, apart from
the few weeks in Freewater. Still, the place was changed.
Guests' horses and carriages lined the pathway at the front
of the house. The house was lit up, candles burning in every
window. There was the tent. Mistress had talked about that
wedding tent for about year.

"That tent will be the talk of the county. We'll do it up
and have everyone there to see it. After this wedding there
won't be a bride in the county who'll want a little dinner in
their dining room," she chimed. Mistress had made us all
half-crazy with that tent and her wedding.

The wedding folks were already there. A few were
walking about outside the house and talking on the grass.
I pulled my straw hat down over my ears. *Walk.* I told my
body. *Walk like you did every day before Freewater. Walk like
you're meant to be here and no one will see you.* That's what I

did. But this time, my back hurt and my neck ached. Nothing felt right. My old invisible ways left my body in pain.

The kitchen was up ahead. I could see lamplight in the window. Mama would be there. I moved quick to the shadow under the kitchen window, put my back against the wall, and listened. It was quiet. That's what I'd hoped. By now, dinner had been put out, and even the cake would have been served. Mama should have been done for the night.

Under the windowsill, I whistled our sound, *whee hoo, whee hoo*, the same one she'd heard a thousand times. I waited to hear her return whistle. But nothing came. I blew again. Nothing.

Around the corner, I pulled the kitchen door. It was empty. Each pot was already washed clean, all the plates were neatly stacked. The kitchen smelled of Mama. Like fresh-swept earth. The only thing left behind to let you know that a wedding had been served was one big tray. On it were small cookies and cakes. The last of the sweets. *Where was Mama?*

"Boy!" The sound cut through my wondering. Every hair on my neck stood up. *Don't see me. Don't see me.*

"Boy! You hear me?" the voice said again, louder.

I froze. A man was standing there in a suit crumpled at the waist, after a long day of sitting. A wedding guest. He didn't know me, nor I him, but that didn't matter.

"Yes, sir," I whispered, hoping he'd forget he'd seen me.

"Bring them cookies and things into the tent. My kids been whining something terrible for more. Bring 'em," he said.

I stared at the tray of cookies.

"These cookies?" I asked in a whisper.

"You heard me," he said. He wiped a bit of sweat from his brow. "Boy, it's hot in here!"

"I'll make them nice for you," I said. "Then I'll be along with them shortly."

The man peered down at the tray.

"They seem fine to me, bring 'em now," he said.

I picked up the tray.

"You come on with me—I'm not having you passing out these sweets to every single body before you get to my table," he said.

"Yes, sir," I said. I walked to the tent and the man pushed me in.

I'm not certain which was louder, the noise from all the people in the tent or the screaming in my head. *Don't go in! Don't go in!* But there was nowhere else to turn.

I squinted in the lamplight and smoke. The flowers I'd tended all spring were on the tables. I'd likely touched each bud and begged for them to grow, to keep Mistress happy and us safe. And grow they did. Now I saw them, all my little flowers, and it felt like the stupidest thing to have spent my time thinking on.

Then there were the people. I'd say Mistress Crumb had been right about one thing. This wedding was like nothing this county had ever seen. On more than one occasion I'd peeked through windows at dinners and small parties they'd had, all neat and quiet. This wasn't anything like those. There was loud, raucous laughing and talking and dancing. People were acting strange.

"Go on." He pushed me, pointing to a table clear across the tent. Neither of us could hardly see it through all the people moving, talking, smoking, and dancing. There wasn't a single place in the swamp as scary as the walk to that table.

A cloud of cigar smoke mixed with breath and body heat hung over everything. I bowed my head, tried to forget my slick wet hands, and started walking straight to the table, excusing myself every few feet as people stepped in my path. *Get to the table, then turn around and leave. That's all. Get to the table, then leave. I am invisible. Clear as glass.*

Old Joe was in the corner, holding a whiskey pitcher. There were field hands moving and fidgeting in their new clothes, a heap of servants I'd never seen before, but there was no Mama. A pitcher in each hand, Anna, looking less than happy as she stared at the crazy crowd, was zigzagging her way through the tables, stopping to pour drinks, and heading in my direction. There was no mistaking when she saw me. Her eyes flashed and our arms brushed. I wanted to turn and tell her that I'd come for her and everything about Freewater. But neither of us said nor did anything. She'd just passed me when Master Crumb called out, "Stop the music! I have an announcement for my Viola." A bit of drunkenness slurred his words.

The raucous went quiet as Crumb spoke.

"The missus and I thank you all for being here tonight. Our little girl is off to start her own home. We know she'll miss Southerland." He chuckled at himself. "We see all these fine gifts you've given these two. Well, we want to make sure Viola takes a bit of home with her as she goes." Master Crumb continued. "I see from all the empty plates that y'all enjoyed the food. Well, Viola's been enjoying this food her whole life, and we want to keep it that way. So, sweetheart, tonight we're giving you our cook to take to your new home. She'll go with you this very evening so that every day of your new life, you can think of your family here at Southerland."

"Stokes!" called Crumb to the tent flap.

The whole world stopped as Mama came into the tent.

76

Sanzi

"I'M GOING," SANZI ANNOUNCED AS SHE GATH-ered her sling and bow.

"G-g-going?" said Billy.

"Listen, Wild Child, he said to wait," said Ferdinand, sitting up in the boat.

"I'm not waiting for Homer when I could be in there and back before he even knows I left," said Sanzi.

"Why do you always have to do that?" asked Juna. "Why can't you just let Homer do what he said? Why do you have to go off and break all the rules just to be the bravest one?"

"You don't understand anything. I have to get the tools," said Sanzi. Shame heated her neck and face.

"But if you w-w-wait, y-y-you can go with h-h-him," Billy reminded her. He was stalling. Buying time and watching the forest for Homer.

"What if he can't get to his mama and that Anna girl or if he changes his mind and decides he can't get the tools? Then we'd have nothing," said Sanzi. "I'm not staying here when I know I can get what we need."

"What if *you* get caught?" asked Ada.

"I'm not getting caught. Sounds like there's people where Homer and his mama are, but nobody's going to the toolshed for the wedding. I'll be in and out fast and without anyone noticing," said Sanzi.

Ferdinand made a brooding face but shifted over and flipped himself out of the boat.

"I'm going," he grumbled.

"You t-t-too?" said Billy.

"You can come if you want, but I'm going," said Ferdinand. Billy looked away, as if hoping the darkness would hide his fear. He couldn't move with it.

"I don't need you to go," said Sanzi.

"Oh no? You don't know one thing about plantations. You're liable to get us all caught. Besides, I told you before, I'll get my own knife," said Ferdinand.

"D-d-don't, Sanzi. D-d-don't," said Billy. It was all he could say.

"Homer said you should stay here," said Ada. "What if Stokes sees you?"

"I ain't worried a lick about this Stokes," Sanzi shot back.

Ada turned to Billy and said with a straight face, "She's crazy."

"Sanzi, we need to stay together," Juna pleaded.

"Stop worrying, we'll be back. And with plenty of tools to show you," said Sanzi as she ran toward the woods with Ferdinand in tow.

The forest was nothing like the swamp, Sanzi thought. It was cleared out and dry, without vines or bush, and with trees straight, narrow, and standing at attention. Things became even stranger once they passed through the trees and entered the cleared land of Southerland. Sanzi stopped. Covered in nothing but short grass, the naked land felt like it didn't belong to the earth. It was an empty place. Like all the trees had died and the animals had gone off to heaven and left only the sound of crickets and cicadas. Almost no sound at all. None of it felt right.

There wasn't a good place for tree hiding. No bushes to block you from view. Moonlight hit the ground unobstructed. But none of that mattered when she saw the large white house in the distance.

"This your first time seeing anything like that?" asked Ferdinand, as the two stood staring at it.

Candlelight flickered in each window. Garlands of flowers were wrapped about the two pillars in the house's front, and small lanterns lit a path from the house to the large tent that stood beside it.

"It's big. Why you suppose they make it so tall? These white masters must be like giants," said Sanzi, beginning to wonder about the enemy she might face.

"No, they ain't tall. The house has up and down floors with stairs to get up to the top," said Ferdinand.

"How do they cut their wood so thin you can see

through it?" asked Sanzi. Despite herself, she couldn't help but ask.

"That ain't wood, it's glass. Now come on! If we get caught, the last thing you're gonna care about is glass," said Ferdinand, pulling Sanzi's arm.

"You can see through it." Sanzi shook her head, dubious about the idea. And for the first time her stomach turned in fear about what else she didn't know.

"Come on," said Ferdinand. "I'm thinking the outbuildings are down that small hill."

Sanzi followed, and soon they found a white shed. In fact, all of the five sheds down beyond the small hill were painted white.

"Which one?" whispered Sanzi.

"That'll be for us to find out," said Ferdinand as he headed west toward the nearest one. Sanzi ran after him.

Ferdinand already had his ear to the wall by the time Sanzi got to his side. With one hand to his lips, Ferdinand signaled for Sanzi to be quiet as he pushed the first door open.

A flutter of quick movement. Something or someone was in there. Ferdinand jumped back, letting the door fall closed.

77

Sanzi

SANZI HEARD THE CLUCKING FIRST, THEN THE scratching of claws and the flapping of wings. With another push, she swung the door open. Chickens. Sanzi knew this type of bird; a few had been brought to Freewater by Suleman and others.

"You sure did jump from some chickens," teased Sanzi.

"I didn't jump as high as you," said Ferdinand.

Running in the moonlight, they went to the next shed. Shirts and sheets hung on a line strung from one wall to the other. They were so white they glowed blue when the light from the doorway hit them.

"Laundry," said Ferdinand.

"How you suppose they get so much cloth?" asked Sanzi as she stared mesmerized at the ghostlike shirts.

"Don't know?" Ferdinand shrugged.

"This is the biggest pot I've ever seen," said Sanzi. Her voice echoed in the cauldron.

"Stop all that and come on! We don't have all night," said Ferdinand.

The third shed was larger than the rest. It was set apart

on a sloped hill. They ran across the far lawn to get to it. After seeing a shed for chickens and one for clothes, Sanzi half wondered if the next shed would only be for rope or for plants. She swung the door open.

Darkness. This was the darkest shed of all. Its heavy door rattled as it closed behind them. Arms outstretched and groping, Sanzi felt her way forward, stopping when her foot hit something cold and hard. Tools?

"You see anything?" whispered Ferdinand.

She touched the metal. It was small, about the size of her hand. Flat on the top and bottom and with holes through the middle.

"I don't know. Maybe this is some kind of tool," said Sanzi. She put it in her bag and went farther into the room before stepping on something else.

Sanzi bent down. "Go hold the door open so we can see."

Ferdinand stumbled his way back to the door. "There's more stuff on the floor over here," he said.

Soon the door creaked open and Ferdinand stood where the moonlight came in.

"A bowl," said Sanzi. *Mama would like this,* Sanzi couldn't help but think. There was something soft beside it. She picked it up and held it in the light.

"A blanket," said Sanzi.

Then another thing that was even softer; she held it up.

"That's a pillow," said Ferdinand.

"A pillow?" asked Sanzi.

"This don't seem like no toolshed to me," whispered Ferdinand into the darkness, "as a matter of fact, it seems like there's—"

"Look!" said Sanzi. Her eyes followed the moonlight coming in from a gap in the shed's wooden walls. It bounced off a small ax and another large blade hanging on the far wall. Right next to them were two knives almost exactly like Ferdinand's.

"Tools!" said Sanzi.

"Sanzi, we should get outta here," said Ferdinand.

"I've never seen so many tools!" said Sanzi.

She pushed to the wall, took down one of the knives, and held it.

"Hey, you come here and hold the door so I can get a knife," said Ferdinand.

"I've got it," said Sanzi, holding it up.

"I told you, I can get my own knife," said Ferdinand. "Now hurry up!"

"Boys, don't you go anywhere," said an unfamiliar gruff voice. "I'm coming back with my harmonica and I'm gonna play that song, I tell you."

The words were loud like stones hurled into the dark shed, and with them were hard footsteps, and a loud voice.

"I'm gonna make y'all eat your words!" the voice yelled again.

"Ferdinand," whispered Sanzi.

He didn't answer. Instead, the shed door clanged shut and Ferdinand disappeared into the darkness. Apart from the tools on the wall, Sanzi could hardly remember anything about her surroundings. Only after stumbling about in the dark did she hit the cold hard metal of a large planting hoe. As the door swung open, she dove behind it.

Lamplight drenched the shed. In the middle of the light stood a man. When Sanzi was little and she'd asked her papa about the color white, he pointed to the clouds. He said there, there is white. So, when they said, *white man*, Sanzi thought it would be a man with face and arms and feet cut from the clouds.

This man wasn't. He wasn't even the color white. He was more pink or maybe the color of bark when you first cut it— tan. But not white. His hair was brown and stringy like the wet end of an ear of corn. He had on more cloth than Sanzi had ever seen on one person, and he had big shoes, not like Turner's. These shoes went up his leg. The man held the lamp up high, swinging it in one direction then the other. Sanzi ducked down low to the ground as the light swept overhead.

Determined to find his harmonica, the man placed the lamp on the floor and eyed his trampled belongings.

He stopped. "Someone's been in here!" he yelled.

He swung around, sniffed the air like he was hunting, then flashed his light across the room.

"Well, what have we got here?" he said.

Sanzi had seen Ferdinand's face a thousand times, but there was nothing familiar about the face she saw hiding in a corner of the shed. Fear had changed it—twisted it into something unfamiliar.

He tried to scramble for the door, but the man in all the cloth caught him. Ferdinand swung his knife stick, but the man grabbed it and pulled him to the ground by his hair.

"Where do you think you're going?" said the man with a wicked laugh.

78

Homer

I DIDN'T HEAR PEOPLE CHEERING. I DIDN'T SEE Miss Viola jump up in her white cloud dress and throw her arms around Crumb. It felt like I was at the bottom of the well where there was nothing but darkness.

Mama walked slow. She had on a traveling shawl and a clean apron. She held her gaze straight ahead and was not looking at anything or anyone.

She was trying to disappear. I could tell.

They put her on a stool right next to the table with the other gifts. Bowls and plates, crystal and glass, and Mama.

"Now, let's all be merry!" said Crumb, and the band began to play. The people danced and talked like they didn't even know the world had ended. From across the way I could see her sadness. *Oh, Mama!* As if she heard my thinking, she surveyed the room and her eyes stopped on me. They got big as the dinner plates set beside her. *Mama.* She found me.

"Keep moving!" said the man behind me. Blocks of wood may as well have been tied to my feet. *Mama.* She was there and she saw me. I moved one step after the next until I reached the table. Sitting there were two boys with a frowning woman who had to be their mother.

The boys were similar—same round faces with big bellies coming out of their untucked shirts. Both grabbed for the sweets on my tray. Each tried taking more than the other. The tray tipped and cakes and cookies slid right into the boys' laps and onto the floor. Their yelling must have reached God himself.

Ever seen a cat catch a mouse? When it's about to pounce you can't help but watch the mouse—it's life or death for the creature, but for you, it's just something to watch. Well, right then, I was the mouse. Every eye was on me, watching, half curious to see what would happen next.

"Forgive me, sir," I said. I dropped to the floor and tried collecting the cookies, grateful to have the tablecloth cover me.

"What's going on over there?" I heard Mistress say.

"This clumsy little darkie spilled cookies all over my boys," said the man.

"Mr. Crumb, go see what's going on over there!" said Mistress.

My heart stopped. His heavy shoes were coming my way.

"Boy! Get from under there!" said Crumb.

I stayed there, hands digging into the grass on the ground. What could I do now?

"Don't worry, Master. I'll see to him." It was Anna. She ducked under the tablecloth.

"I came to get you," I whispered. "You and Mama." Words gushed out of me.

She put her finger over my moving lips. Little cakes and cookies lay around us. She took my tray and started piling the cookies onto it, then put it back in my hands.

"Come from under there!" Crumb said.

"Stay!" whispered Anna. "Master, I'm having him clean every bit of it up. The boy's new, he don't know how to do things. Please let me fill your whiskey glass," she offered.

"Yes, more of that whiskey is just what I need. If the boy can't serve, get him outta here, now!" said Crumb.

"Yes, sir," said Anna.

This was it. I'd be seen and caught.

Then I heard it: A loud crash stopped everything. Like a log had fallen and hit glass. Most every person in the tent gasped.

"Oh, my Lord! The gift table!" shouted Mistress.

"What?" said Crumb.

"Quick, get her off there!" cried Mistress.

"The darkie cook fainted!" said one person.

"Ain't never seen nothing like it!" said another.

"Daddy!" I heard Miss Viola yell. "My gifts! She's ruined my gifts!"

"No, no," said Crumb. "We'll make sure to take care

of everything! Don't you worry." His shoes went running away.

Anna kicked me under the table. I needed to leave. I needed to leave right then.

I picked up the tray and stood. Mama was across the way, on the floor. Miss Nora was there patting Mama's face, with Old Joe beside her. Most everyone was curious and looking over the broken gift table.

A couple of cakes and cookies were left on my tray, so I held it flat and started walking toward that tent flap without looking back. There was still a crush of people. I pushed forward. About twenty paces from the flap, I heard him.

"I'll take a couple of those," Stokes said.

Not me. He couldn't mean me. I kept going.

"Boy! You hear me?" said Stokes. He definitely meant me. I pulled my hat down, turned around slow, and held up the tray.

"Yes, sir," I croaked.

His hand swiped across my tray, taking all the cakes and cookies, along with the bits of dirt they'd collected from the ground.

"Boy! Fetch me some more whiskey!" he said.

"Yes, sir." Face to the ground, I turned to leave. His eyes felt like pins on my back.

Fifteen paces to the tent flap.

I felt the pins sink deeper into my back as I tried to find a way through the people in my path.

Twelve paces to the tent flap.

I prayed that I'd disappear. That I'd melt into the crowd.

Then I heard him.

"Homer!" he yelled.

79

Billy

"I DON'T THINK THEY'RE COMING RIGHT BACK," said Ada. Time had passed like molasses spilling from a jar. Slowly.

Juna fidgeted about, peered into the forest around the boat, hoping to catch sight of Sanzi's, Homer's, or Ferdinand's return. But there was nothing but the sounds of impatient swamp birds and animals chirping, tweeting, and growling.

"What if something happened?" Juna asked Billy.

Billy had remained silent. He was certain his hunter was there waiting for him to say just one word. Instead, he sat dreaming himself back to Freewater.

"Billy, did you hear me?" asked Juna.

Reluctantly, Billy's mind returned to the boat.

"I h-h-have to go after them," said Billy. It was the last thing he wanted to say, but he knew it had to be said. The only thing that frightened him more than going into a plantation was the thought of losing his friend to one.

"S-s-stay here with Ada. I'll go. I know p-p-plantations, I think I could find them. I'll g-g-go."

Before Juna could argue, Billy swung his long legs out of the boat and set off.

80

Sanzi

SANZI WATCHED AS THE MILITIAMAN GROPED about the floor, found a piece of rope, and sat on top of Ferdinand to tie his hands behind his back. Satisfied, he stood up to look over his hostage.

"Get up, boy!" the man shouted.

Ferdinand sat up.

"Which plantation you from?" asked the man as he shone the light on Ferdinand's face. "You don't seem like one belonging to Crumb," he said. "Heck, I'm betting he'd pay nicely for you."

Ferdinand sat in silence, staring into the dark of the shed.

"Boy, you best answer me when I talk to you!" said the man. Without another thought, he raised his fist back and swung it hard into Ferdinand's temple. All the tree hiding, patrolling, and dreaming had not prepared Sanzi for seeing violence. In that moment, she realized that violence was as foreign to her as the glass, or the blue-white shirts. It was another thing she'd never seen.

Ferdinand made no sound, but he toppled over like a

368

tree. Sanzi gasped. The man heard it and swung around. It didn't take long for him to see Sanzi.

Standing over her, he shouted, "Get up from there!"

Every muscle in her legs shook as she stood. The weight of the knife's wooden handle pulled at Sanzi's hand.

"Look at you. You're positively wild," he said, reaching for her. Sanzi had only one thought: Make sure he didn't strike her the way he'd struck Ferdinand. When she raised her hand it was a reflex to save herself.

Sanzi swung the knife. She swung it hard across the pink-faced man's body and sliced him right through all that cloth on his arm. A big red stripe of blood showed itself.

In that instant, the two held one thing in common: Neither could believe what had happened. He stared, shocked, at the blood.

"You cut me!" he yelled. Sanzi swung again, this time striking his leg.

He fell to the ground writhing in pain.

She backed away, entranced at the sight of him. What had she done? It was Ferdinand's voice that awakened her.

"Sanzi!" He said it in a voice she'd never heard. A whimper. Like a small cub who'd lost his way.

Ferdinand held up his tied hands and she cut the rope free. The two ran, pushing open the shed door.

Just outside the door were three more militiamen, laughing and talking.

Oh no! More of them! Sanzi thought. She didn't have time to be brave or strong. Instead she pushed past them and ran as fast as her legs would take her, with Ferdinand right behind her.

Sanzi could hear their voices echoing across the field.

"What on Earth!" one of the men exclaimed.

"She cut me! She cut me bad! Get after them!" the militiaman shrieked.

Ferdinand and Sanzi sprinted across the grass lawn between the sheds toward the small hill. Only thoughts of the waiting canoe in the river were on their minds.

"Over there!" a militiaman shouted.

The loudest sound Sanzi had ever heard was a thunderclap in a great storm when she was small enough to fit on David's lap. That storm sent floods. The waters rose high enough to cover the higher ground of Freewater. For a time, all of Freewater lived in the meeting place. Sanzi swore it was the loud thunder that broke the sky and let loose the great rain.

The clap of the gun from behind Ferdinand and Sanzi sounded like that thunder, but it was loud enough to break ten skies.

The bullet missed her but Sanzi's heartbeat stopped, as did her legs, and down she fell, hard, to the ground. The boom of the gunshot also rang in Ferdinand's head but it made him run even faster, oblivious that he'd left his partner behind. Sanzi tried to stand up and catch him, but then an arm pushed her to the ground.

"Gotcha!" said the militiaman, standing with his pistol drawn over her.

"Yeah, you're both gonna be sorry," the militiaman said.

"Stop!" came a voice from the night.

Billy stepped into the moonlight with a courage that came from seeing his friend in need.

Billy! thought Sanzi.

"Whatcha say to me, boy? I'm coming for you next!" said the man.

No one saw the whirl of Billy's sling, but they heard the stone as it hit the man's chest. A scream tried to escape his throat, but as it did, another stone came and struck his head. He fell to the ground. Ferdinand ran back and grabbed the man's pistol.

"Stop!" called two more militiamen from behind.

Sanzi rolled over and grabbed her sling and stones. The feel of it in her hands was comforting and familiar. As she launched her stone at the voices and shadows, Sanzi knew it would hit its target. It was the first thing she knew since she'd left her canoe on the river. She was reloading her sling when another stone flew past her and a man screamed, then fell.

Sanzi turned to see her sister with her sling in hand.

"Juna," said Sanzi.

"You think they're dead?" a voice asked from the distance.

"It's all right, A-A-Ada," said Billy.

Ada stepped into the clearing.

"They ain't dead, but we best stop them from coming after us," said Ferdinand.

It took all of the vine rope Sanzi and Juna had wound about their arms and waist to tie up the unconscious militiamen.

"Nice shot," said Ferdinand to Billy. Billy nodded and stared down at the three militiamen, a testament to his own bravery.

"You too," Sanzi said to Juna. Her sister smiled.

"Thanks," Ferdinand said to Sanzi. She handed him the knife. There was no irony in his voice, only respect.

"We best get out of here," said Sanzi.

"What about Homer? He didn't come back with Mama," said Ada.

"Come on, Homer will f-f-find his way," said Billy.

Ada shook her head. "What if they got more soldiers up there?" With that, she went running up the hill.

"Ada!" called Billy.

"What if she's right?" asked Sanzi.

"Don't see there's much we could do about it," said Ferdinand.

"I don't know, but she's right, we should at least see," said Sanzi.

They ran behind Ada to the top of the hill.

They crouched down, with the big white house and the tent beside it in view.

"I don't see a-a-anything," said Billy.

"You can't tell much from here. Homer could be any-where in there," said Ferdinand.

"Look!" Ada pointed into the distance.

In the shadow of the moonlight, he walked across the open grass. Walking as if he was in his own backyard. Slow and sure. His bow was tied to his back.

"Suleman," whispered Sanzi, and she took off across the grass toward him, with Billy, Juna, Ada, and Ferdinand in tow.

81

Homer

PART OF SURVIVING SLAVERY IS HABIT. YOUR body needs to know what to do without even having to think about it. My body was full of slave habits. I bow my head and clear the way when white folks cross my path. My stomach will jerk at the sight of a whip.

And my body stopped dead in its place when Stokes called my name.

Before I could press on, he'd grabbed my scratchy new shirt. Stokes licked his lips.

"Looks like Mistress Viola isn't the only one to get a present today. Master Crumb will be wanting to see the likes of you." He started pulling me toward the gift table where Crumb and his family stood. My plan was ending.

There's no knowing about the light that being free brings you until you lose it. I was surrounded by fine clothes, flowers, and pretty things, and yet I may as well have been walking into my own grave. All I knew was that I didn't want to go back. I couldn't go back. There was no being smart, no thinking things through, and no disappearing

374

myself away. Freedom was the only thing my body understood. I swung my arms and kicked at Stokes.

"NO!" I said over and over.

To be honest, I didn't even know what I was doing until
Stokes struck me dead in my face.

Twinkling stars danced around my eyes and I started to
fall back.

82

Sanzi

ONLY A FEW YARDS FROM HIM, SULEMAN acknowledged Sanzi's approach with one swift movement. He pulled an arrow from his quiver, loaded his bow, and aimed at her. Everyone yelped.

Everyone except Sanzi. She halted.

"Suleman," Sanzi said.

He looked at her and sniffed. "Far from home, aren't you," he said, lowering his arrow.

"Are you here for a raid?" asked Sanzi.

Suleman almost smiled. "Well, I have business to attend to," he said. "It looks like you all have business of your own. I think your friend could use some help," he said. "Have you come ready?" asked Suleman.

Sanzi stumbled. This was the moment she'd dreamt of, but she could only think of all she'd gotten wrong. The bow didn't even feel like it was hers anymore.

"Let me see it," said Suleman, and he motioned for her weapon. Sanzi handed it to him. "Not bad," he said, looking it over. "But..." he said.

He pulled a thin string from his pouch, restrung her bow, and tied it taut.

"Now you're ready. Remember, breathe and see the target here." He touched a fingertip to the center of her forehead. He pulled matches from his shirt pocket and handed her three long arrows.

"I don't know if I can," said Sanzi. The last time she'd held a bow everything had gone wrong.

"You made it this far, you can," said Suleman. "Here, I'll show you," he said. He lit a match to his arrow, loaded his bow, and aimed toward the tent. As he was about to release, a shot rang out. *BANG!*

A rifle's bullet pierced the night, shot over the grass.

"Suleman!" Sanzi cried, throwing herself over his body. The two fell to the ground. The others went running.

"It's okay," Suleman said. "Are you hit?" he asked.

"No," said Sanzi.

"It's time for me to get back to work," said Suleman, scanning the field. "Run, your friend needs you." And he pressed several matches into her hand and gave her more arrows. He took his bow, turned, and shot his arrow into the night toward the gunshot.

A yell rang out. It was the same militiaman she'd cut. Suleman fired again and went running into the night toward the scream.

Sanzi looked at the matches and arrows in her hands. She could do it. With pieces of cloth from her shirt, she wrapped the arrows, then struck a match. She lit the arrowhead, pointed it toward the tent, and fired. The arrow swooped high in the air, then arched down toward the tent's top. She lit another arrow and fired again.

83

Anna

ONLY A FEW SAW THE FIRST ARROW FLY.

Guests who'd left the confines of the tent for a bit of summer air and gossip looked up and thought it was a distant comet or tiny meteor. It moved quickly and the flame on the arrow's end trailed orange and red in the evening sky. One guest pointed and the others watched as the arrow soared high, then descended and struck. They ran around to see where it could have landed. All of them were caught in the merriment of the evening, unable to fathom the possibility of danger. Then another arrow came. And another.

Anna saw none of this. But as she served her whiskey and gazed hopefully at the sheep and puffy clouds stuck in the rafters, she saw the first arrow pierce the tent ceiling, burn a hole in the white fabric, and fall into the table centerpiece below. Delicate baby's breath petals were set aflame. Guests at the table let out small, puzzled yelps at the arrival of a mysterious arrow. Perhaps it was part of the reception's entertainment? Anna thought otherwise.

Worry didn't really start until a hail of flaming arrows landed on the tent's top. Plate-sized fire holes pockmarked the entire tent. Tablecloths ignited, and flowers and dresses were set aflame. All at once, as if an alarm sounded, several yelled and ran.

Anna did neither. Instead, she watched as fire rained down from the sky.

84

Homer

I WOKE UP YELLING AND KICKING. EVEN though Stokes had knocked me out, my body remembered that I'd decided to fight.

"NO! Let me go! Let me go!" I screamed as if I'd never screamed anything in my life. My fists and feet knocked Stokes back and I pulled free.

Stokes roared and came after me again, but this time, a crush of people ran right between us, hollering, "Fire! Fire!" and paying me and Stokes no mind.

I was crunched between fancy satin dresses and starched suits stampeding to the tent flaps. I stood up and pushed along with them. Stokes tried reaching for me, but the crowd trampled over him.

I didn't stop for anything or anyone and clawed my way out of that tent. Behind me, I could hear Stokes yelling, "Stop him! Stop him!" But for the first time, no one heeded a word he said.

Outside, I ran and ducked behind some shrubs and out of sight. I'd made it, but where was Mama? Where was Anna? As I coughed and tried to catch my breath from the smoke, I watched people running out of the tent. They howled and tried to put out the fire on their clothes, or ran toward the Big House or to the stables, determined to leave. Others couldn't run fast enough, got trampled, and lay hurt on the ground. Mama wasn't with them.

Viola, the bride, came out of the tent stumbling, dress torn and burned. She stopped and stood dazed, watching her wedding reception burn to the ground.

Mrs. Crumb raced about, wringing her hands, yelling at the flames, "Our wedding, our beautiful wedding!"

Mr. Crumb came out of the tent next. Stokes, Rick, and Ron were close behind him. The fire had sobered Crumb up. "Stokes and you two! Get over here and get water on this fire," he yelled.

"I saw that boy Homer!" Stokes hollered, his head turning in every direction searching for me. I ducked down even lower.

"I don't care if you saw Father Christmas himself, get some buckets and water before this fire takes my house along with this tent!" Crumb commanded. Crumb grabbed three buckets, passed two to Rick and Ron, and began fetching water from the well and heaving it onto the burning tent. I'd never seen him work so hard! Stokes looked around one more time, then ran off looking for buckets.

Where was Mama? I crept from behind one shrub to another shrub, peeking around hoping to see her. Then

I heard it: a scream. Mama's scream. It was coming from inside the tent. I had to go back. I pulled my hat down and ran toward the tent flap, pushing past everyone trying to run out.

Inside, flames and smoke filled the air. Tablecloths were burning; dark smoke covered everything. The scream came again. I ran toward it, ducking just as large burning pieces of tent rained down from above.

Then I saw her—two knocked-over tables had her pinned down.

I pushed one off her.

"Mama!" I called.

"Homer, oh my dear Homer, you're here. You're here," Mama cried. "I can't move!"

With all of my strength, I pushed the second table, but it was much bigger and heavier than the first. It wouldn't budge. Flames fell from overhead and caught the tablecloth on fire.

"Homer, the fire!" yelled Mama. I needed help. Something to unwedge Mama from the table. There was a chair behind me. I picked it up, held it high, and smashed it on the ground. The wood from the chair leg could be enough.

I wedged the leg under the table and pushed.

Mama screamed but this time the table moved and finally she was set free. "You did it!" said Mama, and she hugged me so tight it took my breath away.

I grabbed her, put her arm over my shoulder, and ran for the tent flap, but now the entire entryway was in flames.

We couldn't go that way.

"We gotta go under the tent wall," I said. We ran to the far side of the tent, and I began digging under the cloth, a hole big enough for us to fit under. But as I dug, I heard a tear. I looked up and just above me, an ax blade tore through the cloth and it opened wide. In the gap stood Suleman.

"Suleman!" I said.

"I think your work is done," he said, looking from me to Mama. "Your friends are out there," he said, pointing. "Run to them."

"Aren't you going to come?" I coughed.

"Not yet, I still have business here," he said, and with that he went walking into the flaming tent.

"Come on, Mama!" I said, and the two of us took off running into the night.

85

Anna and Nora

ANNA STOOD JUST OUTSIDE THE TENT AND watched the chaos around her. Nothing had gone as she'd planned. Yet, in a flash she remembered her wish that fire would rain down on Mrs. Crumb. The fruition of this made her certain that even more precious dreams could be fulfilled this evening.

She made her way through the running guests and smoke and headed with determination toward the larder, knowing exactly what was needed.

Hay covering the bags was no matter. Anna pushed it away. The food, clothing, and even the small stuffed baby doll were all intact and untouched. More important, she dug her hands into the bag Nora had packed and Rose had hidden and felt for the thin, dry parchment.

Holding it up to the moonlight peeking through the larder's slats, Anna couldn't read a word of the script on the paper but she was unconcerned. She knew it spoke of freedom. She stuffed it into her apron and turned to leave.

"*Where* do you think you're going?" said Stokes as he grabbed her dress collar.

Anna began to struggle and tried to run.

"Oh no you don't!" said Stokes as he pulled her from the larder and back toward the house.

"Stop!" A voice came from behind.

Stokes swung around. Nora was there.

"Let her loose," said Nora, in a clearer voice than she'd ever used.

"Now you've got some words?" Stokes laughed. "Little lady, ain't no way I'm going to let one of these darkies run off. So you go on back to the kitchen where you belong," he sneered.

This time Nora didn't use any words—instead she ran at him. Perhaps it was surprise, or the whiskey maypop water that finally set in, that slowed his response. Regardless, he froze. Nora rammed her body into him, and his hand let loose of Anna's dress.

"Why, you!" he yelled. But now there was no stopping Nora and Anna.

The two wrestled him, grabbing at his arms and legs until he fell flat on his back, unconscious. Then Anna and Nora both jumped on top of him.

Shocked by their effectiveness, they looked at each other, for a moment sharing something in common—a sense of relief.

In a flash Anna saw Stokes, the man beneath her, turned into a big bug. Ugly but smashable. Anna looked to her left, and stretched out before her was an illuminated golden path headed right into the tobacco fields and toward freedom.

"I'm going. I have to," said Anna.

"I know," said Nora, seeing Anna for the first time. "I'll hold him."

Anna stood up and ran, but not before grabbing the two cloth bags. Nora looked down and perhaps she also saw Anna's vision because suddenly the man that had scared everyone at Southerland looked small. Small enough to sit on. So Nora did.

Anna looked at Nora. For the first time Nora saw true happiness in her eyes.

"Goodbye," Anna said to Nora, and she ran off.

86

Homer

"WHAT ABOUT ANNA?" I STOPPED RUNNING AND turned to Mama. I'd broken my promise again.

"I don't know. She could be lost in the middle of all that," Mama said, looking at the smoky tent.

Then I saw her. I almost didn't recognize her in Nora's nice gingham dress. Anna carried two cloth bags on her shoulder and a piece of paper in her hands, and she was smiling as if finally things were as they should be. She rubbed the scar on her arm, then she waved her paper in the air and ran for the tobacco fields. I waved back.

"I think that girl really is going North." Mama smiled.

I nodded. She just might find freedom, and I'd never forget her.

Then I heard it. "*Eeeoop, eeoop.*" Our call. I grabbed Mama's hand and we went toward it. It was Ada who spotted Mama first, and off she ran to her.

"Mama!" called Ada. Mama took Ada in her arms and hugged her tight, then kissed her forehead. Ada closed her eyes and relished the feeling.

Mama looked around at all of us.

"Mama, these are my friends, Sanzi, Juna, Ferdinand, and Billy," I announced. It felt good to say.

"We have to go," said Ferdinand. He'd had his fill of Southerland.

"Yes," echoed Juna, and they all started making their way toward the small forest.

But Sanzi, being Sanzi, wouldn't move.

"Wait. We didn't get the tools—we came all this way and we didn't get what we need. We can't go back without them! Isn't everything just sitting there now?" said Sanzi.

We all looked at each other. She was right.

"Stokes, Crumb, and the rest are with that fire," said Rose.

"Come on!" said Sanzi, and she made a run for the outhouses.

We each took an outbuilding. Sanzi and Ferdinand returned to the toolshed. I went with Mama to the laundry, and we all bundled up shirts, sheets, knives, axes, soap, matches, grain, and more. Whatever we could fit in our hands or carry on our backs.

We ran for the boat. As we did, we saw Suleman, his back laden with a tablecloth full of plates, bowls, serving spoons, trays, and anything else the wedding tent had to offer. What's more, he was not alone.

Enslaved souls of Southerland and McGrath plantations, having witnessed the unthinkable in the midst of chaos, saw a window of freedom open. Some stayed, but many ran.

"I think we've done our work!" chuckled Suleman as he saw Sanzi, her arms full.

"Let's go home," said Juna, and for once, Sanzi couldn't agree more with her sister.

When we reached the forest I saw Two Shoes, with Minnie in his arms and his wife at his side.

"We thought we'd try going with you," said Two Shoes. For the first time I didn't feel afraid talking to Two Shoes. I knew what he'd done and what he'd chosen.

"Yeah, it's time we got back to Freewater," I said.

After traipsing through the forest, we reached the boat. It was only then I noticed that we were in the very place where Ada and I had first jumped.

This time we were with Mama.

87

Nora

NORA STOOD IN THE SHADOWS OF THE BIG House, watching Rose, Homer, and Ada run into the night.

Her heart ached. Old Joe was sitting nearby watching their departure, too. Nora walked over to him.

"I suppose you'll be missing Mrs. Rose," Old Joe said with a sigh.

"Why don't you go, too?" asked Nora.

"Sounds like you found your words. That's good. Maybe you could use those words for some good around here," Old Joe said. "Me, I'm too old to make that journey. Besides, I have my own uses being here." He smiled mischievously. "And I'll know they're out there for every day I have left on this earth."

"Now what?" asked Nora as she watched the chaos unfolding around them.

She began walking about, surveying what was left of the wedding. What she saw was strange, and for her, unexplainable. The dizzying, boisterous effect of the maypop water and whiskey wore off, and in its place finally came the outcome Anna had sought, sleep. Like a heavy blanket, drowsiness descended on the guests as they sought out their carriages and horses to ride away from the disastrous wedding. Some fell asleep right on the lane. Few made it home before they succumbed to the need to stop and slumber. A guest or two who saw the self-liberated souls run for the forest thought to chase them, but their feet were weighed down with sleep that prevented them from reaching even the first forest tree before they came to a standstill and closed their eyes to snooze.

Nora returned to the larder, where she found even Stokes was still sound asleep on the ground. Finally, she joined her mother, father, Viola, and Rick and Ron in fetching water to put out the tent fire. Embers and smoke filled the air as the fire began to smolder, leaving only ash behind. They worked until exhausted and the buckets of water felt too heavy to lift and their eyelids felt even heavier to keep open and, apart from Nora, sleep overcame all of them right where they stood.

88

Suleman

SULEMAN WAS PLEASED AS HE LEFT SOUTHER-
land. He was accustomed to being alone when he worked.
This time was different.

At the river's edge he uncovered two hidden canoes that
he pushed into the water beside Sanzi's. He was prepared
to help the runaways into the boats and lead them to freedom as he'd done many times before, but he paused and
watched his new, young guides.

As if it were natural and meant to be, Homer, Billy, Juna,
Ferdinand, Sanzi, and Ada all helped the ten new souls run
for freedom. They directed them into the boats and rowed
them down the now-familiar river. Ferdinand cut walking sticks for each traveler to use as they made their way
through mud. For the first time Billy stopped imagining
his hunter and led the way to opening the hidden door on
the water. Juna and Sanzi swung their slings to hunt food
for everyone when they sought refuge in Suleman's tree
den. Homer didn't hesitate when he led them zigzagging
through the field of wooden stakes, and all the while Ada
told them about how to fly on the sky bridges.

Suleman watched it all.

"Plantations, beware, we have some young people ready to set us all free," he said. The group of newly minted rescuers laughed, but they looked at one another and wondered.

Billy and Juna

IT WAS MORNING WHEN THEY MET THE SKY bridge. Billy and Juna were the first to cross, far enough ahead of everyone to be on the bridge alone for a moment.

"Juna," said Billy, stopping. So much had happened, he knew he could do most anything.

Juna stopped and saw him. Even on the waving, narrow bridge, Billy stood taller than he ever had before. She felt a bit taller herself.

"I j-j-just wanted to g-g-give you s-s-something," said Billy, unbothered by the stuttering sound of his words. He knew it was not a sign of his own bravery.

When Juna saw the bracelet, she smiled. The morning sun cast its warm, pinkish-yellow light on them as they stood in the sky. For Billy, it was the perfect moment.

"I was wondering when you'd finally give it to me!" She laughed and hugged him and kissed his warm cheek. "It's beautiful," she said, adding it to her wrist.

Sanzi

SANZI AND SULEMAN WERE AT THE SKY BRIDGE ladder when he stopped and said his goodbyes.

"Where are you going?" Sanzi wasn't sure what to say, but as she watched him leave, she knew the moment needed words.

"My place is out here," said Suleman. "Take this." He pulled his long bow from his back. "You're brave. I knew it the day I saw you chasing butterflies without a care."

Sanzi smiled. "You remember," she said.

"I remember. One day, you might need this more than me," Suleman said. He handed the bow to her.

Then he was gone.

Sanzi watched him go, sure that one day she'd find him again. Then she clutched her bow and began making her way up the peg ladder. By the time she reached the top, most everyone had gone ahead of her. She was on the sky bridge alone. She clutched her new bow and rubbed the smooth handle of her knife. Then through the quiet she heard the call.

"*Swoot, click, click, swooot!*" It was her mother's call for her. For once, Sanzi didn't groan at the familiar sound. In fact, it felt like home reaching out across the bridge. Her eyes swept the distance. Mrs. Light and David were waving. Sanzi's heart leapt and she lifted her head to the sky, and clear as the tinkle of crystal, her call rang out in return.

"*Swoooooot, click, click, swoooooot!*" She ran, sending out her call over and over again.

"*Swoooot, click, click, swoooooot!*" At the platform on the bridge's end, where the morning light shone on them above the canopy, Sanzi fell into her parents' arms. Mrs. Light held her tight, crying and repeating, "I prayed to the swamp that she would return you to me."

When they got to the bottom of the peg ladder, there were more hugs and tears for Juna and the others. Sanzi pulled out her knife and showed everyone her new bow. She had envisioned this moment a million times, but now dreams of her heroic speech and recounting tales and adventure faded from her memory. She was proud, but not in the way she'd always imagined.

"Mama, I saw everything," Sanzi said.

Mrs. Light pulled her daughter close, nodded through tears, and said, "I know, I know."

Then Sanzi said what she was most proud of. "I made it back, Mama. I made it back home to you."

91

Homer

I'VE NEVER FELT FREER THAN I DID CROSSING that sky bridge in the pink sunrise. Ada was flapping her arms in front of us as she made her way to Big Tree. Mama was wide-eyed.

Once we were down on the ground, Mama was at my side, her head turning and wondering about this new place, as everyone came to hug us and welcome us back.

We were in Freewater. We were home.

A Note from Amina

Enslaved women, men, and children found a multitude of ways big and small to resist and escape bondage. We usually learn about them escaping North or to Canada. Lesser known are those who found refuge deep in the swamps and forests of the American South and even began secret communities.

Research and historical literature refer to these secret communities as "maroon communities" and the people who resided in them as "maroons." Although *Freewater* is from my imagination, it's inspired by the Great Dismal Swamp and the enslaved souls who found refuge and freedom within its confines. At its peak, the Great Dismal Swamp covered over fifteen hundred square miles and stretched from Virginia to North Carolina. True to its name, the swamp was an inhospitable and almost impassable tangle of vegetation and marsh. Yet people escaping enslavement found ways to survive within it.

First Indigenous communities used the swamp as a hunting ground and communal space and relied on it for protection from European colonization. Then potentially thousands of enslaved people escaped there as early as the 1700s until the Civil War.

Some passed through the swamp as a stop on the Underground Railroad on their way North, while others made lives for themselves in secrecy. A formerly enslaved man who lived in the Great Dismal Swamp before running away to Canada described his experience in a narrative published in 1859 by James Redpath, *The Roving Editor:* "There are families growed up in that Dismal Swamp that never saw a white man and would be scared to death to see one. Some runaways went there with their wives, and their children are raised there." It is difficult to know exactly how many communities formed in the swamp and how long each survived. *Did the maroons live together as in Freewater, or did individuals and families live separately?*

Although we don't know for sure, historians and archaeologists have been working to uncover this information.

Another researcher, historian Dr. Sylviane A. Diouf, studies America's maroon communities in the swamps and forests of the American South, including in Virginia, Georgia, North Carolina, South Carolina, and Louisiana. Her work on the Great Dismal Swamp showed evidence that maroons were there potentially for decades. Diouf uncovered one early 1800s report describing a woman and her six children seen in the center of the swamp. In another, Diouf recounted the story of a Northern soldier stationed near the Great Dismal Swamp during the Civil War, who reported seeing a family of nine emerge from the swamp's interior. Their seven kids had never laid eyes on a white man. These accounts of children and families in the swamp set my imagination on fire, and *Freewater* was born.

How did the deep swamp maroons live? Accounts reconstructed by post-Emancipation swamp dwellers describe cabins, some on stilts over water, others on land and built from mud, sticks, and bark. For sustenance, people living in the swamp gathered fruits like grapes, as well as honey, roots, and herbs. They hunted and raised wild hogs and cows, and captured squirrels, ducks, otters, quails, and more. They even cultivated land with corn and sweet potatoes. They likely wore fur, animal skin, and treated bark.

Diouf discusses that although some runaways escaped to areas deep in the Great Dismal Swamp, many stayed on the borderlands within the swamp but near plantation lands. They survived off their surroundings when possible, but also by stealing from nearby plantations and businesses. Borderland marauders like Suleman caused great trouble for landowners. They stole all sorts, from cattle to cornmeal, for their survival. Living in the borderlands also enabled them to keep in contact with relations still in captivity.

Not all enslaved people arrived in the swamp as runaways. Many were brought there for work to build canals and ditches, and for logging and shingle making. Long before his presidency, George Washington sought to make his fortune as founder of the Dismal Swamp Company, a venture that aimed to drain the swamp for land cultivation using enslaved labor and ultimately to build a canal. It was brutal work. Some ran off from these camps and, like Ferdinand, found refuge deep within the swamp. Some runaways were said to have informally worked for these swamp companies (who were desperate for labor) in exchange for food, necessities, and money. This was a risky proposition, but it enabled some formerly enslaved people to survive. Moses Grandy, who was enslaved while working in the Great Dismal Swamp, used his labor to purchase his freedom. His poignant slave narrative, *The Life of Moses Grandy*, is a peek into the life of those forced to labor in the swamp.

Archaeologists have dug on the elevated lands of the swamp, also known as islands or hummocks, to uncover more evidence of Indigenous and African American life. Archaeologist Dr. Daniel Sayers of American University has found remnants of cabins, clay pottery, stone implements, and more dating back hundreds of years. He's even found traces of lead shot, gunflint, and what he believes to have been a fort erected to protect and defend their encampments. Imagine that!

Enslaved men, women, and children also ran away to start maroon communities in parts of the Caribbean and Central and South America. Some of these communities were so well protected and defended that they continue to exist today. In Jamaica, the maroon community of Moore Town (Nanny Town) in the eastern highlands grew so large and strong that it engaged in battle. The enslavers they fought were finally forced to sign a treaty with the maroon community, which gave it autonomy from the British government.

This history is a reminder that wherever African enslavement existed in the Americas, a culture (and even communities) of extraordinary resistance was always present.

Acknowledgments

I WAS FORTUNATE TO HAVE A SUPPORTIVE community to help see me through this work. Many thanks to my amazing mentor and friend Kathi Appelt, for her insights, encouragement, authorly wisdom, and a million other things. To my fabulous and fearless agent, Emily van Beek. Thank you for daring to dream big with me. To James Patterson and Jimmy Books for your steadfast support. To Laura Schreiber, for seeing the promise of this book, and for your insightful early editorial hand. To Alexandra Hightower, for your sharp and clear editorial eye and your endless guidance as we worked to bring *Freewater* into the world. To Victoria Stapleton, Cheryl Lew, Bill Grace, Mara Brashem, Annie McDonnell, Tracy Shaw, Olivia Davis, and the whole crew at Little, Brown Books for Young Readers, for your amazing work. You've made a wonderful and nurturing home for *Freewater*. Thanks to We Need Diverse Books for all you've done to support me and other authors of color. To Dr. Sylviane A. Diouf for your invaluable research on the American maroon communities. To Dr. Daniel Sayers, for your research on the Great Dismal Swamp.

Thank you to friends Kaija Langley, Leonard Muse, and Karen English for your great input.

To my Luqman family and my Dawson family for being my best cheerleaders.

To my mom, who was the first to speak my dream of becoming an author.

To my husband and dear friend, Robert, for your endless well of confidence, vision, and positivity.

Zachariah Dawson

Amina Luqman~Dawson

is a writer and mom. She's written freelance for newspapers and magazines. She's also authored a pictorial history book, *Images of America: African Americans of Petersburg*. She most enjoys writing for kids. *Freewater* is her debut novel. Amina, her husband, and their thirteen-year-old son reside in Arlington, Virginia.